W9-AQH-125

PIE TOWN

Center Point
Large Print

Also by Lynne Hinton and available from Center Point Large Print:

Christmas Cake
Wedding Cake

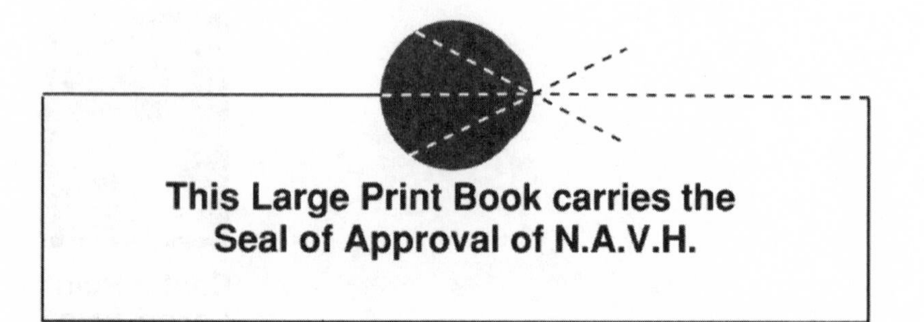

PIE TOWN

LYNNE HINTON

CENTER POINT LARGE PRINT
THORNDIKE, MAINE

This Center Point Large Print edition is published
in the year 2011 by arrangement with
William Morrow, an imprint of HarperCollins Publishers.

This book is a work of fiction. The characters, incidents, and dialogue are drawn from the author's imagination and are not to be construed as real. Any resemblance to actual events or persons, living or dead, is entirely coincidental.

The text of this Large Print edition is unabridged.
In other aspects, this book may vary
from the original edition.
Printed in the United States of America.
Set in 16-point Times New Roman type.

ISBN: 978-1-61173-167-5

Library of Congress Cataloging-in-Publication Data

Hinton, Lynne.
Pie town / Lynne Hinton.
p. cm.
ISBN 978-1-61173-167-5 (library binding : alk. paper)
1. City and town life—New Mexico—Fiction.
2. Life change events—Fiction. 3. Large type books. I. Title.
PS3558.I457P54 2011b
813′.54—dc22

2011015638

Dedicated to
Jasie Barringer, Carolyn Aldridge,
and Art Barrett,
for open hearts and open homes.
We come to the Land of Enchantment
by way of your hospitality.

ACKNOWLEDGMENTS

The gift of a story is always a blessing. I count those blessings with great awe and respect, believing that God is good and is the source of all the good stories in my life. Sally McMillan remains a presence of light and encouragement. How fabulous for me that my agent is also my treasured friend. The Louisville Institute awarded me a Pastoral Study Grant, which has enabled me to find the time to do research and the writing. Thank you for this gift of time and money. Carolyn Marino and Wendy Lee of HarperCollins said yes. Thank you, Wendy, for your keen eye and good heart. And thank you, Carolyn, for reading my stories.

In the year of finishing this book, I was so blessed to serve Chewelah United Church of Christ as their interim pastor. It was such a lovely place for me to land, and I will always remember my stay in the Pacific Northwest as a time of being hemmed in by mountains of kindness and friendship.

I am always grateful for the friends and family in my life. I hope that I have made sure that you know who you are and how rich my life is because you are in it. Finally, how does a person acknowledge the love of their life? Bob Branard remains the steady and sure heartbeat of my every day. There is nothing he doesn't do to make sure I'm happy and whole and able to write. Surely, there is no greater gift in life than the love of a good partner.

Part I

ONE

They come. The two of them, desperate, longing, alone, and displaced, they come because they are told to come. One beckoned from whispers speaking in lingering dreams, directed by stars and canyon voices. The other, obeying the orders of stern and reasonable men, men of piety and certitude. They come because they know no better, because they have nowhere else that will receive them. They come to settle what cannot be settled. They come to find what it is they miss and what it is they never knew existed.

Neither of them has a sense of this desert, the forests, Cibola or Gila, no knowledge of its wide open plains named, by the Spanish, San Agustin, a feeble attempt to wrangle a blessing in their uncelebrated discovery. They do not know the long winding dry springs, Largo and Mangas Creeks, nor have they walked the road through the tiny village of Quemado, with its famed lightning field, or across the meadows studded with short scrubby pinion pines. They have not lifted their eyes to see Madre Mountain Peak or ridden the dusty trails south to the Baldys,

Whitewater, and Mogolion, following the tracks of elk and deer and lone gray wolves.

They do not know this is hallowed family land, my mother's mother's land, the land of my ancestors and the old ones. They have not learned that this is my family's heritage, Zuni, gathered and scattered along this territory, centuries ago, living here long before the farmers, Catholic and Spanish, moved from settlements north and east to establish villages of their own, and longer still before the Panhandle Texans and southern plains homesteaders came riding into town, laying claim to earth and making borders on property that was not theirs to possess. They do not know that this is the place of aged secret trails and the sacred Salt Lake of my people and their tribes.

This is my home, the place where I took my first breath, landed my first step, laughed my first laugh, and shed my last tear. This is the place where I fell in love with red skies and clear black nights, the sky dotted with stars, and afternoon rains, the smell of sage, and the high-pitched cries of coyotes, the dance of red-tailed hawks. This is the place where I fell in love with silence and one man who knew the name of every flower and seed and who looked at me as if I were the sun. This is the place for which I long even when

I sit among the spirits, float above clouds, glide across galaxies. This is my home, and by the time I came back, and though nothing had changed, it still seemed to me that I had been gone far too long.

These two will never understand, however, that I came not for this place, not for them, and not even for the man who grew bushes of sweet lavender and tall stalks of pink and rose hollyhock. I am here not for the man who thought I was the sun, but for the child who was born broken and unformed, the child who was to take my place but who arrived too early and too fast. I came for him, and as if he had been waiting, he knew me when I first appeared. "Lady," he calls me, the one who was here when he was born and the one who has never left his side.

I doubt he will speak of me to these two newcomers because he rarely talks about me to others, not because he doesn't know me or doubts my presence, but because he believes I am a gift to him and he worries that if he speaks of me casually or too much or to too many people, I might find him indulgent and selfish and leave. I doubt, however, that I ever could. Especially now. Especially as the winds speak of change, the clouds of coming storms. Especially as they arrive.

He is, after all, my connection to all that I lost in death, my link to loved ones and earth and desert, and I am his connection to all that he lost in birth, his link to all that is beyond the land with its low ceiling of sky. And together we rely upon the thin air that somehow offers enough breath and lift for us both, the weaving of our two spirits, and this place we both know best, this place the newcomers seek, this place we both call home, this place known as Pie Town.

TWO

"Pie Town." Father George Morris repeated the words the Monsignor had spoken. He echoed the name of his assignment without allowing for any emotion. He was not pleased, but he had no say in the matter. This was the place chosen for him. This was to be his parish, Pie Town, New Mexico.

His first ministry, his first call, was a three-point charge, three churches to serve as pastor, that was more than a hundred miles from the Catholic Diocese in Gallup and more than a life-time away from everything he had ever known, every place upon which he laid claim, every sight that had become familiar. This was where he was instructed to start a new life, where he would live out what he believed had been dictated by God, discerned by pious and faithful men, and written upon his heart. Here was the place where he would exercise the lessons he had learned, the faith he had been granted, and the service for which he had been ordained.

Everything Father George had prepared for, planned upon, worked toward, it was all about to come to pass in a wide desert county surrounded by Indian land, mountain peaks, long empty plains, wilderness. He knew of Catron County because in his travel to Gallup to meet with the Monsignor, his journey west, he had studied every county in the forty-seventh state. He knew the parishes and the populations. He was hopeful he would be sent to Albuquerque or north to Taos. And even though he had been brought to Gallup and knew he was starting in the western corridor of the southwestern region, he had not expected this.

“Pie Town,” he said again as the Monsignor listened, letting the name of the town pass through his lips once more as if saying it somehow would help lead him to it.

“You will report to Father Joseph, who waits for your arrival. You will move into the parish house just beyond the town limits. And you will begin your duties this weekend. I’m sure Father Joseph will fill you in on the existing ministries of the Catron County parish and all of the details of your call.”

Father George waited.

“Is there something else?” the Monsignor asked. He glanced up at the young priest and then down at the clock on his desk. It was just after four in the afternoon, and he had one more appointment. He was hopeful he would have time for tea before the early evening services he was scheduled to conduct.

Father George shook his head, sensing his

superior's impatience. "No," he whispered. "It is my honor to serve God in this place and to serve you in the ministry of the Church in the state of New Mexico." It was a line he had rehearsed on the train from Cincinnati.

The Monsignor smiled. "I'm sure you will find your first call to be a rewarding one. You serve a diverse congregation. There are Hispanics, Anglos, and Native Americans in the area." He stood up and held out his hand. "We are pleased you are here. There has been much prayer offered on your behalf."

The young priest reached for the extended hand and bowed. He understood it was time for him to leave, that there was nothing more to say. He backed away, his head still lowered in reverence. When he reached the threshold, he stepped out into the hallway, pulling the door behind him, closed his eyes, and breathed out. "And so it begins," he said, turning to walk away.

Father George Morris hailed from Grove City, Ohio. Before accepting this call to New Mexico, before the train ride from Cincinnati to Albuquerque, the bus to Gallup, and the taxi to the diocesan office, George had never been farther west than Dayton and no farther south than Beckley, West Virginia. He began seminary, also in Ohio, at age sixteen, without even finishing high school, and had never met a Native American or spoken a sentence in Spanish. At age twenty-four, a senior in seminary, he had requested a mission call, an opportunity to serve the Church in a developing country. He thought it was the will of God for him to leave the United States, leave the seductive ways of Western civilization, the wily temptations of such a secular society, and minister to simple and eager parishioners. His mentor and the other priests at the seminary, however, thought otherwise.

They did not know the reason for the young man's request, had no knowledge of the details leading to his discernment process. They asked, but never learned, why he wanted to leave the country. And so, in the end, they did not agree with him. It had been unanimously decided by all those issuing the calls of young priests, making ministerial assignments to the recent graduates, that Father George Morris should stay stateside for at least eight years before being sent to serve in the mission field, which was considered too far away from supervision and community.

Father George walked down the hall, away from the Monsignor's office, and shook his head. He was remembering the decision handed down by his mentor, the denial of his request to go to Haiti or join the Dominican Order in Trinidad. "How much farther away from Western civilization and supervision could I be than I will be in Pie Town, New Mexico?" He spoke out loud and then glanced around, making sure he was alone. He knew his tone was sarcastic and resentful. He certainly did not want to be found ungrateful or recalcitrant by his superiors in his first call. He knew that no matter what had been decided for him, created for him, after everything that had happened during his last year in seminary, this was to be his place of service, his place to exercise his vows and prove that he was capable of the authority bestowed upon him.

Father George headed out of the office in Gallup and to his sleeping quarters in the back of the building and wondered what the Monsignor knew about him, wondered what records had been kept by his mentor, what letters had been sent from Ohio to the Diocese of the Southwest, what conversations had been shared. He wondered if this was punishment or opportunity.

With one night left before he was to begin his ministry, he decided he would go to the chapel for private worship. As he entered the small room, where candles lining the wall flickered with the prayers of the sinners and saints from Gallup, Father George genuflected, made the sign of the cross, and moved to the altar. He knelt, alone in the chapel, and spoke the words one more time. Part intercession and part petition, it was the name of his own salvation. "Pie Town" was all that he said, and it was the evening's final prayer.

THREE

"Pie Town." Trina woke from a deep sleep, whispering the name of the place from her dream, a name that brought her ease and delight, a name of a place that made her smile. She wiped her eyes, saying it again, "Pie Town," and glanced around. She was in a strange house, waking to nothing that was familiar.

She could see that she had been sleeping on the floor of a small clapboard house, in the front room, a woodstove lit and burning. Trina sat up from her pallet of quilts and blankets. "Hello," she said, hearing nothing from inside or outside of the cabin. She reached down and felt rags wrapped around her feet, stiffness in her thighs. That was when she recalled that she had left Tucson and had been walking for at least three, maybe four days. She lost track of the time after she left Globe and headed onto the San Carlos Indian Reservation. Her last memory of the walk was a truckload of men passing her alongside the road, Highway 60, she thought, seeing the brake lights, watching the vehicle as it stopped and began backing up.

She had jumped across a fence, run beyond the highway, out into the desert. And she had walked for miles, following only the stars and heading away from the faint sound of traffic. She must have collapsed, she thought, and wondered, as she looked around her at the walls of the rustic dwelling, the sparse furniture, the stacks of catalogs, and the worn planks in the floor, who had rescued her and what was going to be expected from her. Turning to her side, Trina noticed her backpack leaning against the wall. She reached for it and opened the top to see that nothing had been stolen. She looked inside the front pocket, pulled out her wallet, and counted her money. Not a penny was missing.

She pushed off the covers and stood. Her legs were wobbly, and she knew, without seeing, that the bindings had been wrapped around her feet because they were blistered and raw. It was painful, but she managed to walk toward an adjoining room, an old and well-used kitchen. An icebox had been pushed into one corner, a table with two chairs was in the other. There was a sink, a small stove, a kettle set on one eye, steam pouring from the spout, and a few cupboards, their doors latched.

Trina glanced out the window and saw an old woman not very far away, bent over, picking berries from a bush. High canyon walls loomed behind her. The woman turned and raised her head slightly just as Trina noticed her, just as if she had been waiting for her guest to wake up and call for her, and then she stood up. She smiled and nodded and turned to walk back to the house.

"Hi," Trina said as the woman entered the kitchen.

She did not respond. She walked over to the stove, took the kettle from the eye, and dropped the berries into a cup. She poured water over them and handed the cup to Trina. She nodded, motioning the young woman to drink.

"Is this tea?" Trina asked and tipped the cup to her lips and took a sip.

"Tea," the woman repeated.

Trina thought the taste was slight and bitter, but it warmed her. She took another sip.

The woman sat down at the table, and Trina followed, sitting across from her. The woman wore a thin gray braid of hair that circled the top of her head. She had dark brown skin and narrow eyes, broken yellow teeth, obvious when she grinned.

"Did you find me?" Trina asked. "Did you bring me here?"

The woman did not answer.

"I don't remember what happened to me. I was walking from Tucson."

"Tucson," the woman repeated. "You walk from Tucson."

Trina nodded. She remembered the phone conversation she overheard from the balcony at the Twilight Motel before she left, Conroe's betrayal, the way a heart sounds when it breaks. She left without a fight, without an explanation, without hearing an excuse. She packed a few clothes in her backpack, took one hundred dollars from his wallet, a bottle of water, and a flashlight, and left the motel, left her life with the smooth-talking man from Abilene and started walking.

"Where am I?" Trina asked.

The woman lifted her chin, folded her hands as if she were holding a teacup, bringing them to her lips, motioning Trina to keep drinking. She wore bracelets on both arms, silver with large blue stones.

Trina followed the instructions and finished the tea. The warmth of the liquid, the unknown contents, seemed to calm her.

"Are you Indian?" she asked as she placed the cup on the table.

"Apache," the woman answered.

"Am I in Arizona?" Trina asked, trying to remember the map she had read at her last stop, trying to remember what direction she was heading.

"Apache land" came the reply.

Trina recalled that out of Globe, she had started walking east on Highway 60, heading in the direction of New Mexico. From there, she was trying to get back to the last place she lived, get back to Texas. It had been dark, and then she remembered the truck and the group of men she had seen earlier that evening at the service station where she had stopped to eat a bowl of soup, how the brake lights on the truck flashed and how it moved in reverse, how the men smiled and rubbed their hands together when they saw it was her alone on the road.

"I left the highway, started walking through the desert," she said, not sure why she was explaining herself to the woman since it appeared she did not speak English. "I don't know how far I walked."

"Apache land," the woman repeated. "White Mountains," she added. And then she got up from the table and walked into the other room. She returned with an old map and opened it for Trina to examine. Standing next to Trina, she pointed to the Apache Reservation, along the southeast corner of Arizona, in the Natanas Plateau. Trina had walked to the Salt River Canyon.

She smiled and reached over to Trina and patted her on the belly. She spoke words that Trina did not understand, and Trina assumed her hostess was asking her if she was hungry.

"Breakfast," Trina said. "Yes, I would like something to eat."

The woman grinned. She walked over to the icebox and pulled out a plate of bread and grabbed a jar of honey from a cupboard. She placed them in front of Trina and nodded.

Although she was embarrassed to be eating in front of the woman, eating what was probably the only food in the house, Trina could not stop herself. She ate three pieces of bread before she felt full. The woman only watched, nodding in approval. "I was so hungry," she said, shaking her head, surprised at her appetite, surprised at how good the morning meal tasted. "I have some money. I can pay you for the bread."

The woman shook her head as if she understood. "I fix you shoes," she said. "To keep walking."

Trina didn't respond. She remembered she was wearing sneakers when she left Tucson. The red ones with the narrow soles. She watched as the woman left the room again, returning with a pair of buckskin moccasins, old ones with magazine paper stuffed in the heels. The strings were made of dark leather. "You take these," she said and placed them on Trina's lap. "You take these shoes to Pie Town."

Trina was surprised. "Pie Town. I dreamed about Pie Town," she said. "I dreamed I was going to Pie Town, New Mexico. I saw it on the map at Globe. It's straight east on Highway 60, the one I was walking on." She studied the old woman. "How did you know?" she asked. "How did you know about my dream? How did you know that was where I was going?"

And without answering, the old woman clapped her hands together, the bracelets sliding down her arms, opened her mouth wide, and laughed out loud.

FOUR

Oris Whitsett pulled up in his driveway, parked, and opened the door on the driver's side. He slid his legs over and stood up. He was wearing an old dress shirt and nothing else but socks. He licked a finger, held it up to calculate the direction of the wind, and then nodded, lifting his chin in the direction of his next-door neighbor, who was watching.

Millie Watson, a widow since the 1980s, was rolling her emptied trash can from the edge of the road to the back of her house. She stopped when she saw Oris pull in. They had been friends for as many years as they had been neighbors in Pie Town, and that had been about half a century. "Oris," she said rather politely. She glanced over his head toward the mountains. "Wind's picked up from the north. Means a change in weather. Likely we'll have rain this week." She waited. "You forget something?"

The old man looked down, shaking his head.

"Got mud all over myself when I fell down in the cornfield out at Earl's. He was irrigating. I couldn't get dirt all over the seats, so I took off my britches. You know I haven't even had this Buick a month." He smiled. "Have I shown you the trunk?" he asked.

"About four times," Millie answered.

"It's big," Oris noted.

Millie made a kind of clucking noise, shaking her head, as she steadied herself over the trash can. She usually walked with a walker. "You went way out to Lemitar this morning? You must have left before dawn."

"Four o'clock," he answered. "Before this wind picked up."

"You get any corn?" she asked, sounding very matter-of-fact.

"A couple of bushels," Oris answered. "He's charging more this year. Said he needed a new tractor." He scratched his chin. "You want yours now or you want me to shuck 'em for you?"

Millie studied her neighbor. "I'd prefer you put on some pants." She turned back to face the direction she had been heading. "I can come for the corn after dinner." She wheeled the can ahead, walked through the gate, and placed the garbage can by the back door. She went into the house, leaving Oris outside by himself.

He walked around to the other side of the car

and was leaning inside, grabbing his pants and shoes from the floorboard when his daughter, Malene, drove past and skidded to a stop just beyond the front of his driveway. She threw the engine in reverse, made a hard turn to her left, and pulled in behind her father's new Buick.

She flew out of her car, looking much younger than her fifty-plus years. "Jesus Christ, son of the Living God, Daddy, have you gone and lost your mind for good?" She hurried toward Oris, pulling off her sweater and, once she got beside him, throwing it around her father's waist.

"Do not drive up here using that kind of language, Missy," he said, twisting to try to face her as she yanked the sweater sleeves into a knot behind him, his butt still uncovered. "Your mother will not have it."

"What my mother will not have is your ass hanging out for the entire neighborhood to see." She glanced around to notice who was watching. She shook her head. Fortunately, it appeared as if everyone who lived near her dad was away from home, everyone it seemed except Fedora Snow, who lived directly across the street and was clearly peeking out her front window. Malene smiled and waved, moving in front of Oris.

"I told you Fedora threatened to call the police on you the next time you did something crazy." She rolled her eyes and faced her father. "I bet she's calling Roger right now."

Oris looked at the house across the street. As he peered in that direction, the curtains fell shut where his neighbor had been watching. "Fedora Snow didn't pay her phone bill. She can't call the sheriff because she doesn't have a phone." He flipped his third finger up, knowing he was still being watched.

"Jesus, Daddy!" Malene grabbed her father's hand and pulled it down. "Am I going to have to get you a room in the Alzheimer's unit?"

Oris yanked his hand away from his daughter and reached down, grabbing his pants. He stuffed the sweater, still tied around his waist, inside them as Malene tried to shield him. "You can't put me in your fancy nursing home because I have it written in my will that if you try to put me away I'll take back the land I gave you when you got married."

"Daddy, that was thirty-five years ago that you gave me that land. I sold that parcel and the house we built on it after Roger became sheriff. You can't get that land back because it's a business zone and Frank has his garage there and Midford built the pool hall behind it. It's gone. It's been gone. And I'm tired of you threatening me with it." She sighed, backing away from her fully dressed father. "Here," she said, letting out a long breath, "let me help you with the corn." She walked around to the rear of the car while he opened the trunk with his key, and she pulled out a basket. “Looks better this year,” she commented, steadying the container against the car and holding up an ear, studying it.

“Quite a trunk, right?” he asked.

Malene just rolled her eyes.

“Actually Earl’s brother from Socorro already got the best of it. I didn’t even know the corn was ready until Fred told me at the diner. By the time I got there, most of the ripe ears had been picked.” He stood behind his daughter and reached for another basket. He lifted it up, and the two of them walked toward the rear of the house. “But with the wind picking up, I guess it’s a good thing I went this morning.” They placed the baskets at the back door. Malene turned.

“What was it Mama used to say about early morning winds in summer?”

“Breeze before noon, storm coming soon,” Oris replied, quoting his wife.

Malene smiled and headed toward the car.

“Aren’t you staying?” he asked, surprised to see her leaving.

“I got to go to work, Daddy,” she explained. Her voice sounded tired, heavy. “I already had to split my shift. I was up all night with Alex. It’s his legs again.”

Oris glanced away. He knew about the continuous aches and pains of his great-grandson. The little boy had been born with spina bifida, and he had been in and out of the hospital for most of his ten years. Malene was a certified nursing assistant who worked at the local nursing home and had become the primary caregiver for both her grandson and her father. Angel, Alex's mother and Malene's daughter, had left Pie Town about a month after Alex was born. No one knew exactly where she was.

"You want me to go over there and keep him company?" Oris asked. Alex had around-the-clock care, services the state offered through its health care program, but Oris still stayed with the boy quite a bit. They were close.

"Frieda's there until I get off work at seven." Malene stopped and glanced back at her father. "Just you stay out of trouble, would you?" She shook her head. "Please, just keep your clothes on when you're outside." She turned and headed to her car. She opened the door and could see the sheriff's car pulling around the corner. She yelled back at her father, "Looks like you're wrong about Fedora paying her phone bill. I'm going to have to let you handle this with Roger. I'm already half an hour late." She got in and cranked the engine. She backed out, waving at the sheriff who stopped his car on the street in front of the house.

Roger got out and nodded at Malene as she pulled away. He rested his hands on his hips and glanced over at Fedora Snow's house. He could see her peeking out the window, and he raised his chin at her, waiting to see if she would come out of her house. When she didn't open her door, he wiped the sweat from his forehead and headed up the driveway toward Oris. He could see the old man from the street. Oris had walked to his car and taken a third basket from the trunk and was heading to the back door. As Roger passed the Buick, he noticed a remaining small cardboard box of corn, and he grabbed it and closed the trunk.

"*Buenos días*, Oris," Roger said as he got near him. "You've been out to Earl's early," he commented. "I didn't even know it was picking time."

"You didn't know because you don't pick corn, and anyway, just because you're sheriff doesn't mean you know everything." Oris studied the younger man. "Fedora got you on her payroll like she does Stan Ortez? Funny, though, because it looks like he does all the yard work, so what's she paying you for?"

"She claims you're performing lewd and lascivious acts in your front yard." Roger placed the box of corn next to the basket and pulled a toothpick from behind his ear and stuck it in his mouth. He stood in front of Oris.

"Fedora wouldn't know a lewd and lascivious act if she participated in it," Oris responded.

"What's that hanging out of your zipper?" Roger asked.

Oris glanced down. He had forgotten that he had put his pants on over his daughter's sweater. He unbuttoned his pants, yanked off the sweater from around his waist, and threw it on the back of one of the patio chairs by the door. He then zipped up his pants and buttoned them, and then he sat down on the chair and pulled a basket of corn in front of him. "You gonna just stand there and write me a ticket, or you gonna sit and shuck?"

Roger smiled. He pulled the other chair around and sat down. He reached down and grabbed an ear of corn. "Malene didn't look too happy," he noted as he pulled the husk away from the ear.

"Malene doesn't get enough sleep," Oris responded. "She tries to do too much," he added. "Thinks she can save the world, and yet she couldn't even save her marriage."

"That was a long time ago, Oris," Roger said. "Why don't you give her a break?"

"Because when a man and a woman promise before God and their witnesses to love each other until death they do part, I expect that they're telling the truth." He yanked the papery layers from the ear of corn he was shucking in one long pull, twisted them so that they came off when he got to the end, and threw the husk down on the ground in front of him. He slid his fingers along the ear, removing the silver threads, and then placed the new corn in the basket.

"She meant it when she said it," Roger replied, leaning over and putting his clean ear of corn next to the one Oris had shucked.

"Well, meaning it and honoring it are two different things." Oris reached for another piece of corn.

Roger slid his hands along the front of his pants and tapped his foot. He slid around a bit in his seat.

"You still trying to quit smoking?" Oris asked, having noticed the fidgety behavior of his visitor.

"I am not trying. I have quit," Roger said in response.

"Still think about it, though, don't you?" Oris grinned as he continued to yank and pull at husks. His hands worked like a machine.

"Yes, Oris, I do."

"When I was a boy, we rolled up corn silk and smoked it." He glanced over at Roger and winked. "You can have all that you want," he said, pointing with his chin at the husks and threads piling up around his feet.

"Never quite got the taste for corn smoking," Roger commented, recalling how his grandfather had let him inhale from a homemade cigarette when he was a boy. He had coughed the rest of the day from that one hit.

"Yeah, your generation is soft," Oris said.

"Can't smoke corn. Can't work a field. Can't stay married."

Roger smiled. He knew his former father-in-law would have to come back to his favorite topic. He was still upset about his daughter's divorce. "You're right, Oris. You're always right." He stood up from his chair and stretched. He reached in his front shirt pocket and pulled out a stick of gum. "I figure Malene already read you the riot act, so I'm not going to say anything about Fedora's complaint." He unwrapped the gum and stuck the piece in his mouth, wadding up the wrapper in his hand and sticking it his pocket. "But don't make me have to drive out here again this week," he noted. "I might just have to arrest you next time."

"Tell Fedora Snow to mind her own business," Oris responded.

"Don't incite her, Oris," Roger said, and he turned to walk to his car.

"You know Alex is hurting again," Oris said.

Roger turned around. He looked down and nodded. "Yes, Oris, I know. I'm on my way over there now." He faced the older man. "I suppose I'll see you at the birthday party?"

"I'm making my famous hot buttermilk cornbread to go with the cowboy beans," Oris replied. "And I bought Alex one of those new computer games he likes so much, ordered it off of the Internet over at the library in Silver City."

Roger smiled. "He'll like that." He turned around. "Just make sure to wear pants," he said, waving as he walked away.

Oris grinned, yanking the husk from another ear of corn. He watched in silence as the sheriff's car pulled away from the front of his house and moved down the street.

FIVE

"Sheriff, it's Loretta."

Roger had just pulled up into the driveway of Malene's house. He turned off the engine, reached over, pulled the radio transceiver toward his mouth, and pressed the button on the side. "Yeah, Loretta, Roger here." He released the button so he could hear what the dispatcher had to report. There was a lot of static because he was almost out of range. The equipment for the sheriff's department in Catron County was older than the sheriff.

"Fedora Snow is on the phone and wants to know if you arrested Mr. Whitsett."

Roger shook his head and blew out a long breath. "Tell Ms. Snow that her neighbor has promised not to walk around naked outside and that I saw no reason for an arrest." Without thinking, he reached for his shirt pocket. Having a cigarette at this time in the morning was typical for the sheriff. He chewed hard on his gum.

"She threatened to contact the state police" came the squeaky reply.

"Well, tell her she's more than welcome to notify other authorities, but also inform her that she needs to quit calling the police for non-emergencies and that it's not the state officers who are keeping her phone connected."

There was silence from the other end.

"You really want me to say all that?" Loretta asked.

Roger sighed. "Loretta, I don't care what you tell her, just don't call me again with her messages."

"Okay, over and out, Sheriff."

Roger returned the mouthpiece to the receiver and looked up at his ex-wife's front porch. He shook his head. It was filled with flowerpots overflowing with marigolds and petunias, red hot pokers and peppermint. There were jars of water with stems and pieces of green plants and plastic containers of black soil, probably embedded with seeds for the garden she would never grow.

He got out of the car and walked around to the rear of the house and came back pulling a water hose behind him. He turned on the sprayer and watered every pot except for the couple in the corner near the door filled with the plants and flowers already dead. He dropped his head in a kind of funeral prayer.

He knew Malene loved to try to grow things —she got that from her daddy—and every year she spent a week's pay buying annuals and perennials from a nursery down in Socorro, trying to add a little color around her house, trying to start a garden in pots on her porch, and every year she killed everything because she always forgot or didn't have time to water.

He finished spraying the plants and pulled the hose around the side of the house. When he returned to the front porch, he began pruning, pulling off some of the leaves withering on the bluebells and marigolds. He hated to see any plants or flowers suffer, and he figured that once again, for another summer, it would be up to him if Malene was going to keep anything alive and growing.

"Hey, Grandpa, you come to arrest me?" Alex was in his wheelchair just inside the screened front door.

"That's exactly why I'm here. I'm arresting you and your grandmother for the murder of all of these flowers." He threw the dead leaves in the yard and wiped his hands on the front of his pants. "I thought you were going to make sure she watered them this year," he added as he pulled open the door. He leaned in and gave his grandson a hug.

"She always forgets and leaves the hose where I can't reach it," the little boy explained, sitting up in his seat to receive the greeting. He handed his grandfather a can of soda and then leaned back and put his electric wheelchair in reverse. "Besides, she knows you'll take care of them."

Roger took the soda, walked in, wiped the sweat from his forehead with his handkerchief, and then stuck it in his back pocket. Even though it was still early, it was hot in Pie Town. "Frieda in the kitchen?" he asked, glancing around the corner.

"She's cleaning up my bedroom," Alex replied. "I was late getting up this morning," he added.

Roger nodded. "Thank you for this." He opened the soda, smiled, and then took a sip, wiping his mouth with the back of his hand. "I heard you had a bad time last night again."

Alex moved his chair forward and then in reverse and then forward again until he was directly across from the sofa in the front room. He shrugged. "It's just my legs again," he replied. "But I feel better now."

Roger walked into the den behind him and sat down on the sofa. "You are the trooper," he said.

"And you are the sheriff," the little boy replied.

They both smiled at the familiar lines they shared with each other.

Roger had been a steady and faithful presence in the life of his grandson even though he and Malene had been divorced years before he was born. Throughout their marriage and even after it was over, they had fought about a lot of things —about which side of the tracks to build their house, the profession he chose, how to care for their aging parents, what to do with their recalcitrant daughter—but once Alex was born and the diagnosis of spina bifida had been given, and then once Angel left, they had never fought again.

It was as if all of a sudden they both realized and accepted that their arguments were of no consequence, and the truth was, they both equally and deeply loved their grandson. Agreeing about that one true thing, their love for Alex, seemed to temper any possible reason they might ever again find to fight. Roger never even fussed very much over Malene's pitiful attempts at growing a garden. It didn't matter anyway, and Alex was right: they all knew Roger would once again end up watering and caring for every plant and flower she bought and stuck in a pot. Gardening had become like everything else they did together, easy and without explanation or argument.

Alex lived with Malene and she was his primary caregiver, but not a day passed without Roger stopping by to visit the little boy at home or talking to him on the phone or having lunch with him at the diner in town. Alex was the light of more than one person's world. And between Malene and Roger, and with Oris and his neighbors, the nurses who worked with Malene and the officers who worked with Roger, the priest and people from church, Alex was parented and grandparented and loved and watched over by everybody in the little town. He was the child the entire village raised. He was the soul of Pie Town.

"Sheriff Benavidez, I didn't know you were here." Frieda had rounded the corner.

"Hey, Frieda." He stood up in respect. "I just stopped by for a drink of grape soda and a wink at my grandson."

The older woman reached up, smoothing the sides of her hair, and smiled. "Alex is late getting up today," she commented.

Roger nodded as he sat back down. "I heard he had a rough night."

"Those legs of his," Frieda said with a clucking noise. "If only we could find something to stop that aching." She mouthed words that Roger knew to be a prayer while she made the sign of the cross, finishing with her fingers touching her lips.

Alex shifted gears on his wheelchair and backed up a bit. He faced Frieda. "I'm ready to do my math now," he announced.

She smiled. "I'll get the computer set up," she

said. She turned to Roger. "It's always good to see you, Sheriff." She nodded and walked out of the room.

"Math, huh?" Roger asked when she was gone. "I thought you were a science whiz. And why are you doing schoolwork in the summer anyway?"

"I like school," he answered. "And now I'm taking pre-algebra," Alex added, shifting his chair again to be closer to his grandfather.

"Pre-algebra?" Roger repeated. "Are you old enough to take pre-algebra?"

"When I pass the test in a couple of weeks, I can start taking algebra in the fall," the young boy responded with a grin.

"Well, I don't know where you got those skills," Roger noted. "It certainly wasn't from our side of the family." He placed his drink on the table in front of him, reached in his pocket, and took out the pack of gum. He sat forward, holding out the pack to Alex.

The little boy reached over, pulled out a stick, opened it, and popped it in his mouth. "Big Red," he said, naming the gum while he chewed.

Roger nodded. "Best chewing gum in the world."

Alex grinned.

"By the way, I saw your great-grandfather this morning. He's making buttermilk cornbread and cowboy beans for your birthday party." Roger took a stick from the pack and added it to the one he was already chewing, placing the pack back in his pocket.

Alex nodded. "It's a Pie Town tradition," he said. "Goes with the green chile stew Ms. Bea always makes." He chewed a bit more as the two sat in silence. "And the Spanish rice Mrs. Watson always brings." He paused. "You think Mom will make the party this year?" he asked.

Roger hesitated. He reached up and took the can of soda, finishing the drink in one long sip. He didn't answer at first.

Angel had been gone for more than ten years. She missed her son's party the previous year and the year before that. She had returned to Pie Town on his birthday about five years earlier. Alex had been in the hospital, and she didn't find out until she got home. She drove over to Albuquerque to see him, but he had been in surgery when she arrived. She left before he awoke. That was the last time she had been home.

Roger kept up with his daughter through friends in sheriff's departments across the state. The last he heard about Angel, she had moved up north, to Taos. She was working at a bar, living with some hippie. But that information had been delivered about a year before. He wasn't sure if she was still there or not.

He shook his head. "I don't know, Alex," he answered, rubbing the back of his neck. "Last time I talked to her, she didn't have a car or a phone."

There was a pause. They both listened to the noises outside. A dog was barking somewhere off in the distance, and they could hear the traffic from Highway 60. Frieda was humming in the back bedroom.

"Don't worry, Grandpa," Alex said, sounding much older than his almost eleven years. "She just needs to be somewhere else. Besides, I have a feeling there will be plenty of friends at the party, maybe even some new ones."

Roger looked at his grandson, wondering how he could be so forgiving, so understanding. He knew that the boy had a lot of people in his life who loved him, played with him, took care of him, but Roger knew there was never anyone who could take the place of a child's mother.

Everyone tried to pretend Angel wasn't necessary to Alex's growing-up, wasn't crucial to his healthy development. They tried to act like the town and family together were somehow enough, could somehow make up for her disappearance. But deep down everybody, especially his grandparents, worried that a boy without his mother, a boy abandoned by his one known parent, a boy as insightful and sharp and fragile as Alex, would always question and probably always mourn her absence.

"You want a clown or wagon rides this year?"

Roger asked, changing the subject away from talk about Angel. "Or have you gotten too old for that kind of thing now that you're taking algebra?"

Alex smiled. "I'd like music," he said. "The softball game and everybody we love laughing together and dancing to music."

Roger studied his grandson. He worried about the boy. He worried about his health and his disability, how he would grow up suffering so much. But in his short life, and unlike everyone else around him, Alex never appeared to be bothered by the way things were. He seemed to never regret what everyone else thought was missing.

"Then music you will have," Roger responded. "Because your grandfather does know some of the finest guitar pickers in Catron County."

"And that is probably because my grandfather *is* the best guitar picker in Catron County," the boy noted.

"You trying to sweet-talk me into letting you stay up all night for your birthday?" Roger asked as he stood to leave. "Because you know bribery is a misdemeanor in this state."

Alex grinned. "And you would know that because you are the sheriff," he said, backing up his wheelchair so his grandfather could pass.

"And you are the trooper," Roger responded, rubbing the boy's head as he walked out the door.

Alex moved his chair to follow him. "Don't forget the plants out back!" he yelled as Roger made his way off the porch.

And Roger threw up his hand to wave goodbye, picked up the hose he had left at the side of the house, and moved around the corner to finish the task of watering his ex-wife's neglected and scattered garden.

SIX

"No red icing." Malene spoke sharply into the receiver. "That red dye is not safe. I don't care what the FDA approved." She slipped the mouthpiece away from her lips. "I'll be right there, Mrs. Henderson," she said to the patient who was pulling on the edge of the counter at the nurses' station where Malene was on the phone. The older woman was trying to lift herself out of her seat. As soon as she stood, the alarm on her wheelchair sounded.

"Mrs. Henderson!" Malene called out. She dropped the phone and ran over to her patient. She got to Mrs. Henderson just as she wobbled but before she fell. Malene carefully placed her back in her seat. She turned off the small alarm clipped to the wheelchair and pulled a belt around her patient. "You cannot get up without help!" she shouted, tightening the belt. "You're going to fall again!"

"I just want my yellow pill," Mrs. Henderson said. "It's time for my yellow pill." She waved Malene away. "You people never give me the pill at the right time."

Malene pulled the wheelchair away from the station and placed her patient next to the wall, facing where she had just been trying to stand. "You had your pill at lunchtime, Mrs. Henderson," she said, her voice softer this time. "It was the yellow one, and you have it with meals. Please just sit over here for a bit while I finish my phone call," she added, "and then I'll take you back to your room. Your show starts in ten minutes. I'm trying to get Alex a birthday cake."

"Alex has a birthday?" The older woman perked up. "That sweet boy. How old is he now?" she asked, sounding clear and alert.

"He'll be eleven," Malene replied, walking back to the phone. She picked up the receiver and heard a dial tone. "They hung up," she said.

"Alex is the son of an angel, and he brings me the evening light."

Malene smiled. Like everyone in Pie Town, the residents at Carebridge loved Alex. Malene often brought him to the nursing home with her when she worked the second shift. He played bingo with the patients and helped serve meals.

It was his job to turn on the table lamps for every resident after dinner and say good-night. "That's exactly right, Mrs. Henderson. Alex brings us light." She placed the receiver back in the cradle. "Oh well, I guess I'll have to call back."

"What kind of cake are you getting?" Christine, one of the other nursing assistants, had walked into the station. She was young, just out of community college, and she often worked alongside Malene. Even though she was young enough to be Malene's daughter, they were friends.

"It should be yellow!" Mrs. Henderson yelled out. "A yellow cake with an angel."

"She say that she didn't get her pill?" Christine asked, noticing the patient next to the wall.

Malene nodded. "What is it with her and that yellow pill?" she asked. "Why does she get so worried about not taking that one?"

Christine shrugged. "I don't know. Maybe that's the one she thinks is keeping her alive."

"I can hear you," Mrs. Henderson noted, glaring at the two women talking about her. "Take me back to my room. My show is starting."

Christine rolled her eyes in the direction of Malene and walked over to the patient. "How many times has Erica been married?" she asked, referring to a character on the soap opera her patient watched. She had become familiar with the characters and the plotlines.

"Enough to know better than to jump in bed with that Adam Chandler again, I'll tell you that."

Christine released the brake on the wheelchair and pointed her patient in the direction of her room. "Well, maybe what Erica and Adam have is real love and it just takes two or three times to get it right."

"You should quit watching soap operas, Mrs. Henderson, it will turn your brain into mush," Malene called out to the woman as she was being wheeled down the hall.

"You should know better than anybody, Malene, that my brain is already mush." Mrs. Henderson's voice trailed away.

Malene smiled. She picked up the phone again and dialed the number of the grocery store. "Deli, please," she said, and she was connected to the bakery section.

"Hello, it's Malene Benavidez."

"Oh right," the woman on the other end responded. "No red icing," she recalled. "Did we get cut off or something?"

"Yes," Malene answered. "I'm sorry. It was my fault. I had to take care of something. Okay, so it's a full sheet cake, chocolate with white icing. And it should say, 'Happy Birthday Alex.' " She paused. "Do you have any little toy guitars?" she asked, thinking about the gift she and Roger were getting their grandson.

"Nope, just cowboys and balloons, a princess,

and a couple of Disney characters" came the reply.

"Can you make a guitar?" Malene asked.

"You mean out of icing?"

"Yeah, can you draw guitars on the cake?"

There was a sigh on the other end. "I can't, but I can get Ronnie to do it. He's real good at making pictures on cakes. He's an artist. He comes in early. I'll leave him a note."

"Perfect," Malene said.

" 'Happy Birthday, Alex.' Chocolate with white icing. No red. And some guitars somewhere on the cake." The girl in the bakery confirmed the order.

"Guitars on the corners, yes, and that's it," Malene noted.

The phone line went quiet, and Malene figured the girl was adding up the cost or writing down instructions. She didn't interrupt.

"It'll be ready for pickup Saturday morning."

"Thank you," Malene said and hung up the phone. When she turned around, Roger was standing in front of her, on the other side of the nurses' station.

"Hey," she said, looking surprised to see her ex-husband. He stopped by Carebridge on occasion, but usually he called first.

"Hey, Lena," he replied, calling her by the nickname he had given her when they were teenagers.

"You arrest Daddy?" she asked, wondering if that was why he was there to see her. She picked up a couple of folders and placed them in a file drawer beside her. "I can't make bail, so he's just going to have to wait it out behind bars."

"Nah, I didn't lock him up. He promised to keep his pants on from now on." Roger slid his hands into the back pockets of his pants. "Besides, I didn't want to have to do all that paperwork." He paused and then commented, "You didn't look too happy when you drove off." He was grinning.

Malene shook her head. "I really don't know what I'm going to do with him." She straightened up the papers around her. "I still don't know why he bought that new car. The one he had was fine."

"You know Oris. He likes a new Buick," Roger replied.

"Yes, I know Oris. I know Oris better than anybody, and I know he doesn't have the money to go buy a brand-new car."

"Oris has got more money than most," Roger noted. He glanced around, nodded at a few patients who were sitting close by. He called out their names, since he knew everybody at Carebridge. "I still think he's got some squirreled away that he hasn't told you about."

Malene had been managing her father's affairs since her mother died, and that had been not long after Angel was born, when she and Roger were married and they thought they would be able to handle anything. Her brother had joined the army just after he graduated from high school, and he was always on some base out of state. When it came to handling their parents, whether it was their mother's illness and death or their father's financial situation, Malene was the one in charge. She rolled her eyes at Roger. "If he had anything squirreled away, I can promise you that it's gone by now."

Christine came around the corner. "Hey, Sheriff, you taking a break from busting criminals?" she asked, punching him in the shoulder as she passed him. She moved into the station behind the counter with Malene.

"I came to get your payment for that speeding ticket you never paid," he replied, teasing her.

The young woman smiled. "I don't know what you're talking about," she answered, sounding very coy. "I never got any speeding ticket. Danny gave me a warning."

"Danny let you off the hook because you batted those big brown eyes in his direction and because he has a big crush on you, but I'm the sheriff, and I saw you speed past the work zone, and I say you need to pay." He pulled his hands out of his pockets. "And why don't you give that boy a break and go out with him?"

"Because Danny White was born and raised in

Pie Town and that's the only place he wants to live. I'm aiming for better things," she said. "I got places to go."

"And just where are you planning to go?" Roger asked.

"I'm not sure yet. I just know I don't want to stay here," the young woman answered.

"Why?" Malene asked. "What's wrong with Pie Town?" She was working on updating her patients' charts.

"What's wrong with Pie Town?" Christine repeated the question and stared at her coworker. "Are you kidding me? This place has nothing to offer somebody my age." She considered what she was saying. "Shoot, it doesn't have anything to offer somebody any age. There's no stores, no decent restaurants, nothing to do. You can't even get a cell signal unless you climb Escondido Mountain. There's not even any pie, for Christ's sake. All they serve at the diner for dessert is brownies! Why would anyone want to live in Pie Town?"

Malene shrugged. "It's a great place to hike and ride horses and be outdoors," she replied.

"When's the last time you hiked a trail or rode a horse?" Christine asked.

"If I had time it would be a great place to do those things," Malene responded. "But regardless, it's got more to offer than just that anyway."

"What else?" Christine asked.

"It's safe," Roger answered, tapping his badge.

"Right," Malene agreed. "And the folks are nice and helpful. You won't find this small-town generosity in a big city."

Christine laughed. "This town is not generous. You ever asked anybody for a loan in Pie Town?" she asked. "And as far as the folks being helpful, when's the last time you tried to organize them to do something for anybody? You remember what a hard time we had trying to raise money for a van for the senior center?"

Malene thought about the question. "Well, as a community, we are a little uncooperative, I'll give you that. But everybody knows everybody, and you can't get lost."

"A little uncooperative?" Christine repeated. "We can't agree with each other about anything. We don't hang holiday lights because some people want snowflakes and others want Christmas trees. We don't have a July Fourth parade because some people claim we're still oppressed by a government and that we're not really independent. We can't have a library because everybody wants to say what books get put in there. It's like we take pride in not getting along with each other in this town. I think everybody ought to sell their land to the government, let them bulldoze Pie Town, and build some more radio towers like they did near Magdalena. At least then we'd be sending out some signals in the world other than indifference and orneriness."

"Oh Christine, it's not that bad," Roger chimed in. "We get along on some things. We accepted the state's stimulus money to repave the highways."

"Yeah, but didn't we have to pay it back because we could never decide on a bid from a construction company?" It was Malene who asked.

"We can still have it when we make a decision," he replied.

"See what I mean?" Christine said. "It's like the only time we get together is for Alex's birthday parties. Beyond that, we got nothing here, and I'm just saying, as soon as I save up enough money I'm heading out of this godforsaken place."

"Well, before you leave town, just make sure you pay your ticket," Roger said. "Or I'll send Danny to find you and bring you back."

"Yes sir, Sheriff." She stood at attention and saluted Roger. "Now I know why Malene divorced you—because you are no fun at all!" She grinned at the two of them. "I'm going to give Mrs. Otero her meds," she noted and walked out of the station. "You let me know if he's harassing you," she called out to her coworker. "I'll call the deputy."

Malene laughed. "So what's up?" she asked, wondering why her ex-husband had stopped by.

"I went by the house after I saw you to check on Alex."

"Was he out of bed?" Malene asked.

Roger nodded. "He wanted to do math," he answered.

"He is very smart with his numbers." Malene studied her ex-husband. "What's wrong?" she asked. She knew her ex-husband rarely did anything without thought and purpose. She could see that he had come to the nursing home to talk to her about something. "Was everything all right?" she asked. "Was Frieda there?"

Roger nodded reassuringly. "He's fine," he answered. "Everything was fine." He paused. "You know, you need to water those plants twice a day," he commented, recalling the pitiful shape her flowers and vegetables were in.

"I know," she said. "You tell me that every year."

"And every year you don't listen."

Malene was used to the lecture, and she waited for more of his speech on plant care, but Roger didn't say anything else about it.

"He asked about Angel," he finally explained. He stood up straight, dropped his arms by his side, and shifted his weight from side to side. The toothpick dangled from his lips.

Malene knew that Roger had quit smoking and that he had been without a cigarette for almost four weeks. She also knew that was a record for him. Because she had been with him when he had tried before to quit, she knew he was chewing on anything he could find. He liked gum and toothpicks best, but she had known him to chew on pieces of hay and the ends of pencils when he was desperate. Malene didn't respond.

"You think I should try to find her?" he asked. He rested his hands on his hips, waiting for her reply.

Malene didn't answer right away. She thought about Angel, how much like her father she was, how much he loved her. She had his frame, his dark hair and eyes. Angel had always been a spitting image of her father. Malene looked away. She knew how much he still missed her.

When Angel was a little girl, the father-daughter duo had been inseparable. He doted on her night and day, bought her everything she ever wanted, taught her everything he knew about riding horses, fixing a car engine, reading animal tracks. She was the biggest tomboy in Pie Town, and there was nobody more important to their daughter than her father. When Angel became a teenager, gave up those childish games, learned to drive, and started making her own way, it had been hard on Malene, but it had been harder on Roger. He hated watching his little girl grow up. And unfortunately she didn't do it well or easily.

Malene and Roger had argued before their divorce, but their fights had been nothing like the fights he had with Angel when she turned fifteen and started hanging out with the Romero boys and that girl from Omega. Those fights lasted two years, and then she was pregnant and then she was gone. And Roger and Malene and their marriage and Angel's little boy were all left in the wake of their daughter's destruction.

Malene shook her head. "I don't see the point, Roger," she finally replied. She went back to filing papers, straightening up the area around her.

"I could just check to see if she's still up north. I can call my buddy up there, and he could stop by the bar, the last place we have on record where she worked, and just ask a few questions." He hesitated.

She glanced at the clock. It was getting late and she still had six sponge baths to complete and eight beds to change. She had to finish charting her daily duties and still work on a new admission scheduled to arrive before she left. She faced her ex-husband. "Alex always asks if his mother is coming to his birthday parties. He asks if she's going to come at Christmas and at Easter and how to send her a card at Mother's Day." She shrugged. "He always asks, but he never seems devastated when she's not there. Disappointed maybe, but not devastated." She picked up the folders that needed her notes. "Just let it go, Roger. She knows it's her son's birthday. If she wants to show up, she will." She looked down at the forms she still had to complete. "I'm way behind. I got to get some work done."

Roger slid the toothpick from side to side in his mouth. "Yeah, I know. I'm sorry I bothered you. You're right. I know. I need to leave her alone. I guess Christine is right. This town isn't for everybody." He pulled out the toothpick, seemed like he wanted to say something else but didn't, stuck the toothpick back in his mouth, and nodded his good-bye. He turned to walk away.

"He ask you about the music?" Malene spoke before he got too far down the hall.

Roger turned around and nodded with a smile. "There will be music," he replied and turned around again.

"See you tomorrow, Roger," Malene called out.

He nodded and kept walking, while Malene opened a folder and picked up a pen.

"He still looking for Angel, trying to bring her home?" Christine was back from giving meds to her patient.

"He'll never stop," Malene replied. She jotted down a few notes and picked up another folder.

"Is that why you broke up?" Christine asked. She sat down in the chair next to Malene.

Malene turned to the younger woman. She shook her head. "No," she answered. "That wasn't why we broke up."

Christine waited for more from Malene, but her colleague kept working on her files. Christine sat down and pulled out the schedule for the following week. She hadn't noticed before that it had been completed. "I got six shifts," she said, going over the next week's assignments and sounding perturbed. "I told Shirley I only wanted five."

"We're short-staffed again," Malene noted. "I'm working six too. They're trying to hire somebody."

"Hiring somebody and keeping somebody are two different things," Christine said. She put the schedule back in its place beside the phone. "Well, I guess I can use the money, right? So why did you break up then?" she asked, returning to the earlier topic of conversation.

Malene finished her charts and placed them back on the chart rack. "I got a lot of work to do, Christine," she replied.

The younger woman could see that she was being dismissed and that Malene wasn't going to answer any more of her questions about her former marriage. She had never really given a reason for the divorce, and Christine was always curious. She watched as Malene hunted for her supplies to give baths. "Doesn't matter anyway," she said. "You might as well not be divorced. Y'all act like every married couple I know. You're worse than that couple on Mrs.

Henderson's soap opera." She found a bath cloth on the counter, picked it up, and threw it at Malene. "I say, you should just get back together. Then maybe he wouldn't come around here so much and you'll quit being so bossy."

Malene took the cloth and folded it, adding it to the supplies she had gathered. "Thank you, Christine. I'll keep your advice in mind the next time I have a minute to think about Roger and me." And she headed out of the nurses' station and down the hall to finish her work.

SEVEN

"It makes a little rattle when I rev up the engine." Oris was talking to Frank, the town mechanic. Frank had his head under the hood, listening for the noise Oris had called about earlier that morning when he made an appointment for an oil change.

"Hit the gas again," Frank called out, and Oris bore down on the pedal.

Frank waited a second and then finally pulled his head out and closed the hood. "I don't hear it, Oris. It sounds fine." He wiped his hands on the rag he had hanging from his back pocket, then held the rag and waited. He was tall, and he wore his black hair in a long ponytail that hung down his back.

"Listen again. I swear there's a rattle." Oris was seated behind the wheel of his new Buick. He revved up the engine again and waited.

Frank shook his head, confirming what he had just said—he couldn't hear anything.

"I thought you Indians could hear things the rest of us couldn't." Oris turned off the engine and swung his legs around, placing his feet on the ground. It was hot and he was sweating.

Frank walked over to Oris. "That's your wife's people, Zuni, they're the trackers, the ones with good ears. For us, it's just another myth, Oris, just like the one that claims we aren't good at business. You owe me twenty dollars for the oil change." He stood next to the open door. Frank was Navajo, and his family had been in Catron County for generations.

"I was told that my oil changes were free for the first year of ownership," Oris responded. He stepped out of the car. "You see the size of the trunk?" he asked.

Frank rolled his eyes. He had seen the trunk.

"If you take it back to the dealership in Albuquerque. Do I look like I sell Buicks here?" Frank asked, glancing around at his garage.

Oris reached into his back pocket and pulled out his wallet. He fished out a twenty-dollar bill and handed it to the other man. "What happened to the good old days when we traded in tobacco and animal skins?" he asked, putting his wallet back. He yanked up his pants and stuck his thumbs in his belt loops.

Frank took the money and stuffed it in the front pocket of his coveralls. He wiped his hands again and returned the rag to his back pocket. "We got screwed is what happened. Now it's cash only, my friend." He winked at Oris.

"How's your mother?" Oris asked. "I haven't seen her since the graduation." He recalled seeing all of Frank's family when Frank's son graduated from high school. Even though Oris didn't have any young people in his family finishing school, he liked to attend the special ceremonies. He went every year just to see how the children had grown.

"My mother and all my family are well, thank you," Frank replied. "They don't travel much in the summer. They stay up in the mountains where it's cool."

"And your boy," Oris hesitated, trying to recall the name. "Raymond," he remembered. "He still heading off to the army later this month?"

Frank nodded. "Getting ready to go to boot camp, and against my better wishes," he answered. "But what's a father to do?" He shrugged.

Oris leaned against his car and then pulled away because of the heat. "He'll get a good salary, learn a decent trade. It's not all bad, the military I mean."

Frank didn't respond.

"Could be worse," Oris noted. "Could be screwed up on drugs, locked up in jail, living with hippies in Taos."

Frank looked at Oris. They both knew he was talking about his granddaughter Angel.

Frank had not asked about Alex's mother in a long time. The news never seemed to change, and it always appeared to be an uncomfortable topic for Oris, and Angel's parents, Roger and Malene. At first, everyone in town thought she would give up whatever she was chasing and come home. They all agreed it was just that she was trying to figure things out, needed a little break from Pie Town, suffered from postpartum depression, or was trying to find the baby's father. But that was ten years ago. Frank, like most of the others in town, quit asking about Angel once Alex was old enough to understand the questions and understand his family's embarrassment or discomfort in answering them.

He nodded at his older friend.

"Ah, but that's the way of being young, isn't it?" Oris asked, not expecting an answer. "Lord knows I did my share of stupid things when I was a teenager." He laughed and shook his head. "And if my memory serves me, seems like you did a stint in the army. Doesn't look like it screwed you up too bad."

Frank glanced down at the ground. "There

wasn't a war when I signed up," he said. "The worst thing I saw in four years was some of the recruits suffer from heat stroke at boot camp. I was stationed in North Carolina and Georgia. It was just boarding school for me. Raymond's likely to face a whole lot more that I don't think he's cut out for. He's soft."

Oris considered Frank's assessment of his son. "The boy might surprise you, Frank," Oris concluded. "Could turn out to be a hell of a soldier. My boy's done okay."

Frank just looked at Oris.

" 'Course, it doesn't matter anyway, everybody has to find their own way. Seems like I remember you telling Roger that a few years ago."

Frank nodded, remembering the conversation he had with the sheriff when Angel left town after Alex was born. He and Roger had been friends since they were kids.

"I suppose you and his mother have carried him strapped on your backs for as long as you can," Oris added.

"I guess you're right about that," Frank responded.

Neither of the men spoke for a few minutes, and then Frank glanced up at the sky behind Oris. "Looks like yesterday's storm is finally coming in," he noted. "Or bad company."

Oris didn't even turn around to look at the sky. "I'm not falling for that Indian crap. If you can't hear the rattle in my engine, I'm not going to believe that you can read the sky for a weather report or ghost sighting."

Frank shrugged. "Suit yourself."

The two men glanced at the street. A car was turning in their direction.

Following it with their eyes as it stopped and pulled in, they both recognized the car and the driver.

"Mrs. Romero needs her tires rotated," Frank said, acknowledging his next customer.

Oris watched as the car pulled in behind his Buick. He turned back to Frank. "Mrs. Romero has had those tires since the 1980s," he commented. "Seems like to me they need more than just rotating."

Both men waited as the woman steered her car around them and then stopped beside Oris's, parked, and stepped out. "Hello, Oris," Mary said as a greeting to the man she had known all of her life. She was carrying her purse on her arm. She was wearing a pink dress and high-heeled shoes.

"Mary," he said in reply. He made a slight smile. "You going to a wedding?" he asked. "Or did you get dressed up for Frank here?"

"It's Wednesday, Oris," she replied.

He waited, not understanding her reference. "What? Nobody gets married on a Wednesday?" he finally asked.

She made a *humph* and turned to Frank. "Can you fit me in?" she asked the mechanic.

"Of course," Frank replied. "Oris, always a pleasure," he said as he nodded at his other customer. "You should get out of this heat," he said to the older man, whose face was reddened by the sun. "It's not good for white skin."

Oris wiped his forehead but stayed where he was. "I'll see you at the birthday party," he said, referring to Alex's weekend party. "Hey, how about bringing me a soda from your cooler?" he asked. "A little service can go a long way with customer loyalty."

Frank grinned and walked over to Mary's car and sat down in the driver's side. The keys were still in the ignition, and he cranked the car and pulled it into the open garage bay.

Oris stood at his car next to Mary Romero. "So you're going to have to help me out here, Mary," he said. "What happens on Wednesday?"

"I go to Mass in the morning, and then I drive out to be with Clarence," she replied, appearing as if she didn't care to talk to the man questioning her.

"Mary," Oris responded, trying to sound sympathetic, "Clarence is dead."

"I know Clarence is dead!" she shouted, pulling her arms around her waist, her purse slamming against her hip. "I go to the cemetery and eat lunch with him every Wednesday," she explained.

"Somebody serves food at the cemetery?" he asked, appearing bewildered.

She blew out a long breath and rolled her eyes. "Not that it's any of your business, but I take my own lunch, an enchilada and some chips," she said.

"You take Clarence anything?" Oris asked. "Or do you just eat in front of him making him even more envious of the fact that he's dead and can't have lunch?"

A young boy, a summer worker at Frank's garage, came toward Oris and Mary with a couple of cans of soda. "Mr. Frank says you owe me two dollars." He handed them the drinks.

"Well, for God's sake," Oris complained. He pulled out his wallet and got two one-dollar bills. "You should find somewhere else to work, young man. Frank Twinhorse is a bad influence."

The boy shrugged and turned away, stuffing the bills into his pockets.

Both Oris and Mary popped open their drinks and took long swallows.

"So what were we talking about?" Oris asked. Before Mary answered, he recalled the conversation. "Oh, that's right. You're eating lunch at your husband's grave, and you were getting ready to tell me what you take him to eat."

"He likes posole," she answered.

Oris smiled. "Well, now that's the truth," he noted. "Green chile on the side?" he asked.

Mary turned to face the man. She seemed to

soften. "Of course, green chile on the side. How else would I serve my loving husband?"

Oris laughed.

"You used to eat lunch together every week," she said, recalling the friendship her husband had with Oris.

He nodded. "At the café. Tuesday special. He'd get his posole and green chile. I'd have a burger."

"He used to tell me you were always trying to find somebody to pay for your meal." She laughed and took another swallow.

"That is not true. Clarence is the cheapest man I ever knew. I was always having to pick up the check for him." He shook his head. "He said he never had any money because you spent it all on shoes."

They both glanced down at the woman's shoes. They were dressy sandals, and they looked new.

"I have my own money," Mary said. "Always have. And besides, you're the one who's cheap," she added. She glanced behind Oris. "Except for your cars, Oris Whitsett. When did you buy this one?" she asked.

Oris looked behind him at his new Buick. "Got a nice trade-in a few weeks ago, down at the dealership in Albuquerque. She's a beauty, isn't she? You should see the size of that trunk." He took a sip of his drink, wiped his mouth with the back of his hand. "A man is only as good as the car he drives."

Mary shook her head. "Clarence said you wasted a lot of money buying so many cars and trading them in."

"Clarence drove a pickup truck that didn't have a floorboard. He never bought a new car his whole life."

"Clarence liked tractors," Mary commented, remembering her husband and how he spent his money.

Oris nodded. "Well, yes, he did. Clarence did not mind forking over money for expensive farm equipment." He turned to Mary. "He ever take you out in his tractor?" he asked.

Mary rolled her eyes. "I wear high heels, Oris. I don't ride in tractors."

Oris laughed, drinking some more of his soda.

"I remember when the four of us used to go out. You always had to drive. Do you remember that?" she asked, but before he could answer she added, "Alice was so beautiful. She always got so dressed up for dinner."

Oris didn't respond at first. He just nodded his head. "She was like you about that," he noted. "Alice loved to get dressed up and go out."

Mary took a long swallow. She reached in her purse and took out a tissue, blotted her lips.

"So, you waiting here for Frank to finish and then driving out to the cemetery?" he asked, glancing up at her.

"Yes, I was planning to wait," she replied.

"Well, why don't I drive you?" he asked. "Maybe I'll stop and get a burger, and we can eat together and really piss Clarence off." He smiled.

Mary knew Alice was buried in the same cemetery. She guessed that Oris wanted to go so that he could visit his wife's grave. "Did you take the driver's test this year?" she asked, eyeing him closely.

"I did not," he answered. "But I've been driving seventy years, and I've never even as much as run over a skunk or landed in a ditch."

"There's a first time for everything," Mary said.

"Not in my new Buick," he replied. "You're safe as a Catholic schoolgirl at choir practice."

Mary smiled. "I'll just go and tell Frank that I'll be back to pick up the car."

Oris nodded and finished his soda. He crushed the can and tossed it in a garbage can near the building. He was back at his car not long before Mary. They both got in, and he started the engine and backed out of the driveway.

After stopping at the diner for his lunch, Oris headed down Highway 60, toward the cemetery located about ten miles out of town. They had made the curve, just past the cutoff to the dirt road that meandered down to the creeks, just a couple of miles from their destination, when Oris swerved and slammed on his brakes.

Another car, coming from the opposite direction, had suddenly veered into his lane and Oris almost hit it.

The two of them, Oris and Mary, were so shaken by the near miss, so rattled by what almost happened and didn't, that they never even noticed who was walking on the other side of the road. They never saw the girl who stood watching the entire event, the one standing in the dust, her thin arms wrapped around her belly, the girl who seemed to come out of nowhere. Neither of them saw her standing near the other car, the one that almost hit them, now stopped, which, just like the girl, had been heading right straight into the center of Pie Town.

EIGHT

Father George Morris was driving the car loaned to him by the Diocese of Western New Mexico. He didn't have a vehicle of his own. This one was a clunker, an old station wagon given to the church by a woman on her deathbed. The parish priest in Gallup tried to give it back, knowing her husband or sons would need it, could sell it, or would certainly use it, but the woman insisted that the car belonged to the church.

In turn, the priest gave it to the diocese and

they also tried to return it to the rightful family. But once the dead woman's decision had been made, no one, not her spouse or children or siblings, would take the car back. They claimed that the car was cursed and that it bore the spirits of the woman's dead parents. The family claimed that she gave the car to the church not because she was charitable or wanting to show her gratitude, but because she was trying to save the rest of her family from the fate she had suffered. Nobody wanted anything to do with that car.

Of course, no one at the diocese had given this information to young Father Morris. He thought the car was a perk, an added benefit for all new parish priests in New Mexico. He figured it was intended to be used for providing transportation to church members and for parish activities. He thought the car needed some work, a good cleaning, maybe a tune-up, but he was happy to have the vehicle and accepted it with humility and grace.

Once he got on the road, he experienced some difficulty getting the hang of managing pedals and gears—he hadn't driven a car for more than seven years—but after an hour he finally remembered how it was done. He turned on the radio, found a Catholic station, and rolled down the windows since the air conditioning was not working.

Father George was hoping to make Mass on that Wednesday, his first day, but he had been held up at the diocese filling out some last-minute forms and had called to inform the older priest who was covering for him that he wouldn't arrive until late that evening.

It was just about lunchtime when he opened the map that the Monsignor had given him to see how far down Highway 60 he would travel before coming to his first parish and the rectory where he would live in Pie Town. He had made better time than he expected and was hopeful he could grab a bite to eat when he got into town. He glanced down just for an instant to study the map, but it was an instant almost too long. When he looked back up, he had drifted into the other lane, almost running into a brand-new silver Buick, the driver and the passenger screaming as he veered back into his lane. He was so shaken up by the experience that he pulled to the side of the road and stopped. In the rearview mirror he could see that the Buick hit the brakes as well, but then kept going in the opposite direction.

He dropped his head on the steering wheel and prayed a short prayer of thanksgiving. When he raised his head a girl was standing right in front of his car, staring at him through the windshield. He watched as she walked around to the driver's side.

"Hey," she said. "You okay?" She leaned down to see into the car.

He nodded quickly, his white-knuckled fingers

still clutching the steering wheel. “I looked away and almost hit that car,” he confessed. He glanced up at the young woman who was peering at him through the opened window and then quickly faced ahead. She appeared to be not much older than a teenager. She was wearing shorts and a tight T-shirt, strange-looking moccasin shoes, and carrying a small but bulging backpack.

“I know,” she responded. “I watched you.”

Father Morris looked around. He didn’t know where this girl had come from.

As if she understood his confusion, she explained. “I was walking. I was just behind over there.” She turned, casting her glance behind the car.

Father George peered into the rearview mirror, as if he would find something marking where she meant. “I was trying to read the map,” he explained without making eye contact.

She stood up. She dropped her backpack and stretched her arms above her head, and this time the priest was watching. Her shirt came up a bit, and he was sitting right beside her exposed midriff. He blushed, cleared his throat, stared straight ahead, wondering how he could make his exit.

“So, are you lost?” She reached in her pocket, pulled out a tube of lip balm, rubbed her lips, put the tube back, and then bent down again, picking up the backpack and balancing it on her back.

He fiddled with the map, without looking in her direction. "I think I'm okay," he answered, noticing that she now smelled like cherries, like cherry gum he used to chew when he was a boy.

" 'Cause I'm a good navigator," she explained. "I could get you where you're heading. I've got experience in that kind of thing."

Father George could easily see what she was asking. He felt his heartbeat quicken. He couldn't remember the last time he had sat in a car with a young woman. The idea made him very uncomfortable, but before he could say anything, before he could explain that it wasn't a good idea for them to travel together, she had walked around the car and was opening the passenger-side door.

"I, I . . ." he stuttered, something he hadn't done in months, a childhood malady that had disappeared with puberty but came back briefly while he was in his last year at seminary. "I, uh, don't think I can let you ride with me." He finally got the whole sentence out.

The girl stood with the door opened and leaned in. "Why not?" she asked.

The priest felt the line of sweat beading across his top lip. "I, I . . ." He stuttered again. "I don't have insurance for riders." He lied. He knew it as soon as the words left his mouth, he lied. He had told himself never again, and now, quick as taking his eyes off the road and almost wrecking the car, it had happened again.

"Oh," she said, standing up straight outside the car. "Well," she paused, "I guess it's a good thing I don't care about that." She took off the backpack, threw it behind the front seat, jumped in, and shut the door. "I'll also put some air in your tires when we get to town. Your right front one is a little low."

Father George turned to the girl, trying to think of a way to get her out of the car. He could imagine the scandal he would cause upon his arrival at his first parish with a young woman, not much older than a teenager, seated next to him in his car. A young woman scantily clad. A young woman hitchhiking. A girl putting air in his tires. He turned a bright shade of red as he considered what the other priest would think when he drove into town with her in his car.

"Trina," she held out her hand to shake. "I'm Trina, and I'm going just up the road to Pie Town. You don't mind giving me a lift, do you?"

Father George inhaled, muttered a prayer under his breath. "I'm George," he said, taking Trina's hand. "Father George Morris," he added.

"Then, Father George Morris, we only got about ten minutes before we pull into Pie Town and likely never cross paths again." She pulled her hand away and grabbed the map from the priest. "Now, where is it that you're headed?" she asked. "And is it a wedding or a funeral?"

He seemed not to understand the question. He glanced down at his clothes and suddenly realized she was asking because he was wearing his clergy collar and his black shirt and pants. She had obviously assumed he was on his way to officiate at some service.

"Oh, neither," he replied. "I'm just starting my new job."

"Fabulous," she responded. "I plan to start a new job today too." She smiled. "Or maybe tomorrow, since it's a bit late now." She noticed the clock on the dashboard. It was after one o'clock. "And where is your new job?" she asked. "Not that I would really know," she said. "I'm from Texas." She leaned back against the seat and closed her eyes. "God, it feels good to sit down," she said. She looked over at the driver. "I've been walking for two days," she added.

"Where are you coming from?" he asked. He had not yet taken the car out of park, and the engine was still idling. He wondered where her family was, how long she had been traveling alone.

Trina considered the question. She wasn't quite sure how to answer. She was from Texas, but had just come from Tucson, having left the man she thought had finally taken her away from everything bad in her life, everything broken and wrong. And then there was the Indian woman in Apache land who was part of the reason she was moving east and slightly to the north.

"Well, that's not as important as where I'm going." She reached up and placed her hands behind her head. "Don't you think it's where you're going that's more important than where you've been?"

The priest considered the question. He finally let go of the steering wheel. "I guess you could have a point," he responded. "So then, why are you going to Pie Town?" he asked, not sure why he was engaging in conversation with the talkative young woman. He mostly wanted to figure out a way to get her out of his car.

"I just heard about Pie Town, New Mexico, and decided it was a town I needed to visit. Just sounds friendly, don't you think?" She closed her eyes, trying not to think about Tucson, trying not to think about her dreams and hopes all wrapped up in a smooth-talking man from Abilene.

"Pie Town," she repeated. "Sounds nice. I mean, who doesn't like pie, right?" She decided not to mention the dream and the woman who read her mind. Trina turned to the priest, who wasn't answering, and then began glancing around her, lifting her nose in the air. "This car smells funny, don't you think?" she asked, sniffing.

Father George sniffed as well. "I don't smell anything," he replied.

Trina looked behind her. "It's something," she said. "Smells like a funeral parlor I was once in. Like fruit that's too ripe."

Father George raised his nose and smelled again. He shook his head. "No, I don't notice anything."

The two of them sat in silence for a few moments.

"So, Father George Morris, are you going to put her in gear and get back on the highway, or are we going to sit here on the side of the road while everyone passes and stares, thinking we're up to no good." She winked at the priest. She liked knowing she made him uneasy.

He blushed. "I'm not comfortable driving," he explained. "It's been a while since I drove."

She shrugged and leaned in his direction. "Oh well, that's okay. You want to scoot over and let me?" she asked, sitting up, holding on to the steering wheel as if she expected him to slide under her. "I'm a good driver," she commented. "I started driving a truck with my granddaddy when I was eleven. I even helped drive a big rig across Highway 10."

"No, no . . . what?" He was confused and tried pushing her away. "I'm not scooting over," he acknowledged, sounding very shocked by the suggestion.

She sat back in her seat. "Fine, have it your way, Padre," she said. She folded her arms across her chest. "But you're not really thinking about putting me out to walk eight miles in this heat, are you?" she asked. She glanced out the window. "And I'm pretty sure it's going to rain. Did you see those clouds? It's trouble ahead, for sure."

He didn't respond.

She raised herself up, trying to make eye contact with the driver.

"I mean, leaving a girl to fend for herself in a hundred degrees, all alone, without water or good walking shoes, that's a bigger sin than sitting close to her, right?" She studied the man.

He sighed, knowing he was beat, knowing he had no choice, and put the car into gear. He closed his eyes and crossed himself. "You need to put on your seat belt," he instructed.

She smiled, clapped her hands together, and reached beside her to pull the belt across her waist. It clicked, and he pulled onto the road.

"You're young to be a priest, aren't you?" she asked as they drove along.

"It's my first parish," he replied. "You're young to be hitchhiking, aren't you?"

She shrugged again. "I wouldn't say that. I've been hitching rides since before I learned to drive. It's not such a big deal where I'm from," she said. She pulled her legs up and placed her feet on the dashboard.

"Texas?" Father George asked. He watched where she put her feet and considered saying something about the inappropriateness of it, but decided against it.

"That's right," she responded, slapping her thighs, thinking about her home state, her hometown, deciding not to take the trip down memory lane. "So, you never told me where you're headed," she reminded him.

"Pie Town too, I guess," he answered. "It's one of my three parishes, and I figured I would start there. It's the one with a parish house." He loosened up a bit as they drove down the highway.

"You'll live alone?" she asked.

He nodded. "That's usually the way it works. A few of the ladies in the church cook and clean, but unless there are sisters in the parish, nuns, I mean, then I live in the house alone."

"You get a whole house to yourself and a cook and a maid?" Trina asked, her tone one of surprise.

Father George considered how his arrangement must sound to a layperson. "I guess that's about the way of things," he answered.

"Damn," Trina responded, without seeming even to notice that a curse word had just escaped her lips. "That's pretty sweet. Last place I lived, there were three of us sharing a two-room apartment, and that's the most space I've ever had. When I was kid, we always had a bunch of people staying around, sleeping on the floors, on the sofa, on the back porch. Then, in the foster homes, well, there were so many kids in those houses, you were lucky just to have a place to sit at the table to eat."

George didn't answer. He just glanced over at his passenger, wondering about her upbringing, wondering from what circumstances she had emerged. "So, Trina, how old are you?" he asked, trying to sound fatherly, trying to erase the discomfort in his voice as well as in his thoughts. There was something about the girl that troubled him.

"Twenty," she answered. "Not that it really matters."

"Why wouldn't it matter?" he responded.

"I think age is just a way we use to judge people. You hear how old somebody is, and based on their answer, you decide that they must be a certain way. If we never knew the ages of each other, maybe we wouldn't be so, I don't know, critical."

"But sometimes the age of a person does tell us a lot about them. A twenty-year-old hasn't had the same experiences as a forty-year-old. She hasn't seen all the things that an older person has." He turned to Trina, suddenly remembering himself at twenty, not so many years before, remembering parts of his youth he had tried to forget. He turned back to face the road.

She studied the priest. "I figure I've seen more

than most forty-year-olds. I figure I've seen more than most anybody." She pulled at the seat belt stretched across her lap, lifting it away from her body.

"Aren't you going to be hot wearing that black outfit out here?" she asked, changing the subject.

Father George glanced down at his shirt and pants. He hadn't really thought about any alternatives to the orthodox attire he was given. Priests in Ohio, at his home parish and at seminary, wore only black pants and a black shirt. They had robes and other clothes for particular services and events, but on most days a priest wore his black. "I'm sure I will be comfortable where I reside and work," he replied.

"You're not from around here, are you?" she asked. "What, the Midwest maybe, huh? You're too pasty to have grown up in the desert. You got a snakebite kit and water bottles?" she asked. "Boots?"

Father George smiled. "I thought it didn't matter where you're from," he teased. "I thought it only mattered where you're going."

She nodded, enjoying the banter. "Well, that's true, but if you're not from here, there are things you have to learn pretty fast or you won't make it."

"Yeah, and what are those things?" he asked.

"Boots are better than shoes when it comes to stepping on rattlesnakes. It's bread, not water, that takes the sting out of spicy food, and never give up your water rights or leave home without a gallon of it in your backseat." She stretched her right arm out the car window.

Father George turned to the young girl and thought about her instructions. "You learn all this from experience or did somebody teach you this information?"

"A bit of both, I guess. I saw a boy get bit by a rattler right on the ankle. He had on some fancy ball shoes, trying to impress a girl riding by on a horse. His daddy whipped him raw when he found out he wasn't wearing his boots out in the field. The doctor visit and medicines cost him more than he made all month." She paused. "Boots cover your leg about as high as a snake can strike," she noted.

The priest didn't respond.

She continued. "The spicy food tip I learned on my own after taking a bet from one of my cousins that I could eat a jar of peppers, and the stuff about water I just heard the old folks talking."

Father George thought about her answer. He wasn't sure if she was serious or not, but he did think her suggestion of keeping some water with him wasn't a bad idea. He turned back to face the road just as they passed the sign that read, WELCOME TO PIE TOWN.

"We're here!" Trina said, sounding excited,

sounding as if she had arrived at some point of safety, some destination of possibility.

Father George wiped the line of sweat off of his top lip. He took in a deep breath, trying to calm his stomach as he felt it do a long, exaggerated flip.

And just like that, the clouds broke and the rain fell.

NINE

Roger was at his usual table, the one in the center at Pie Town Diner, when the station wagon pulled into the parking lot. Alex was sitting across from him. They had just ordered lunch, and they were watching the storm as it rolled in. They ate most of their noon meals downtown at the diner, but they especially enjoyed eating there on Wednesdays. The Wednesday special was chicken and dumplings, and Alex loved chicken and dumplings. He never missed a Wednesday unless he was sick.

"We have guests," Alex reported as the car came to a stop in a space just by the front door. Like most of the residents, he knew everybody in Pie Town and what kind of car they drove, so he knew when there were travelers and strangers passing through. “You think they just stopped because of the rain or are they here for pie?” he asked Francine, the waitress who was still standing next to the table, and then grinned.

Everybody in Pie Town was used to the tourists driving Highway 60 from Albuquerque to Phoenix who stopped at the diner and asked for pie. With a name like Pie Town, it was a reasonable expectation. The town got the name in the late 1920s when a man settled in the area, selling oil and gas to the cowboys and travelers passing through the territory. He also started baking pies, selling coffee and other snacks, and finally decided to call the stop Pie Town. The next owner of the store added a post office, and with that addition, the name became official. For a very long time, the place was known for its baked goods, its chili con carne, and its fruit pies, but unfortunately, since Fred and Bea had taken over the store and café, now the Pie Town Diner, it no longer served very memorable desserts. Fred and Bea served great daily blue plate specials like dumplings and chicken-fried steak. Bea made the finest tortillas in the county and fixed a green chile stew that even folks in Socorro claimed was the best around. Both Fred and Bea were excellent cooks, but neither one of them was very good at making pies.

When they bought the diner from the previous owners, two sisters from Santa Fe who thought they'd make a go of selling pies and baked goods, they tried to keep up the tasty tradition in addition to serving meals, but they just never seemed to get the hang of crusts and fillings. They gave up trying to load up the menu and the pastry counter with pies and just settled for cooking what they knew best. Nobody in town seemed to mind. Most everyone was sort of glad to get rid of the sisters and the bakery and have a real place to eat lunch.

Francine looked out the window, saw the car with its wipers still moving, and stuck her pencil behind her ear. "If they're here for the pie, they'll be disappointed," she said, answering Alex about the potential request for pie. "Fred made brownies for dessert."

"And they aren't very good either." Another customer, Bernie King, a rancher, piped in. He had finished his lunch and was just getting up from his seat at the counter.

A couple of other customers sitting near him laughed.

"I heard that," Bea called out from the kitchen.

"Good," responded Bernie. "Maybe you should do the desserts from now on or get something from the bakery at the grocery store."

"You don't have to eat here, Bernie." Fred had now entered the conversation. He was yelling from the kitchen. Everybody in the diner could hear him.

"Yeah, where else do I have to go?" he asked. He stood at the cash register and waited until Bea came out and took his money. She was wiping her hands on the bottom of her apron.

"There's always the vending machine at the gas station," Roger noted, joining in the conversation. "The Twinkies are good."

Bernie turned to Roger. "Yeah, it looks like you should know about that," he said, patting his belly. "Don't you have a weight limit as sheriff? Aren't you supposed to be able to run a few miles and do a hundred sit-ups or something?"

"Just have to be able to shoot annoying ranchers," Roger answered. "And so far, the Twinkies haven't interfered with that."

Everybody laughed.

"Well, I reckon I need to hush then," Bernie said as he handed Bea cash to pay for his lunch. "Alex, watch yourself," he said to the young boy. "Don't spend all of your time with your grandfather. He's a bad influence, I don't care what kind of badge he wears on his shirt." He winked. "I'll see you at the party. Hopefully, this storm will be done and gone by Saturday."

"Yes sir, Mr. King, I'm sure it will," Alex said. "I look forward to seeing you too."

"By the way, who's making the cake?" Bernie asked.

Roger shrugged. "That's on Malene's list, not mine."

"It's chocolate," Alex said.

Bernie smiled and nodded. "Sounds good already," he responded.

"You getting up the band?" Bea asked Roger.

"That's my assignment," Roger replied.

"Try not to play too much of that raunchy music you tend to be so fond of," Bernie said. "I'd like to bring a date." He got a toothpick from the dispenser by the cash register and stuck it in his mouth. He placed his cowboy hat on his head.

"Bernie, if you bring a woman with you to Alex's birthday party this weekend, I'll make sure we play nothing but church music." Roger knew the same thing that everybody in Pie Town knew about Bernie. He was a big talker, but he was way too shy to ask any woman out on a date. He was in his sixties and, as far as anybody knew, had never been out with a woman.

"Why don't you bring Ms. Francine?" Alex asked. He looked up at his waitress, still standing beside the table. "You're coming to my party, aren't you?"

Francine appeared surprised to hear the question, and she blushed. "I, I am planning to attend your festivities," she stammered. "But I will need to leave early because I have to drive to Albuquerque that evening to visit my sister." She glanced up at the rancher, who quickly looked away.

Everybody seemed to notice the awkward exchange, and there was a pause in the conversation.

"Well then, Bernie," Roger said, "I'm afraid you'll have to get your hymns at church on Sunday. It's raunchy music at the party Saturday night." He smiled at Francine. He knew what nobody else in Pie Town knew. She was in love with Bernie and had been for a number of years.

Francine smiled back at Roger. She had confided in him a few years ago when he had driven her home after her car broke down. He had promised his silence about the matter, and as far as she knew, he had kept his word. She doubted that Alex had made his suggestion because he knew anything about her feelings for Bernie or had heard anything from his grandfather.

The rancher suddenly seemed to be at a loss for words. He stood by the counter, shifting his weight from side to side. He slid his hands into his pockets. "Okay, I guess we'll be seeing you all." And he waved at everyone, grabbed his umbrella by the door, and headed out into the parking lot. He stopped and waited until the two strangers Alex had seen earlier were getting out of the car. He held up his umbrella near the door while the driver emerged. A man stood up next to Bernie, receiving the shelter from the rain while the passenger jumped out and ran to the door of the diner. She waited for the driver.

"You think Bernie's going to tell them to go somewhere else?" Alex asked.

"Not if he wants to eat here again," Bea replied, watching the two in the parking lot. She closed the register and headed back into the kitchen.

Roger turned around to see the strangers. He watched the young woman as she stood near the door. She stretched her arms high above her head, her T-shirt rising, exposing her stomach. He glanced over at Francine, who looked down at him, lifting her eyebrows. Roger smiled and turned back to watch as the driver stepped out from under the umbrella. Because of the black shirt and the clerical collar, it was immediately clear he was a priest, and Roger and Francine looked at each other again, this time both of them raising an eyebrow. The priest shook hands with Bernie and headed toward the front door.

"You think that's the new guy?" Alex asked, referring to the priest. Everyone in town had expected him to arrive sometime that month.

"I suspect so," Roger replied.

"Seems young," Alex commented. "At least younger than Father Joseph."

"Honey, God is younger than Father Joseph," Francine responded.

Roger studied the two newcomers as they stood outside under the awning at the front door, the priest waving to Bernie. "You're right, he does look green behind the ears, and he has a pretty young passenger traveling with him, don't you think?" He turned back around and winked at the waitress, who was still watching the three people outside. "Wonder what Father Joseph would say about those two?" he asked.

"Shoot, Father Joseph's eyesight is so bad, he wouldn't be able to tell which one was his replacement if they were standing right in front of him." Francine shook her head. She glanced down at Alex. "You want a little cherry soda with your lemonade?"

Alex smiled. "Yes, thank you," he responded.

Francine nodded and walked behind the counter to the beverage station. "Order up," she called out to Fred as she placed the order at the counter that was the opening to the kitchen. "The sheriff's grandson wants extra dumplings."

Fred walked over to pick up Francine's order. "I got hot sopaipillas too, Alex," he called out to his favorite customer.

Alex backed up his wheelchair and turned around to face the restaurant owner. "Thank you, Fred," he said. "You're the best."

"You save a sopaipilla for me?" Roger asked.

"You get tortillas like everybody else," Fred replied. "I don't want to be accused of trying to bribe the sheriff."

"Nobody has to know, Fred," Roger replied.

"I'll know," Alex chimed in. "And I will talk."

"Sorry, Roger," Fred said. "Can't afford to get busted. No sopaipillas."

Roger smiled as Alex readjusted his chair under the table. Francine brought over their drinks just as the priest and his passenger entered the diner, shaking the rain from their hair and wiping their feet.

Roger watched his grandson as the boy followed the pair with his eyes. "It's not polite to stare, son," he noted.

Alex kept watching the two.

"Alex," Roger called out his name, trying to get the boy to look away from the strangers.

"She looks a little like Mom," Alex said softly, as if he was talking to himself, as if he had been expecting someone, but just not her.

Roger studied his grandson and then glanced over to take a closer look at the young woman he had seen in the parking lot. He turned back, watched his grandson, and took a drink from his glass of tea. "I don't know, Alex." He hesitated. "A little maybe," he conceded.

"No, she really does," Alex insisted. "I mean, she's smaller than Mom, but she has her smile, and she fidgets like her." He kept eyeing them.

Roger turned back at the door. The girl, smiling, pointed to a booth, and the priest joined her. He nodded and smiled nervously at Roger and Alex before taking his seat across from his companion. Roger returned the greeting.

"The priest seems kind of anxious," Roger noted to his grandson. "Maybe Bernie did tell him not to eat here."

"If he's the priest, then who is she?" Alex asked.

"I wouldn't know," Roger answered. "But I'm pretty sure she isn't a nun."

Alex smiled. He had noticed the girl's tight T-shirt and the short shorts too. He shrugged. "Maybe she's just thinking about being a nun," he responded, "and he's helping her make up her mind."

"Then she's not anything like your mother," Roger noted.

"Lunch is served," Francine announced as she set the plates in front of Roger and Alex. "You want honey for your sopaipillas?" she asked the boy.

"No, I like to dip it in the juice," he replied.

"That's the best way," the waitress said. "Roger, you want anything else?" she asked.

Roger shook his head. "Nope, it's all just right."

The two of them started eating as Francine went over to take the orders of the newly arrived couple.

"What made you tell Bernie to ask Francine to your party?" Roger wanted to know.

Alex shrugged his shoulders and chewed a few bites of dumplings and biscuit. "I just thought it would be nice. They seem to like each other, but neither one of them acts like they know how to talk to each other." He turned back around to look at the patrons in the booth.

"So, do you think she's here to stay?" Alex asked his grandfather, referring to the young woman who had entered the diner with the priest.

"I wouldn't have a clue" came the response.

"I like her," Alex noted. "I like her looks. I like that she came in with him. I like that she picked him and us and this diner." He took a big bite of dumplings and grinned.

Roger smiled.

"Let's invite them to my party," Alex suggested. "I think that would make it perfect."

And Roger nodded at his grandson with a hint of worry on his face, wondering if the boy was still anxious for his mother to come home.

TEN

"Try not to look so nervous," Trina said to Father George. "It makes you seem like you've done something wrong." She reached over and pulled a napkin out of the holder. She spat the stick of gum she'd been chewing into the napkin and then balled it up. "And Father George, I suspect it's been a while since you did anything wrong."

"Thanks for the advice," he responded, surprised by her comment. He straightened his fork and knife on the table in front of him, placed the napkin in his lap. He tried not to glance around.

Francine walked back over to the table and placed two drinks in front of them. "Your food will be out in just a minute," she told them. She kept staring at Father George. Finally, she asked, "Are you the new priest over at Holy Family?"

He cleared his throat, sat up a bit in his seat. "I am Father George Morris, and I will be taking over for Father Joseph in this part of the diocese." He held out his hand.

Francine shook it. "Nice to meet you, Father. No offense, but I'm Presbyterian."

He nodded. "None taken," he said.

"I'm Trina," the young woman butted in. She held out her hand to shake Francine's hand as well. "Nice storm," she said, and then added, "I'm looking for a job."

Francine turned to her and took her hand, which was wet. "Always nice to see rain," she noted. She wiped her hand on her apron. "Unfortunately, as far as jobs go, there's not much here in Pie Town," she replied. "What kind of work you looking for?" she asked.

Trina thought about the question. "I don't know." She shrugged. "My last gig was as a dishwasher. Hey, do you need a dishwasher?" she asked, realizing that she was at a diner and could possibly find a job right there.

"You'll have to speak to the owners about job openings," Francine answered.

"Cool," Trina said.

"Are you planning to stay in Pie Town too?" Francine asked, understanding that the priest would now be their newest resident.

"That's the idea," the young girl replied. "This seems like a nice place to settle."

"It seems that way," Francine said, "but it can be a little tricky for new folks." She eyed the girl. "You got family here?" she asked, trying not to sound too nosy.

Trina shook her head. "Don't know a soul here but the priest," she replied, grinning at Father George, who immediately blushed.

"You got a place to stay?" Francine asked.

"Not yet," Trina replied. "Hey, do you know a place I could crash for a while?" she asked. She was not shy about her requests.

Francine considered the question. She picked up the balled-up napkin from the table and stuck it in her apron pocket. "Let me ask around," she replied.

"Cool," Trina said again.

"Order up" came the call from the kitchen.

Francine turned in that direction and then back to her customers. "Looks like lunch is ready." She walked over to the kitchen, picked up the two plates, and carried them back to the table. "Two specials," she noted as she placed them in front of the priest and Trina. "You need anything else?" she asked.

"I think I'm fine," Father George responded.

"You got chile?" Trina asked.

"Red or green?" Francine replied.

Trina shrugged. "Red, I guess."

"Coming right up," Francine said and turned to go back to the kitchen.

"Hey, Little Man, what's up?" Trina spoke to Alex who had been watching the pair since they arrived.

"You should get the green," he answered, referring to the chile. "The red is super hot."

"Thanks," she noted. "Hey, Miss," she yelled out to Francine. "My buddy here says I should go with the green chile. Is it okay if I change my mind?" She winked over to Alex.

Francine nodded in her direction and then spoke to Fred.

Trina turned to her companion, who was bowed over his plate of chicken and dumplings. It was obvious that he was praying, and Trina glanced over at Alex and shrugged. Then she grinned and bowed her head as well. When the priest said, "Amen," she snapped up her head. "Amen," she repeated, rubbing her hands together. "Now, let's eat!"

By the time Francine had brought over the

small bowl of green chile, the young woman had practically devoured everything on her plate. She took the chile and put it on the chicken and dumplings she had left and kept eating. Even Father George seemed surprised that his young companion appeared to be so hungry.

"When's the last time you ate?" he asked her.

She swallowed the mouthful of food. "I don't know." She thought for a minute. "A couple of days. At least it feels like it." She slid more food on her fork. "This is really good. Thanks for the chile tip," she called to Alex across the diner. "Good move on my part. I can't remember being so hungry," she said to George, who was still just watching her eat. "I'm not usually such a big eater."

Alex smiled. He looked at Roger. He had overheard the conversation between Francine and the young woman. "Granddad, I know where she can stay," he said.

Roger studied his grandson. "What are you talking about?" he asked, not understanding. He hadn't heard the conversation.

"She needs a place to stay. I heard her tell Francine. So why don't you let her move into the apartment?" Alex knew that his grandfather had a garage apartment in the back of his house. It was the place where his mother had stayed when she was pregnant and when she had just delivered Alex. Roger had spoken about it on lots of occasions. Because of his disability, Alex had never gone up to see it.

"Alex, I don't know. That seems kind of sudden, don't you think?"

Alex shrugged. "The priest must think she's okay or he would never have let her in his car, right?" he asked. "And she needs a place."

Roger turned around and peered at the odd couple sitting in the booth next to the window. The priest was eating slowly, and the young woman had practically finished. She smiled when she noticed him glancing in her direction.

"You said that you needed somebody to stay there because the cobwebs are taking over," Alex said, reminding his grandfather of something he had mentioned a few weeks earlier. "It would be perfect for her."

Roger turned back and shook his head. "It hasn't been cleaned in years," he responded. And as soon as Alex understood that his grandfather was considering letting this young stranger into the apartment, he wheeled himself over to the table where she was sitting.

"I'm Alex," he said, sticking out his hand.

Trina smiled. "Hello, Alex," she said, wiping her mouth and then taking his hand. "I'm Trina, and this," she nodded over to the priest, "is Father George Morris."

Alex glanced at him. "Welcome to Pie Town," he said.

"Thank you, Alex," the priest responded.

"The green chile is okay?" Alex asked Trina.

"Perfect," she replied.

Alex nodded. "I know where you can stay," he said.

Trina appeared surprised.

"I can't find you a job, but I know where you can stay," he repeated.

"Yeah?" Trina asked.

"Yeah," he replied. He spun his wheelchair around to Roger. "Tell her, Granddad," he said.

Roger cleared his throat, wiped his mouth, placed his napkin on the table, and got up from his seat. He walked over to the table and stood beside Alex. "I'm Roger Benavidez," he introduced himself.

Father George stuck out his hand. "Father George Morris," he responded. "Nice to meet you, Sheriff," he said, noticing the uniform.

"Father George," Roger said. He turned to Trina. "And you are?" he asked with a smile.

"Trina," she replied.

"And so you have charmed my grandson from a distance," he noted.

Trina grinned at Alex, who blushed a bit.

"Is it true that you have a place where I might crash?" she asked.

Roger nodded. "I have a small apartment above the garage in the back of my house. It's not much, but my daughter lived there a while with

Alex when he was a baby. I'll need to clean it up a bit before you move in, but yes, it's available."

"Cool," Trina responded. "But hey, I'll do the cleaning, and then maybe you can knock off a few bucks from the rent since I don't have much cash to start."

There was a pause.

"Actually, I don't have any cash," Trina admitted. "I'm trying to find a job, but I really don't have any money right now."

The two men seemed embarrassed for her.

"I got some cash I can loan you," Alex responded.

Trina reached over and placed her hand on Alex's arm. "I think I can swing my rent if the sheriff here will give me a couple of weeks to raise the funds. But that is a very kind offer."

There was another awkward pause among the four.

"So where's your mom now?" she asked, recalling what Alex had said about the apartment.

Alex looked over to Roger as if he was expecting him to answer.

"Taos," Roger replied. "She's living in Taos."

"Nice," Trina responded. "I love Taos. You been to see her?" she asked Alex.

He shook his head.

"Well, maybe we can go up there and visit

her sometime." Trina smiled. "Maybe when I get a job and can buy a car, I'll drive you up there."

Roger cleared his throat. The direction of the conversation seemed to trouble him.

Appearing to notice Roger's discomfort, Father George spoke up. "Can you tell me, Sheriff Benavidez, how far the Holy Family Church and the parish house are from here?" he asked. "If my directions are right, I shouldn't be too far away, right?"

Roger turned back to the priest, glad for the question. "Right. It's not far at all, just a few miles up Highway 60 and east on Clive's Road. Would you like me to escort you over there?" he asked. "Is Father Joseph waiting on you?"

"I believe that he is," Father George answered. Then he glanced over at Trina and then back to Roger. "But I think that if you can help my passenger here find suitable housing," he nodded over to Trina, "I can locate my new residence."

"Father George was kind enough to give me a ride when I was hitchhiking," Trina explained. And then she whispered to Alex, loud enough for the men to hear. "I think I must remind him of an old girlfriend. I think I make him nervous." She winked, and Father George's face reddened.

"You can walk to Granddad's from here," Alex said, grinning. "If you want, when it stops raining, I'll go with you." He thought for a second about his offer. "Only I can't go up to the apartment with you because of the stairs," he added, looking a bit disappointed.

Trina considered his words. "Well, I bet that if the sheriff comes along with us, we could sling you over his shoulder and get you up those stairs. Maybe instead of giving me a loan, you can help me clean."

Roger glanced down at his grandson. "I think we can find a way to get him up there," he said. He picked up the check from the table. "Let me take care of your meal."

Father George immediately responded. "That won't be necessary. I don't expect any special treatment."

"It's not special treatment unless you get dessert, and based upon the reviews I've heard, you don't want to go there, so let's just call it a 'welcome to your new home' lunch."

Father George nodded. "What? No pie?" he asked innocently.

Roger turned to the kitchen and yelled out to Fred. "Father George wants to know if there's pie."

Fred stood at the window. "Brownies," he yelled back.

"Only pie you can get is down the road in Quemado. But it's worth the drive," Roger explained.

Father George appeared to make a mental

note. “No pie in Pie Town,” he said. “I’ll keep that in mind. Although that does seem a bit odd. Maybe that will change.” He smiled. “Anything else I should know about the area?”

“We’re just small-town folks, not too fancy with our thoughts and not too progressive with our religion,” Roger answered.

“And the best party all year happens to be this weekend,” Alex added.

“Oh, and what kind of party is that?” the priest asked.

“My birthday, and even though there’s no pie, I can promise you there will be cake.” Alex grinned. “And you’re invited.”

Father George smiled. “Well, with such a lovely personal invitation like that, how could I say no?”

“Great,” Alex responded. “It’s always a lot of fun.” He studied the priest. “Can you play soft-ball?” he asked.

The priest shook his head. “I’m afraid I’m not the athletic type, Alex,” he replied.

“That’s all right. You can just watch.”

Father George nodded.

Roger cleared his throat. “Well, with the storm and all, I’ll drive you over to the house, Trina,” he said, “if you’re ready to go.”

Trina took a swallow from her iced tea. She put down her glass, and suddenly something seemed to be wrong with her. She reached for her napkin and held it to her lips as if she might become sick.

"You okay?" Alex asked.

She nodded and placed the napkin in her lap. "Just not used to the chile, I think." She cleared her throat. "Okay then, Father, you are now officially free of me!" She glanced over at Alex. "Well, I mean, unless I become a Catholic." She smiled. "Now let's go see my new digs!" And she slid out of the booth and headed to the front door. "See you at the party," she exclaimed to the priest, even though, unlike Father George, she had yet to be formally invited. "And will you look at that? The storm has passed."

Alex grinned, glancing at the sky, and followed behind her.

Part II

ELEVEN

Every day I go to him drifting in the threads of white clouds that hang above the Gallinas and the Datil Mountains. I fly high above the fields and peaks, lighting always on the familiar landmarks, the places I have walked or ridden in wagons and on horseback. I circle and spin, dipping down, dropping once again to the place where I was born and the place where I died, the place where my beloved lives.

The boy grows so tall now. His voice has deepened. His limbs have lengthened. He is not the child I first remember. He is not the tiny baby, so frail, his spine unformed, his backbone open and vulnerable. He is not the fragile toddler or the chubby child in preschool. He is just on the cusp of change. Boy to man.

The party is thrown in his honor. It is quite the celebration, quite a gathering of joyful souls. It is better than a holiday. They all come, bearing gifts and sweet corn and skillet bread, hot chile and stew. They sing and tell tall tales of his arrival. They laugh and dance and wrap their love around each other. They claim to come for him, but I see their hearts. They also come for themselves, to remind themselves that life defeated death, that this broken child lives beyond what was destined, and if a miracle happened to him, maybe a miracle can happen to them too.

They are here because it brings them pleasure to see him, to be near to him. He gives them hope, shows them possibilities, how to open their hearts. And I can see, even from this far distance, that he too is happy. He laughs. He sings. He is fully in this moment, fully in his life.

She is not there with him, and yet she is. A few worry about her absence, and yet he has found a way to transform the grief and disappointment and wrap it up into a grand welcome for a girl who doesn't even know how to be lonesome for home. They have bonded in a few short days. She will stand with him and he with her, although it is difficult to know for how long. She is only a child herself. But she is of the same spirit as he. She is hard not to like.

I am there, but no one sees me. He knows. I can feel his gratitude as if he thinks I have arranged this celebration, this gathering, her coming. But it is not my place to interfere in the lives of those around him. If it were, I would have gone across the Sangre de Cristos and raised a racket around his mother, making her jump from her bed of addiction and leave to go join them. I would have forced her to stay there, forced her to care, forced her to love him. But that is not my role. I am instead only a presence of comfort, the gentle voice in their minds leading one in the direction they have already chosen. I am the one dancing at birth and the one carrying the dead ones home.

I cannot change the outcomes or the movement of will. I cannot create the choices or dismiss the consequences once those choices have been made. And I cannot change what will happen even if I see it coming, even if I try stepping in its way.

And yet, today I do not think of these things, these things I cannot push away or cast aside. Today I cannot carry the burden of sorrow or the weight of grief. For today is a party, a gift of birth to be celebrated, the gift of life to be honored and enjoyed. There is no time or space for the suffering of tomorrow. Today we sing and we eat too much cake. Today we joke and make music and count the blessings and revel in what we do not know.

I watch from a distance, but I am there. I dance right beside them.

TWELVE

"You drive that station wagon?" Oris had not seen the priest since he had made his way into Pie Town. The old man was Catholic, but he rarely attended Mass. He and Father Joseph and a few members of the congregation had a falling-out when Oris tried to hang lights on the rectory to decorate it for Christmas. The priest and the Altar Guild had taken them down because they all said it wasn't respectable for a parsonage to be covered in colored lights. Oris had gotten angry at the rejection of his gift and quit the church, so he wasn't paying much attention to the arrival of Father George. He did, however, notice the station wagon around town and knew right away that it was the car that almost forced him off the road earlier in the week.

Father George followed Oris's glance out to the school parking lot where he had parked his car. "Yes," he replied. "It's on loan from the diocese," he explained, sounding proud. He turned back to look at Oris. "It's not real pretty, but it gets me where I need to go."

"You get your driver's license from the diocese too?" he asked.

Father George appeared confused.

"You almost ran me off the road a few days

ago. I remember what your car looked like," Oris said.

"Oh my," Father George responded, recalling the incident that happened just as he was making his way into Pie Town. "I am so sorry. I had glanced down at a map to figure out where I was and I just wasn't paying attention. I'm so sorry. You weren't hurt, were you?"

Oris grunted and waved off the apology and the question. "Don't matter. Oris Whitsett," he introduced himself. "Alex's great-grandfather." He had walked out to his car to get ice from the trunk.

"Father George Morris," the priest responded. "Looks like a nice day for a party," he added, trying to sound cheerful.

"Party's been started," Oris barked. "You're late. But wait a minute before you go out there. Let me give you a bag of ice to carry." He peered at the priest. "Don't you guys have comfortable clothes for outside events?"

Father George glanced down at his clergy uniform, recalling what Trina had said to him on the drive into town. He was wearing the same black shirt, black pants, white collar, black belt, and black dress shoes. He did bring a straw hat for the afternoon gathering and was wearing short sleeves. But the young priest didn't own anything other than a few sets of running clothes, pajamas and a robe, one suit coat (black of course), and the four black shirts and four pairs of black pants he had bought when he finished seminary. He thought priests, and especially the new ones, needed to stay in the appropriate attire at every community event. He was hot, but he liked wearing the uniform. "I'll be fine," he responded.

Oris opened the trunk and turned to the priest. "Take a look at that," he said, pointing to the back of the car. "Have you ever seen a trunk that big?" he asked. Then he reached inside a cooler and pulled out two bags of ice. He pitched one to the priest, who stumbled but was able to hold on to it. Oris pulled down the trunk hood and winked at Father George. "Nice catch."

Father George managed a smile, appearing surprised that he had caught the ice. "It's a big trunk," he agreed.

"Holds every suitcase I've got plus a couple bushels of Hatch green chile."

The priest nodded. "So, are you expecting a lot of people?" he asked as the two moved away from the car. He had seen a number of cars on the street and in the parking lot, but he figured they belonged to people using the ball fields and picnic tables behind the elementary school. He wasn't sure how many people would be at an eleven-year-old boy's birthday party in the middle of the afternoon on a Saturday in the middle of summer, but he didn't expect very many. Since he knew he had Mass at five P.M., he figured he would just say a blessing over the meal and then slip out.

As soon as he walked around the corner he realized there were more than just a few family members at this event. Behind the school it looked as if the entire town was present. There were at least a hundred people sitting around tables and under trees, even a big group playing a game of softball. Father George assumed that a lot of people knew Alex and his family, but he had no idea that the boy's birthday was an event the entire town celebrated.

"It's everybody," Father George said, sounding surprised as he stopped to look at the crowd.

"Yep," Oris responded. "Somebody should have told you to cancel Mass tonight," he commented. "Or maybe you'd prefer to do it here? There's enough of us Catholics to be able to follow you from the prayer book. Probably take up a better collection." He kept walking toward the gathering.

Father George suddenly realized that in stopping to glance around he had fallen behind the older man, and he hurried to catch up. "Should I have brought something?" he asked, still cradling the bag of ice.

"Nope, you're a guest the first year. Next year you'll have to make the stew," Oris teased him.

The two of them arrived at the long picnic

shelter just as everyone was running out to the ball field. “Alex is up!” Someone shouted.

“Well, I can’t miss that!” Oris yelled. He threw the bag of ice on top of a cooler and hurried out to the field with everyone else.

Father George stood alone at a picnic table, still holding the bag of ice. He turned to watch what everyone else was running to see. Alex was sitting at home base, in his wheelchair, holding a bat, awaiting a pitch. The priest glanced around and noticed that he was completely alone. He opened the cooler, put the bag of ice inside, and walked to the edge of the shelter just as Alex took his first swing. An older man was pitching slowly to him. It looked like the sheriff, his grandfather, the one George had met when he met Alex.

Everyone seemed to be cheering for the boy. There was a second pitch, and Alex swung at that one too. More cheers of encouragement erupted. The ball was returned to the pitcher, and he wound up and threw the ball again. This time Alex connected and the ball went over second base, landing just short of center field. Alex started moving down that first base line, his chair in high gear. He ran over the corner of the bag and rounded to second. The teenager playing in center field threw the ball over the head of the pitcher, and Alex wheeled on to third. Everyone was cheering for him to keep going.

He was heading to home base when the catcher, a girl who looked to be about twelve or thirteen, retrieved the ball and ran to home to tag him out. When she saw Alex coming in her direction, the wheelchair barreling at high speed, she dropped the ball to her side and watched as Alex made it to home base and was called by the volunteer umpire, Fred, the owner of the diner, loud enough for everyone to hear, *"Safe!"*

Father George smiled as he watched everyone run to Alex. The boy had hit a home run.

"Kinda reminds me of how I used to think about heaven." A voice spoke from behind the priest.

Father George turned around. Trina was standing there. She was wearing a different pair of shorts and a different tight T-shirt, but she looked about the same as the day they met. "You just get here?" he asked, feeling his face reddening. She had some hold over him.

"I had to walk," she replied. "Couldn't find a priest in a station wagon anywhere," she added.

He nodded, turned to watch the crowd still congratulating Alex, then back again to Trina. "What do you mean it's how you used to think of heaven?" he asked.

She headed over to stand next to him. "All those people out there doing something as simple and easy as playing a game of ball. Kids, old people, all of them wanting the same thing at exactly the same time. All their minds together like that, wanting something pure and wonderful, like seeing a little boy hit a ball and be the hero." She shrugged. "Just seems like what heaven ought to be."

Father George looked over at the first person he had met in Pie Town. He felt connected to her in some troublesome way. She reminded him of the things he was trying to forget.

"What about you, Father George?" she asked.

"What about me?" he asked, surprised by the question, worried about what she was asking.

"What do you think heaven will look like?" She had jumped up and was sitting on the picnic table.

"Oh," he replied, and then considered the question. "Pearly gates, streets of gold." He paused. "I haven't really thought much about it, since I spend most of my time just trying to make sure I get there." He turned to Trina.

"Well, it seems to me like you want to make sure it's a place you want to go before you waste your life trying to earn a trip inside." She pulled her legs up, wrapping her arms around her knees.

The priest turned away from the young woman sitting on the table and back to watch the group on the softball field. Someone else was up to bat, and a few people were heading back to the tables.

"Look, a feather," she announced, jumping

down from the table and picking up a small white feather. "My grandfather used to tell me that when you found a feather it meant an angel had passed by." She held it in her hand, sliding it through her fingers, remembering her mother's father, his kindness, the one bright spot in her otherwise dim childhood. "You believe in angels?" she asked as she stuck the feather behind her ear.

Father George glanced down. "I believe in the saints," he answered. "The apostles, Peter, Paul, James, the mother of our Lord, Mary, of course. And I do believe the scriptures make reference to a number of angels who assist our Heavenly Father, Michael and Gabriel being the most familiar."

"I'm not talking about those big scary ones from the Bible who came down in their long white robes, making some grand announcement. I'm talking about now. Don't you have a guardian angel?" Trina asked.

Father George cleared his throat. He placed his arms across his waist and then dropped them by his side. He cleared his throat again.

"It's not a test, George," Trina said, noticing his discomfort. "I just figured with you being a priest and all, you'd have your own by now." She sat back down on the table.

"I have a guardian angel," she explained. "I call her Miss Teresa."

"Like Saint Therese, the Carmelite," the priest acknowledged.

"Who?" Trina asked.

"Saint Therese, the Little Flower," he replied. "She believed that she was like a flower with a mission of bringing glory to God. She was known for her great spirituality. I studied her during a retreat I took in seminary. She brings many believers a sense of peace and serenity."

Trina shook her head. "No, I named her Teresa because that was the name of my best friend's mother when I was a little girl. Miss Teresa Lawson. I called her Miss Teresa. And she was as close to an angel as anybody I ever met."

"And your Miss Teresa died when you were a child?" the priest asked, trying to sound concerned. "So she became an angel?"

Trina glanced up at the priest. "I don't think she died," she answered. "She just moved away." She looked over at the coolers. "Do you think it would be all right if I got a drink?" she asked. She jumped down and walked over to one of the coolers and opened it. "You want a soda?"

Father George turned in her direction. "Thank you, yes," he replied.

Trina reached in and got two sodas. She threw one to the priest, who was not prepared to catch it, and immediately it fell to the ground. "Looks like you could use a bit of Alex's heaven too," she said, smiling. "You were right when you told Alex about your athletic abilities. You're not much of a ballplayer, huh?" she asked.

Father George bent down and picked up the can that had landed near his feet. As he did so, he noticed another feather and picked it up. "Looks like there were two angels here today," he noted, holding the feather out to Trina.

She reached for it as she opened her drink. "Teresa must have brought along a friend," she said. She stuck it behind the other ear. "Maybe yours finally showed up," she added.

"Maybe," he replied, not sounding very convinced. He opened his can, which immediately spewed its contents all over his clothes.

Trina hurried over with a handful of napkins and was wiping them across his shirt, trying to help clean up the mess, just as the crowd of people were making their way back to the tables.

"Well, you two just seem to show up everywhere together." It was Bernie, the rancher who had met the priest and the young woman in the diner parking lot when they came into town. He was leading the group from the field back to the tables under the picnic shelter.

"I know," Trina responded. "It's like we just can't stand being apart."

Father George pulled away from the girl, yanking the napkins from her. Trina seemed surprised at such a sharp response. There was an awkward pause in the conversation.

"Well, I guess that's my cue to leave. I'll go down to the field," she commented and backed away. It was clear that the priest didn't want her around.

"Alex just hit a home run," the rancher commented, aware of the awkwardness between the two newcomers.

"I know. I saw it from here," Trina said. "Pretty sweet." She turned and headed to the field, throwing her hand up in the air to wave goodbye.

The two men watched as she stopped and spoke to the few others heading back to the tables. It looked as if introductions were being made.

"I reckon she's a mess of trouble," Bernie commented. "A girl like that." Father George didn't respond. "You know anything about her?" Bernie asked.

Father George shook his head. "She said she came here because she liked the name of the town," he replied. "I picked her up on Highway 60," he explained, glad for the chance to tell somebody how they met, glad for the opportunity to clear up any ideas about their association. "She was hitchhiking," he added, wanting to make sure the old man heard the entire truth and was able to make a fair judgment.

Bernie walked over to the cooler and took out a soda. "Crazy kids." He opened the can. "What kind of girl hitchhikes in today's world?"

Father George shook his head. "I wouldn't have an answer for that," he replied. "It's not something I know anything about."

Bernie studied the young priest. "Yeah, I reckon that's probably the truth."

Blushing without completely knowing why, Father George took the wad of wet napkins and threw them in the trash can at the edge of the shelter.

"Well, I just hope she ain't got trouble coming with her or after her." Bernie sat back down at a table.

Father George hadn't considered that Trina might have friends who would join her.

"We don't need no more drugs being peddled through here. We had enough of that with the sheriff's daughter and her crew. Thank God they all left or got locked up." He was watching the group of people coming in his direction.

Father George turned to study the rancher. The news of drugs in his parish, in this sleepy little town, surprised him, especially in reference to the sheriff's family. He cleared his throat, not knowing what to say. "It seems like everybody from town is here at the party," he finally said, changing the subject.

"Yep, it's about the only thing this town can agree on, celebrating Alex, having his birthday party out here. I figure you'll learn about our disagreeing ways before long," Bernie commented with a grin. "We ain't an easy town to motivate or resuscitate."

George was about to ask for an explanation, but before he could ask the question the others had made their way into the picnic shelter.

"Father George," called out one of the women, the first one to enter the shelter. She was older, thick around the waist, and hunched over. She pulled herself up to make the introduction. "Good to see you." She stuck out her hand. "I'm Fedora Snow," she announced. "I'm in charge of the Altar Guild," she added. "I'm sure you've seen my name on the programs. I had planned to drive out to the parish to introduce myself earlier this week when I had heard you arrived, but I figured you needed a few days to get settled. I expect I'll have a chance to come by in the next few days to fill you in on how our Guild works here in Pie Town."

Father George smiled and shook her hand. "Nice to meet you, Mrs. Snow."

"It's Miss Snow." Oris had made his way back to the shelter too. "She's never married, although I suspect she's spied enough on other folks' marriages to know what she's missing." He pinched her on the behind as he walked past the two of them, making his way to the coolers.

"Oris Whitsett!" Fedora yelled out, falling into the priest. "You are a sorry son of a bitch!" She suddenly realized what she had said, and in what company, and she immediately turned a bright shade of red. "I'm so sorry," she sputtered. "I, he, I . . ." She struggled with her words. She backed away from Father George.

"Oh, hush up, Fedora," Oris called out. "You might as well let the good father know who he's dealing with. No need trying to act like the saint everybody here knows you ain't." He laughed a bit and took a soda from the cooler. He sat down at one of the tables.

Fedora made a huffing noise and quickly turned to walk to the front table in the shelter, a place as far away from her neighbor as she could manage.

Father George cleared his throat. His discomfort with the conversation was obvious, and he struggled to find a way to change the subject or move things along.

"I'm Malene." A middle-aged woman had walked up from the field with the others. She was pushing an older woman in a wheelchair, and she stopped the chair just in front of the priest and greeted him. "I'm Alex's grandmother and that old geezer's daughter," she explained, glancing over to Oris. "He's a handful, and you should be glad he was forced to leave the church years ago," she added. "And this is Mrs. Henderson." She smiled down at the woman in the chair.

"I quit the church," Oris explained before anybody else could speak. "Nobody forced me out. I just got fed up with all that mumbo-jumbo you say every Sunday and the way the hypocrites always take over."

"Nice to meet you, Mrs. Henderson," Father George said, ignoring Oris. He stuck out his hand to the old woman, and she rolled her eyes and waved his hand away. He hesitated. "Nice to meet you, Malene," he said, turning to her and trying not to appear distracted by the older woman's rejection. "I was just saying what a lovely gathering this is for your grandson," he said.

"Thank you," she replied. "This is Father George, Mrs. Henderson." Malene spoke directly in the woman's ear. "He's the new priest at the church."

Mrs. Henderson shook her head and grimaced.

"Are you from around here?" Malene asked as everyone turned in his direction, curious about his answer.

"Ohio," he replied. "I was born and raised in the Midwest."

Malene nodded. "Then I expect living out here will be a big change for you." She leaned down to Mrs. Henderson in the wheelchair. "He's from Ohio," Malene yelled to her.

"I don't care," Mrs. Henderson yelled back.

Malene shook her head and wheeled the woman over to a table.

"You got any boots?" Bernie rejoined the conversation.

Father George shook his head.

"Well, you're going to need some boots. That parish house has always had a den of rattlesnakes take up residence there every summer," Bernie noted.

"I think you're talking about inside the church," Oris responded. "And you'll need more than boots to handle that brand of venom."

Fedora turned around and made a hissing noise.

"See what I mean," Oris said. "Your Holy Family Church is sort of like this little village."

The priest seemed confused.

"Ain't no pie in Pie Town and no holy family in that church," Oris explained.

Malene locked the brakes on Mrs. Henderson's wheelchair and walked back over to where the priest was standing. "Do you need anything to help make your transition more comfortable?" she asked, ignoring her father's comments.

Father George was glad to focus on something other than the two old feuding neighbors. "I can't think of a thing," he replied. "Father Joseph got everything ready for me, and the house committee has gone out of their way to make sure the refrigerator and cabinets are well stocked." He nodded with a big smile. "Now I just look forward to the opportunity to meet the members of the congregation and learn how best to serve each and every one of you." He had practiced that opening line a number of times, and he thought it came off quite sincerely.

"You need some boots," Bernie repeated. "And just make sure you keep that back door to the sanctuary closed." He turned to Oris, who had sat down beside him. "You remember that time a skunk wandered in there?" He laughed. "Father Joseph tried to shoo the damn thing out and got the whole place sprayed."

"I remember him swinging that incense bucket two or three times before and after Mass for about a month. Still didn't cover up that skunk smell!" Oris slapped his leg.

"We had to dry-clean every altar cloth in the sanctuary, not to mention Father Joseph's vestments." Fedora shook her head. "It was terrible." She placed her hand over her nose.

"You know, I still think Father Joseph sort of smells like that old skunk," Oris commented.

"Daddy, that was more than twenty years ago," Malene responded.

"Still, don't you think he sort of took up that smell?" Oris asked. He turned to Bernie.

"You know, come to think of it, Oris, you might be right. You know how they say people start looking like their pets? It's pretty lonesome out there at the church, way up that long dirt road. Maybe he and the skunk made friends." Bernie winked at his old friend. "Instead of looking like each other, they started smelling like each other."

"I heard of stranger things happening out in the desert." Oris grinned. "It can seem a mighty long ways from town after midnight," he added. "A skunk can be good company even though it can take a lot of Bible reading to get one baptized!" He and Bernie laughed.

Malene shook her head again. "They're just teasing you," she explained to the new priest. "You are only five miles from town, there's plenty of people who'll be coming and going from the church, and with three parishes to serve, I doubt you'll get so lonely you need to take up with the wildlife."

"Still, keep the door closed just the same," Bernie repeated. "Old skunk might come around looking for his best friend. Besides, y'all do seem to dress in the same colors."

The group in the shelter all turned to the priest, noticing his attire.

"Keep the doors closed," Father George played along. "I'll remember to do just that." He smiled and felt the sweat roll down his back. He suddenly wished he had packed more than just the black wardrobe.

THIRTEEN

"That was a fine hit." Trina had made her way to Alex, who was sitting by the dugout as his team took the field.

"Hey, Trina!" he exclaimed. "I'm so glad you made it."

"Just in time to see you score a run," she said with a smile. She reached over and tousled his hair. "Happy Birthday."

"You bring Father George?" Alex asked.

"He was already here," she replied.

Alex glanced over in the direction of the picnic shelter. He nodded, even though he couldn't see who was there. "Y'all didn't come together?" he asked with a grin.

"Now, Alex, what are you trying to say?" she asked, grinning as well.

The little boy shrugged. "I thought y'all made a nice couple," he said. "That you came together to make your home in Pie Town."

Trina rolled her eyes. She knew the boy was only teasing her. "Well, even though we arrived at the same time and might both be calling this place home, I suspect God would have a few things to say about the 'being a couple' part."

Alex shielded his eyes as he squinted up at the

girl. "I think God likes couples," he said. "He did make Adam and Eve, after all."

"That's true," Trina responded. "But I guess the priests have a different idea about that." She leaned over and fixed the mess she had made in the little boy's hair. "I think Father George is scared of girls. Maybe one bit him when he was your age.

"You throw quite a party," she commented as she glanced around at all the people on the field and gathered in groups under trees and back at the shelter. "This must be everybody in Pie Town."

Alex smiled. "They come every year," he said. Then he turned to Trina. "When's your birthday?" he asked. "We can throw you a party."

Trina smiled. "December," she replied. "December 16. Usually it's too cold for a party. Or too close to Christmas." She squatted down and sat next to Alex's chair. "At least that's what they always told me," she added.

"You never had a party?" Alex asked, sounding surprised.

"I always got a card and a bag of candy from my granddad," she replied.

"But no party?" Alex asked. "No cake, no family standing around you singing the birthday song?" He paused. "No candles and wishes?"

Trina shrugged. "Didn't really have much of a family," she answered, and then noticed Alex's concern. "But it's all right," she said, sounding reassuring. "I left home pretty early, so I never gave anybody much of a chance to plan a party for me. Besides, I make my own parties . . . and my own wishes."

Alex smiled. He turned back to see what was happening on the field. "I got my wish already," he said.

"That home run?" Trina asked. "It was a beauty," she said, following his gaze to the field.

"No, not the home run," Alex replied. "They let me hit one of those every year." He smiled. "I always act like it's a big deal, but I think it makes them happier than it does me."

Trina glanced up at the boy. It surprised her to hear what he was saying. "Then if it wasn't the hit, what wish came true?" she asked.

Alex didn't answer at first. He glanced down at Trina. "You," he said softly. "You were my wish this year, and you showed up."

Trina didn't respond at first. She thought about his answer, trying to figure out what he meant.

"You wished for a girl from Texas to come to Pie Town for your birthday party?" she asked.

Alex shrugged and watched the team on the field. "Well, I didn't care whether or not you were from Texas, but yeah," he replied. "I wished for a change in Pie Town, something or someone new to come here, give the place something to think about other than just me and my disease."

Trina didn't know what to say. She was surprised at the boy and his birthday wish, surprised that she had arrived at just the time he was wishing it, and she wondered if he had brought her there. She thought of her own wishes of the past weeks, her own desire to leave everything old behind her, start a new life, and forget all the pain that had followed her from Texas and Tucson. She thought about Father George and wondered what part he had in the fulfillment of Alex's wishes. She thought about the Indian woman she met on the Apache Reservation, the one who took care of her when she collapsed after walking so far, the one who sent her to Pie Town with a new pair of shoes, and the one who seemed to recognize the sorrow and hope and all the rest that Trina was carrying inside her.

"Looks like the game's over," Alex announced, shaking Trina from her thoughts, drawing her attention to the members of the team as they approached. "And we won," he added.

Trina stood up as everyone gathered around Alex, congratulating their only home run hitter. She backed away a bit so there would be room. Roger, Alex's grandfather, walked over to Alex, saw Trina, and headed over to her. He took off his hat and began wiping his face and neck with a handkerchief. "You been here the whole time?" he asked.

Trina shook her head. "Just in time for the big

hit," she answered. "You pitch a mean curveball," she said with a smile.

Roger grinned. "I have my moments," he said. He put his hat back on his head. "Everything okay in the apartment?" he asked. They hadn't spoken since she moved in a few days earlier. His schedule at work and caring for Alex got him out early every morning and home after dark in the evenings.

"I like it," she replied. "It's perfect for me. The bed's soft, just the way I like it, and there's a nice breeze always blowing through the place." She stuck her hands in her back pockets. "I like the little room in the back the best," she said. "Was that Alex's nursery?"

Roger nodded. "He never really got to stay in it," he said. "Alex spent most of his early years in the hospital." He looked over at his grandson. "But Angel," he said, turning back to Trina, "his mother, she wanted him to have his own room."

Trina listened, glancing over at Alex as the other team members came over to congratulate him.

"When she moved in, it had just been a little storage room, a closet. But she emptied everything out of it, cleaned it up, and painted it all those bright colors. She wanted it to be special for him, you know." He slipped his handkerchief into his pocket. "She worked on it a long time, but then after they kept putting him back in the hospital or making him stay down in Albuquerque, she just quit." Roger paused. "She just quit decorating." He blew out a long breath. "Then, when we did get him home, the stairs were just too much. She didn't hang around much after that."

"And now she's in Taos?" Trina asked.

"Last we heard," Roger answered. "She tends to like to wander," he added.

"What about his dad?" she asked.

"Never really knew the answer to that question," Roger replied. "Angel would never say, and we really aren't sure. Although I have my suspicions."

Trina studied the man. "Guess being sheriff means you hear a lot of chatter, huh?"

He nodded. "I hear stuff," he answered.

"Yeah, I suspect so." She stretched her arms out to her side. "But I get your daughter," she noted. "I never stay too long in one place either. I'm sort of a gypsy at heart too. Like to keep moving, you know."

Roger turned to the young woman. He realized that Alex was right. She was very similar to Angel. She didn't physically resemble his daughter very much, but there was something that seemed to connect the two of them. Maybe it was the wandering, maybe it was something else.

"Did you find work?" he asked, remembering that she was trying to get a job at the diner.

"I'm filling in for the dishwasher and the waitress while they take a few days off this month, but I don't think Fred and Bea have anything too permanent for me," Trina replied. She looked over at Roger. "You know of anything?" she asked.

Roger thought for a minute and shook his head. "We can ask Malene." He stopped. "She's my ex-wife," he explained. "She's an aide over at the Carebridge Nursing Center. Maybe she knows something over there."

Trina nodded. "I can do about anything," she said. "I mean, as long as it isn't technical or anything. I don't know much about computers, but I'm good with fixing stuff, and I work hard and I learn fast."

Roger smiled at the young woman. "Did you finish school?" he asked.

"Tenth grade," she answered. "But I read a lot, and I figure I could pass the GED if I took it. I know a lot of kids who took it who had a harder time reading and doing math than I do."

"Then why haven't you ever taken it?" Roger asked.

Trina shrugged. "Never stayed long enough in a place to sign up for it," she replied.

"Well, if you did take it and passed it and wanted to go to college or technical school and could do anything you wanted, what kind of work would you like?" Roger asked. "Can you bake pies? 'Cause we could certainly use somebody to bake pies."

"Nah, I'm no baker." She reached up, pushing her hair behind her ears. "But I'm pretty good with engines, auto mechanic stuff. My grandfather fixed buses for the school system. I used to ride along with him. He taught me a lot and I liked it. He said I had a natural talent for engine repair and that it was something I could be good at because my fingers are real small." She shrugged. "But that was a long time ago, and he was probably just trying to make me feel better about myself." She held out her hands. "And besides, my fingers aren't so small anymore." She slid her fingers into her pockets.

Roger studied the young girl. "Maybe we can find you something over at Frank's. He runs a garage not far from the house."

Trina rocked back and forth on her heels. "I don't know," she replied. "I never did anything by myself. I just did what he told me."

"Still," Roger continued, "no harm asking him if he has work for you. Or if he's willing to train an apprentice."

Trina smiled. "Yeah, maybe so. What about Alex?" she asked.

Roger wasn't sure what she meant.

"What does he want to do when he grows up?" she asked. "Be a policeman like you?"

Roger looked over at Alex. The group was starting to head over to the shelter. He shook his head. "Alex doesn't talk too much about that far in the future. He's had enough setbacks that we all just sort of take it one day at a time. He's good with numbers, and he knows a lot about computers. So I don't know. If he makes it to be an adult, I expect he'll surprise us all with what he chooses to do with his life."

Trina seemed surprised. "What do you mean, if he makes it to be an adult? Isn't he just paralyzed or something?"

Roger lifted his ball cap and scratched his head. "He was born with spina bifida. You know what that is?" he asked.

Trina shook her head.

"It's a birth defect. It means the baby's spine isn't completely formed. He had what is called myelomeningocele."

"Damn, how long did it take you to learn how to say that?" Trina wanted to know.

Roger smiled. "A couple of months," he replied. "Anyway, he had permanent nerve damage from the defect, and he's had a lot of surgeries." Roger shook his head. "He's having more trouble now." He took in a breath, recalling what the doctor had told him during the last hospital stay. "He has more pain, in his legs mostly. And there just seem to be more infections. He gets pneumonia every year." He shook his head. "I don't say this much, but I just think his little body is wearing out."

Trina followed Roger's eyes as he watched his grandson being celebrated by so many people.

"So that's the reason we throw these massive birthday parties. And they just seem to get bigger every summer. I suppose we celebrate his birthday, but we also celebrate having a miracle every year he's still with us." He paused.

"Well, you could say that about everybody, couldn't you?"

Roger turned back to her.

"I mean, don't you think it's sort of a miracle any of us are still here?" She glanced around the field. "You running around with a loaded gun on your belt all the time, going into all kinds of crazy situations, driving too fast at times."

Roger raised his eyebrows at the girl.

"I'm just guessing," she said. "But think about it, you in your line of work, Fred and Bea alone at the diner at all hours of the day and night with their doors unlocked and their cash registers full. And from what I see, half the people at this party look like they're ready to fall over any minute." She slid a piece of hair out of her eyes. "I know there are a few things I survived that I didn't have any business making it through." She shrugged. "I guess I'm weird, but I figure every day for anybody is a miracle." She faced Roger, who didn't respond.

They both looked over at Alex just as the boy turned around. He grinned and motioned for Roger and Trina to join him.

"Guess we need to get moving," Roger noted.

"I suppose so," Trina responded.

And the two of them caught up with Alex, and they all headed in the direction of the picnic shelter.

FOURTEEN

It was after ten o'clock before everyone had cleared out from the party. Malene and Roger were the last ones left, packing up the leftovers and the party supplies, cleaning up the tables, and tying up the trash bags and throwing them in the back of Roger's truck. The moon was high and full.

"Good party," Roger said as he walked up to the shelter from the ball field, a large bag of garbage thrown over his shoulder. He dropped it by his side.

Malene was stacking up another load of plastic dishes and boxing up the condiments. "It was nice, wasn't it?" She stopped, yawned, and sat down at the table where she was working. She decided to take a break. "Alex seemed pleased."

"He was worn out," Roger noted, taking her cue and sitting down at the table across from his ex-wife. "He'll sleep good tonight at your dad's."

"He got so many gifts," Malene commented. "It took Daddy and me at least four trips to get everything in the car." She smiled. "And you know how big that trunk in the new Buick is."

"Yes, Oris has made me look inside his trunk at least three or four times." Roger stuck his hands in his pockets. "Did Frieda drive your van to his house?" He knew Alex's wheelchair couldn't fit in a car, even Oris's Buick.

Malene nodded. "I figured you would give me a ride back," she responded.

Roger nodded. He never minded driving Malene anywhere.

"He is smitten by the girl," Malene said, eyeing Roger, waiting for more information about his new tenant.

"Trina," said Roger. "And I know," he added. "He had his eye on her the first time he saw her."

"That working out, her living in the apartment?" she asked. Alex had told her about the living arrangements right after he met Trina.

"So far. Of course, she hasn't paid me anything yet." He shook his head. "What is it with these young people? You and I had to live at your parents' house for months before we struck out on our own."

"And we had at least enough money saved," Malene recalled, "to pay rent for a year when we finally did move into that little apartment near your office." She shrugged. "Just a different generation, I guess."

Roger waited. "He thinks she looks like Angel."

Malene sighed. "I know."

There was a pause between the two.

"You know, he asked me at least five times this morning if the mail had come. He never said, but I know he was hoping for a card from her."

Roger shook his head and didn't respond.

Malene blew out a breath. "I know that I said not to try to find her, to leave her alone, but honest to God, you think that girl would have called, at the very least, just called to tell her son happy birthday." She shook her head. "Or sent a card. I swear, I tell myself every year I'm not going to get upset, and every year it just burns me up." She looked up at Roger. "We did not raise that girl to be this way."

Roger took off his hat and ran his hands through his hair. This was the conversation that never ended. It was the fight no one could ever win. It was the main reason their marriage had ended. Malene could not let go of being angry at her daughter. He sighed and didn't answer.

"Oh, don't sit there and act like I'm just being

irrational. You could see it bothered Alex that she didn't come. You told me yourself he was asking about her. And you were the one who wanted to go up to Taos and get her."

There was no response. Roger just dropped his glance away from Malene.

"Just let me be mad for a few minutes," she said. "I deserve at least that on the boy's birthday."

Roger looked up and smiled. He loved Malene. He had since they were twelve years old. They had divorced not because he had stopped caring about her or because he fell in love with someone else or because, like so many other married couples, they had just drifted apart. They hadn't even fought all that much. They divorced because they could never seem to agree on how to make their daughter face her addiction and her poor choices and get her to be somebody she would never be able to be.

Malene wanted to use the tough love angle: make Angel pay for her mistakes, make her go to prison and face the consequences of her choices. And Roger, well, Roger realized that he was always trying to save his daughter.

He used every resource available to him as sheriff to try to get his daughter opportunities to do better, to be better, to tow the line, to do the right thing—finish school, come home, get a job, take care of her child. In the end, neither strategy seemed to work. Angel had chosen her own path, and there was nothing either parent could do to force her down another one.

When Angel turned fifteen, she became somebody neither of her parents recognized. And none of Malene's tough love antics or Roger's attempts to arrange for her salvation—the drives from one end of New Mexico to the other to bail her out or get her cleaned up, the favors from lawmen across the state, his efforts to keep her out of prison and in a halfway house or an inpatient facility—none of it worked. Even though Roger knew Malene knew it wasn't his fault, she needed somebody to blame. And so he let her blame him. He figured it was easier than having her blame herself, so he made the decision, not long after Alex was born, when it was clear that Malene was eaten up with anger and bitterness, that he would give her that gift. He would let her hold him responsible. He felt like he was anyway. As angry as Malene was, Roger was guilty. So he took the blame for them both. At least that was something.

The two of them sat in silence.

"The cake was good," Roger finally said.

"It ought to have been," she responded, willing to change the subject. "The grocery store in Socorro lost my order, and I had to drive clear up to Los Lunas to find a cake big enough to serve everybody. Ended up costing me forty dollars for the cake and sixty dollars for gas." She shook her head. "It was supposed to have a guitar on it, but all they had at the Wal-Mart was Disney characters and monsters. I just had them write 'Happy Birthday' and be done with it."

"Alex loved it. And I'll cover the extra costs," Roger offered. "It was worth it."

Malene shook her head. "Nah, it's all right. Daddy gave me some money." She rested her arms on the table. "It was good cake, though, wasn't it? I mean, being one I just picked up without ordering." She leaned against her elbows. "It's a shame we don't have anybody baking around here anymore."

Roger nodded. He remembered the sisters and their bakery. Everybody complained about too many pies and cakes and not enough meat and potatoes, but it was sure helpful for special occasions to have somebody in town who could bake a cake.

"You sounded good tonight," Malene said, referring to Roger's music. He and a group of other musicians had played and sang for about three hours.

"I couldn't keep the strings in tune for some reason, the humidity I guess, but it was fun, and Alex seemed to enjoy the music. I think he was happy about his gift from us. He already knows a few chords, and the size of the guitar is perfect for him." Roger was glad he had sent away for the small guitar. It worked well for someone confined to a wheelchair.

"It was much nicer than I expected. I know I owe you more than you asked for."

Roger shook his head. "We'll just call it even, with the cake and all."

Malene nodded.

There was a pause.

"The new priest seemed to have a good time."

Roger laughed a bit. "I don't think he ever understood which punch was for the children and which punch . . ."

". . . my father got hold of," Malene interrupted. "When did Oris buy liquor?" she asked. "And how did he get it in the punch bowl with no one seeing him?"

Roger shook his head. "I didn't know what was going on until I noticed Ms. Millie going back for her third or fourth cup." He thought for a minute. "Have you ever known her to dance with your father?"

"Not like that," Malene answered. "For a second there I even thought she was going for a stripper's pole."

Roger slid his hand down the back of his head and across the back of his neck. "Now that's something I do not care to witness," he noted.

Malene laughed. "You seemed pretty happy yourself. How many cups of punch did you drink?"

Roger shook his head. "A few more than I needed," he replied. "But not as many as Father George."

"Yeah, I figure he'll have a bit of a headache come morning," she said. "Maybe you should drive up there and check on him, make sure he can make it to his early Mass in Omega."

"You're asking me to babysit the new priest?" he asked.

Malene shrugged. "He seems so young and nervous. And he tries too hard. And he's probably never had more than wine at communion in his whole life. You checking on him is just the neighborly thing to do. After all, it was our party." She paused. "You think he was able to drive back to the parish house okay?"

Roger scratched his head. "Well, since all the deputies were here, at least he wasn't in danger of being pulled over for a DUI." He placed his hands on the table and rubbed his fingers together. His thoughts went to smoking a cigarette. "And I haven't gotten a call about a priest in a ditch, so I'm sure he's fine." He looked at Malene. "What about you? Did you have a little punch?" He winked. He could tell his ex-wife had imbibed. She seemed to have loosened up a bit as the party went on, and he had enjoyed watching her in her relaxed state.

She waved off the question. "Maybe a couple of glasses," she replied. "But that was hours ago.

Now I'm just tired." She rested her chin in her hand. "You thinking about a smoke?" she asked.

Roger leaned back and shoved his hands in his pockets. "It'd be a great time for one right about now."

Malene nodded. "You've done good this time," she commented.

"Almost a month," he noted. "And it's just as hard as it was the first day."

They both laughed. There was a pause in the conversation.

"Full moon," Roger finally said. He peeked out of the shelter and looked up at the sky. "I can't remember the last time we sat alone outside under a full moon." He sat back up and smiled.

"You used to sing to me under the full moon," Malene remembered. "What was that song you used to sing, something about a freckle beside my lips?"

"*Ese lunar que tienes cielito lindo junta tu boca. No se lo des a nadie cielito lindo, que a mi me toca*," he sang.

"You know I fell in love with you because of your singing," Malene said.

"You fell in love with me because I was the only boy you could beat in a footrace," Roger responded.

Malene laughed. "You never were very fast."

"That's not what you were saying by the time we were in high school." Roger smiled.

Malene shook her head. "Ah, to be young again," she said, dropping her head on her arm to rest.

"*Ay! Ay! Ayay! Canta y no llores, porque cantando se alegran, cielito lindo, los corazones.*" Roger sang another line from their song while Malene closed her eyes and smiled.

It was the perfect ending to a perfect day.

FIFTEEN

Father George was drunk. He had managed to drive himself back to the parish house without incident, although he had gone a few miles before he realized he had turned on the windshield wipers and not the lights. He handled the dirt road up to the parish and was able to park the car in the appropriate place next to the house. He had to wait a minute to be able to get out of the car, catch his breath, steady himself, before he could manage to stumble to the door, unlock it, and walk inside. But that was all he could do before the spinning intensified. He hurried to the bed, falling on it.

When he first left the party, he thought he must be sick, coming down with something, since he hadn't knowingly drunk alcohol. However, by the time he had gotten off of the main road and was having such a hard time concentrating while he drove, he knew what was happening. The punch was spiked, and he was definitely intoxicated. He thought the people standing around the bowl of punch seemed oddly delighted that he was enjoying so much of it. He thought it had been a bit strange that everyone stopped talking to watch him as he poured himself a glass. He was not the reason for the tainted drink, but he was certainly an entertaining consequence. The people at the party, members of his parish, had watched their priest unknowingly get drunk. The room spun as George realized what had happened and suddenly remembered the only other time in his life when he had had that much alcohol. Like this one was sure to become, it wasn't a memory he cherished.

George moaned, jumping up from the bed to run to the bathroom. He was going to be sick. "What on earth did I drink?" he asked out loud. After thirty minutes of vomiting up everything he had eaten for the entire day, he crawled to the kitchen, pulled a bottle of water from the refrigerator, and headed back to his bed. He sat on the edge and took a few swallows of water. The room kept spinning. He closed his eyes and leaned forward over his knees, dropping his head in his hands. Voices and bits of conversations floated across his mind.

"Get some boots," he recalled somebody saying. "You two just seem to show up everywhere together," the same voice commented. "You believe in angels?" a girl asked. "Altar Guild . . . that skunk seemed to take up with the priest . . . den of rattlesnakes at the parish house . . . cancel Mass. . . ." The voices just kept resounding, getting louder and louder. He ran back to the toilet.

Father George Morris had been planning to be a priest since he was eight years old. That was the year his family moved into the downstairs apartment in a house that was right beside St. Peter's Church. He discovered the way to the altar on the day they moved in, and once he found that the side door was always unlocked, the one next to the priest's private office, George spent more time at the church than he did in the apartment.

He loved everything about the place. The music, the chanting, the silence, the incense, the candles, the order of things, and mostly the relief he felt when he entered. It became his own private sanctuary, his solace, his home. Since his parents were either fighting or working late hours or drinking until they passed out, neither of them seemed to mind or notice that their only son was becoming so pious. They didn't say a word when the priest would let him stay over for meals or even sleep in the parish hall, or when he made arrangements for the boy to start parochial school. After all, it didn't cost them anything. They were just glad not to have to worry about bus schedules or even teacher-parent meetings, since the priest handled them. George was out of their way, and that was all that seemed to matter to them.

George flourished in the church and in the parish school. In his early years as a student in public school, teachers had assumed something was wrong with the boy. He was too quiet, too sullen, too withdrawn, and they were always having him tested for disabilities or assessing him for special needs. One teacher thought he might be deaf. Another was convinced he was autistic. They would arrange for doctors and clinical trials, and as long as they were free and held during regular school hours, his parents never interfered. They didn't share the teachers' concerns about their son and yet didn't mind the special attention. Since they weren't willing to spend extra time trying to analyze or understand their only child, they were glad to have experts interested enough to try to figure the boy out.

Only when George was five years old did his father demonstrate any special interest in his son. He tried, as he put it to his wife, "to get the boy out of his shell." For weeks he tried teaching his son how to box, goaded him into emotional outbursts, even whipped him when George refused to fight another boy who lived next door. Mr. Morris finally gave up and went back to drinking and playing cards with his friends when George stood out on the porch, locked out for four hours, missing supper and practically freezing to death, because he wouldn't scream out what he wanted. Finally, his mother rescued him, unlocking the door and taking her quiet, unemotional son to bed. Neither parent tried to figure their son out again, leaving the diagnosis and treatments to teachers and school aides and well-meaning social workers.

At the church and the parish school, however, George blossomed. He was still quiet and even-tempered, did not have many friends, and preferred to work alone, but instead of raising suspicions from the adults, his behavior was rewarded and celebrated in this setting. He was coddled by the nuns and set apart by the priest as a special child, even one called by God to service. He had found his place at an early age, and in almost twenty years he had never regretted his childhood or the decision he made. He had even found great love and pity for his parents, and he was grateful that they had moved to that apartment and grateful that they never stood in the way of God's plan for his life.

George lay on the cold bathroom floor, his mouth dry and his head starting to pound. He didn't try to get up.

After seminary, when he finished his studies,

he asked for a call to serve in another country. He believed there was greater reward in serving the poorest of the poor. And he relished the thought of being out of America, away from the influence of television, the Internet, and all things secular. He thought it would be a good fit for him to serve in missions.

George remembered his spiritual director at seminary, who had recommended that George stay in domestic service, noting that the young man might find difficulties in being too isolated. He claimed that George's desire to serve in an undeveloped country was more pathological than spiritual, and he was concerned that isolation for George would be more harmful than helpful. His spiritual director had said that George should wait for a few years, have a bit more supervision, before being sent abroad. The young man had disagreed with his mentor, but in typical fashion for George, he accepted what was handed down to him.

"I wonder what Father Leon would say now," he said to himself. "At least in Haiti I wouldn't have to worry about somebody getting me drunk." He sat up, resting on his arms, and waited for the room to stop spinning.

He thought about what he had said, the words "getting me drunk." He recalled that the other time he was intoxicated it had happened in exactly the same way . . . at the hands of somebody else. He leaned back against the bathroom wall, recalling the only other time he had felt this bad.

After being harassed for weeks for not going out, not joining the other students for anything other than study groups, he had agreed to go with his roommates to Cincinnati to "blow off some steam," as they called it, the semester before they would be taking their final vows. It seemed harmless enough to George. They told him their itinerary. They planned to take in a movie, go to a ball game, spend time at a shopping mall, and sample a few restaurants. Seeking guidance about the idea, George had discovered that even Father Leon agreed that the outing would be a good thing for him to do.

George sat on the bathroom floor and remembered that weekend. For the first night and the first full day, it had been fun. He had found himself enjoying a bit of leisure. The guys had even commented that he looked more relaxed away from school and that the trip seemed to be good for him. And he thought it was. He liked the movie, loved the ball game, even enjoyed being in a shopping mall, seeing all the people. He was pleased with himself and his decision to join his friends, until the last night they were together.

That night was the night, they later confessed, they had made a plan "to get George drunk." It started innocently enough with a late dinner at a nice restaurant. Following the first course, he noticed that his iced tea tasted different. It wasn't the iced tea he was used to. There was a sweet taste to it, syrupy, but it wasn't a sugary sweetness. It was something else. When he wanted to complain or ask for something else to drink, the other guys had convinced him it was fine, and he had ended up having two refills.

Later, when the roommates decided it would be fun to take a cab over to the river walk and find a club to hear some live music, George decided to head back to the hotel. He had told them that he wasn't feeling very good, and after they admitted to him what he had been drinking, and after he had already been to the restroom three times, sick from the drinks, they agreed to go on without him. The plan to watch George get drunk didn't produce the great excitement the others had expected. It was actually quite a letdown. So they believed him when he promised them that he was fine and would be able to find his way back to the hotel.

He recalled that on the last day of the trip, hours after they had missed their bus back to seminary and minutes before they were getting ready to call the police to report that he was missing, he had stumbled into the hotel room, hungover, without his shirt or his wallet, claiming he had no memory of where he had been or what had happened.

After a week they quit asking, quit feeling angry and guilty, and they never knew where George had been, never knew what had happened to him while they were listening to some bad karaoke and flirting with college girls. They also never invited him to join them on a weekend out of town again. Father Leon knew that there was some story to tell, that something had happened, but after three sessions in which George would speak only of his upcoming vows and what would be required of him upon graduation, refusing to answer questions about the trip or what happened, the older priest quit pressing as well. He simply denied the young man's request for foreign service, thinking George needed more time to mature spiritually and socially, more time located near supervision and assistance before being sent somewhere out of the country.

"Is this what you had in mind for me as a priest in the States, Father Leon? You think somebody would have gotten me drunk in Haiti after being there only four days?" He asked the questions out loud again, the words filling up the room. "You think New Mexico is all that much better than a foreign mission field?" He shook his head slowly, careful not to make the pounding worse. "You're the one who needs to get out more," he said. "This is a Third World country."

He pulled himself up from the floor and made his way, leaning against the wall, back to the bedroom. He took a deep breath and removed his clothes and hung them on the chair next to the bed. He pulled aside the covers, reached for his rosary on the table beside him, and crawled in. "Hail Mary, full of grace," he started to pray, and then he stopped. He rubbed his eyes and started the rosary prayer again. "Hail Mary, full of grace, pray for us sinners now. . . ." And he stopped again.

This time he quit praying because he thought he heard something outside. He listened, straining to hear whether the voices were real or just more sounds from earlier in the night that were rumbling across his mind. He opened his eyes. There were voices, he thought, coming very near his window. He clinched his fingers around the rosary and held his breath.

"He's home." It was a whisper, male, very close to his head.

"Shhhhh . . . get away from there." Another voice, female, a little farther away.

"No doubt, if he drank as much as everyone else did at the party, he's dead to the world, I'm sure."

There were footsteps moving away from his window. Father George waited a few seconds, and then he sat up in bed and turned to face outside. He stayed perfectly still as he heard the voices moving farther away, heading in the direction of the church. He took in another breath, suddenly feeling much clearer, and leaned up to pull aside the curtains. As he did, he saw a young couple walking toward the back of the church. They were holding hands, the boy leading the girl. He watched them and was sure that the boy was someone he did not recognize, but the girl he was quite confident he knew.

He dropped back down into the bed, threw the covers over his head, the rosary falling behind the pillow, and closed his eyes, deciding that he wasn't in the mood to deal with young lovers, even if they were trespassing.

SIXTEEN

Trina was dreaming. There was a field, rows of corn, withered and brown like crops late in the season. The stalks were spindly, mostly devoured by grasshoppers, brittle from the summer sun. She walked through the rows, blindfolded, but she was not afraid. She walked, her arms stretched out on both sides, touching the stalks, feeling her way down the row. It seemed like some lesson she was learning, some means of testing her progress. There was someone near her, a woman, familiar, sweet-voiced, and kind, telling her to keep going, telling her that she was almost there. But Trina stopped when she felt the corn no longer beside her but now in front of her, blocking the way she had been going. She felt around, spinning, reaching out, and feeling the stalks in all directions. They were tall and close, and suddenly she was disoriented and could remember neither the direction she had come from nor where she was heading.

"I'm lost," she called out, waiting for the woman to answer. There was no response. "Aren't you there?" Trina asked, hearing nothing. "Wait, don't go, I don't know where I am," she yelled. "Can I take the blindfold off? Is it okay to look?" And Trina was reaching up to remove the covering over her eyes when she awoke to the sound of a knocking on her door.

"Trina, are you awake?"

She shook her head, clearing her mind of the dream that lingered along the edges of her consciousness, the dream she had had since she was a young teenager. She opened her eyes.

"Trina, it's Roger. Are you up?"

"Yeah," she shouted. "Just a minute." And she got up from the bed and hurried over to the door. She opened it, wearing only a T-shirt and panties. "Hey," she said, blinking at the sun, bright and full behind the man standing at her door. She shielded her eyes with one hand.

"Oh." Roger quickly averted his eyes. "I'm sorry to get you up. It's just that I never saw you come in last night, and now it's the afternoon and I hadn't seen any sign of life over here." He cleared his throat. "Alex asked me to stop by." He glanced down at the bottom of the stairs. Alex was sitting in his wheelchair. He waved at Trina.

"Hey, you," she said to the boy, stepping outside the door. "You checking up on me?"

Alex blushed. He could see the girl was not dressed. He just shook his head.

Trina smiled. "What time is it?" she asked Roger.

"Four o'clock," he answered.

"Sunday?" she asked.

He nodded.

"Wow" was all she said. She squinted again against the sun. "That was quite a birthday party, Alex," she shouted down to the boy.

He nodded. "Yeah, it was fun," he replied.

"I'm taking him back to Malene's. We've been to Mass and driven over to Socorro for lunch." Roger studied the young woman. "You need anything?" he asked. "Breakfast, coffee?"

Trina shook her head. "No, I've got some cereal. I'll be fine. Happy birthday again," she yelled down to Alex.

"Thanks, Trina," he called back. "And thanks for the card. It's my favorite."

Trina smiled. "Yeah, the homemade ones are best, I think."

"Okay then, again, I'm sorry I disturbed you. Alex just wanted to make sure nothing was wrong. He . . ." Roger paused. "He was just worried about you," he said.

Trina grinned and winked at the boy. "I like that," she said. "You can check on me anytime," she added, stepping out on the landing and leaning over the stair railing. "And one day we're going to get you up here so you can see what I've done to the place."

Alex nodded. "That'd be nice," he said.

"Good," Trina responded. "Y'all have fun and I'll see you later." She blew a kiss to the boy. "And you too, Sheriff."

Roger nodded and headed down the stairs. He watched as Alex waved again at the young woman. "Thanks, Grandpa," the boy said when he made his way beside the older man.

Roger just shook his head and squeezed the boy on the shoulder as he moved past him. "You and your bad feelings," he said. "I told you she was fine."

"Yeah," Alex responded. "But it was worth the view, don't you think?" He grinned and spun his chair around to follow his grandfather.

Trina watched from the small landing as the two of them moved toward the driveway and got in the van. She opened her screen door and walked back into the apartment. She glanced over at the clock to confirm what her landlord had said. It was four o'clock in the afternoon. She sighed and went back to the bed, heading under the covers. "What happened last night?" she asked herself. And then she closed her eyes and started to remember.

Trina had decided to walk back to her apartment even though several people at the party had offered her a ride. She explained that she liked moonlight walks and that she felt as if she needed the exercise. That had been almost nine or nine-thirty, she thought. She figured it was about three or four miles from the school to her apartment. That was nothing compared to how many miles she used to walk in a day. She hadn't gotten very far, a mile maybe, when the pickup truck stopped in front of her. It was an old Ford, red but the paint faded, short bed, new tires. The engine knocked a bit, and she guessed it was because of cheap gas. She had seen the driver before, in town, the second day she was there. She was walking then too, asking everybody she saw about a job. He had been standing in front of the hardware store when she went in to ask the manager if he had any openings. She felt the boy watching her then, but he hadn't spoken to her. She remembered him from the party too.

She walked just past the driver's side and looked in.

"You want a ride?" he asked. He had dark hair, brown eyes, tan, muscular arms.

Trina smiled. "Where's your girlfriend?" she asked, recalling that he hadn't been standing alone for long in front of the hardware store before a girl came up and stuck her arm through his, the same girl he had been coupled with at the party. She was young, probably not more than fifteen or sixteen.

"I took her home," he answered, grinning.

Trina studied the boy. He didn't look much over sixteen himself. A little arrogant, she thought, but safe.

"So, do you want a ride or not?" he asked again, this time looking straight ahead.

"Is there anything else to do in this town?" Trina asked.

He turned back to her, raising his eyebrows. "I know some places," he replied.

And with that, she opened up his door and climbed over him to sit on the passenger's side.

She was not a whore, like her father called her. She didn't sell sex. She didn't get money or ask for favors when she slept with a man. She didn't think of the encounters she had as business opportunities or some means to an end. She just liked sex. She liked the way she felt as soon as she realized the flirting had begun. She liked the excitement of it, the pleasure it brought, the intimate way she joined with a boy, their bodies fitting so perfectly.

She was not a slut either. She knew that type of girl too. A slut performed sex while always maintaining some hidden agenda. She slept around to gain access to another world or find opportunities to move out of the world in which she felt trapped. Sex for a slut was a way to better herself, make friends, have people she could call on. Trina didn't need sex for money or to prove anything or to escape someplace. She had abandoned her messed-up little world a long time ago, and she hadn't had to sleep her way out of it. She earned enough money to buy a bus ticket out of Lubbock, Texas, and she'd never had to use her body to get anywhere or get out of anything.

It didn't matter what her father had told everybody in town about her. She was smart. She was resourceful. She was fast on her feet. And she never had and she never would come crawling back to him for anything. He rode and broke her mother until she was nothing but a sorry drunk, lost and gone forever, but he would never get his hands on Trina. Not ever. Not again.

The boy she rode with, the one in the Ford truck, was inexperienced, and in the end they only made out, with him getting his first blow job and her getting the pleasure of being teacher to a very eager student.

His name was Rob—more like Robbie, she thought. "Little Robbie, high school darling, the apple of his mother's eye, the pride of his hometown football team." Trina smiled to think of how the boy was bound to be spoken of at home or among his friends. She thought about his girlfriend, a good Catholic girl who would only let him touch her outside her clothes, the one he had promised that it didn't matter that she wasn't ready for sex, the one he would eventually marry and cheat on by the time she was pregnant with their first child. Trina knew all about the Robbies of the world. She had met her fair share of them when she was in high school. A Robbie was the main reason she had left after tenth grade. By the time she had visited California, lived in Phoenix, and worked in Amarillo, she had discovered that there were Robbies everywhere. By the time she was nineteen, they no longer irritated her so much, and in fact they entertained her. After she left Texas for Tucson, she had learned everything there was to know about the Robbies.

Trina rolled over on her side, recalling how he had driven her out to the high school and the field where he played football, the cemetery where he said his baby brother was buried, the path out to a few of the old settlement quarters, mud houses, some of which still stood, and finally to the church, the one place she asked to go, even though she didn't explain, because she wanted to see where Father George was living.

It appeared as if he wanted her to see how easy it was for him to get inside the sanctuary. He had been an altar boy, he explained, and knew where they hid the key. She could see his plan. He intended to take her around back and let her inside, but she really wasn't that impressed with the church or the boy who guaranteed her he could break in. She didn't want to see the sanctuary or steal the communion wine. When they pulled up and she saw the station wagon with the driver's door opened and the headlights on, it became clear, at least to her, why she had wanted him to drive her up there. She wanted to check on the priest. She knew he had gotten drunk on the punch. She knew he didn't realize what he was drinking. And she was concerned. She wanted to make sure he'd gotten home safely.

She got out of Robbie's truck, turned off the pastor's car lights, and quietly closed the door, hoping not to wake him. Robbie was stupid enough to get out as well and stand right beside the window, probably near his bed, and talk loud enough for him to hear. Trina had to pull him away from the house and back over toward the church. She promised he'd get the blow job only if he came away from where the priest was sleeping.

Robbie was happy to oblige at that point. He

led her around back, located the key, found the bottle of wine. She drank most of it, and he had the religious experience of his young life. Trina smiled when she realized that Robbie would never think of church in the same way again. She pulled the covers over her head. She figured Robbie would be back at her door soon enough, and she would have to deal with him and maybe even his girlfriend at a later time. For now, she just wanted to get back to sleep.

SEVENTEEN

"She was still asleep," Roger explained to Malene after she asked if his tenant was okay. They were in the kitchen, Roger and Alex having just come in.

Alex had pestered Malene all morning after Oris brought him home. He wanted her to call Roger and make him go up to the apartment and check on Trina. He got worried as soon as his great-grandfather told him that she had walked home from the party. Oris said he wasn't calling Roger, that if Alex wanted to check on the girl he would have to get his grandmother to make the call. Malene made him wait until after church before she would let him talk to his grandfather about Trina. She tried to convince him that she was sure the girl was fine. If she wasn't, they would have heard something. Alex had heard everyone's excuses and had waited until four o'clock. Roger finally had to do what Alex wanted.

"Granddad woke her up," Alex chimed in. He glanced over at Roger with a big grin.

Roger closed his eyes and shook his head, a sign not to say anymore about the visit.

Malene noticed the exchange between the two. She studied them, watching them for what they might share, but she didn't ask anything else. She didn't mind the fact that her grandson shared secrets with her ex-husband. She actually sort of enjoyed the idea.

"She's okay then?" was what Malene asked.

"Yep," Roger answered. "Did you get everything unpacked from last night?" It was obvious that he wanted to change the subject. He glanced around the kitchen. He didn't notice any of the boxes or coolers that she'd had with her when he dropped her off after the party.

"Oh yeah, she's just fine," Alex added, emphasizing the word "fine." He grinned and then, unable to help himself, laughed out loud.

Roger stared at the boy. He cleared his throat. He wasn't so sure Malene should hear how the young woman had answered her door. He worried that she might keep Alex away if she knew.

Malene waited before answering the question. She kept watching the two of them. "I did it after service, while you were gone to Socorro. We'll just have leftovers for supper, if that's all right." She kept her eyes on Alex. "You okay eating another burger tonight?" she asked her grandson.

"Sure, Grandma, they were excellent. Papa's beans and cornbread were good too."

"Yeah, all that got eaten before I had any," Roger noted.

"Probably me," Alex confessed. "I think I ate two bowls and four pieces of bread."

"And a hamburger?" Malene asked, surprised to hear the boy had eaten that much at the party.

"Yep," he answered. "And two pieces of cake. A growing boy needs his food." Alex wheeled around the table and moved right beside Malene. "Thank you again for the party. It was awesome." He leaned up and Malene bent down so that he could kiss her on the cheek. Then he backed up his chair. "Now I'm going to go to my room to check out my gifts again. I don't even remember everything I got." He waved at his grandparents and headed down the hall.

"You were right, he sure got a lot of stuff," Roger commented. "He'll be busy for the rest of the year with all those games and things."

"Some of the people just gave him money," Malene noted. "I think he must have gotten two hundred dollars."

“This town loves that boy,” Roger said. He stood at the doorway for a minute. “I don’t know what would become of us if something happened.” He shook his head, deciding not to consider such a thing. “So what did you think of Father George’s performance today?” Roger asked Malene, changing the subject. He moved over and sat down at the table and stretched his legs out.

She scratched her forehead. “He seemed a little nervous, got lost in the order of service a couple of times, forgot to pray at the end, but I guess he’ll do okay.” She stood at the counter. She was slicing tomatoes. Her back was to Roger, but she knew he was watching her.

“What was he talking to Miss Snow about before service?” Roger wanted to know. He had noticed the priest spending a lot of time with the president of the Altar Guild. They both seemed upset about something.

“The wine was gone. He thought it was somewhere else in the church, but she told him where it was kept, and they apparently looked everywhere for it. They were both surprised that it was missing.”

“Don’t they keep extra?” Roger asked.

Malene kept her back to the table. She nodded. “Yes, but all three bottles were gone. He finally thought there was a bottle in the rectory. That’s what they ended up using, I think.”

Roger considered this bit of news. “Anything else missing? Was there a break-in?” He was the sheriff after all.

Malene turned to face her ex-husband. “I didn’t overhear that much of the conversation. But maybe you should check it out yourself. You didn’t go over there early to make sure Father George was all right today, did you?” She recalled that she had asked him to look in on the pastor before Mass.

“I called him. He seemed a little hungover, but other than that he was fine. Didn’t mention anything about missing wine,” Roger replied. “Maybe he hadn’t noticed yet.” He thought for a minute. “Hey, you don’t think Father Joseph took a couple of bottles when he headed out?” He smiled at the thought of the exiting priest stealing the wine from the church he had served.

Malene turned back to her kitchen work. “I doubt that,” she answered. “But Miss Snow did seem a little suspicious.” She smiled.

Roger laughed. “Well, maybe I should ride out there this evening, see about changing the locks on the door, talk to him about security issues.” He placed his hands on the table. There was a pause. “He seems awful young, doesn’t he?”

“We’re just old, Roger,” Malene responded.

“I suppose that’s true.”

“But really, how old do you think he is?” Roger asked.

"Twenty-four, twenty-five, I'm not sure," she responded. "I know he was in seminary about five years, and he's been out just a couple of months. I know that this is his first call."

"Well, that much you can tell," Roger noted. "Shouldn't these young men work with another priest before they're given their own church?"

Malene shrugged. "I guess they need all the help they can get," she answered. "The Catholic Church is running low on priests."

Roger nodded. "I hope he can make it here. We're not known for our generous hospitality to new folks."

"What's that mean?" Malene asked, turning to look at her ex-husband.

"Oh, you know, we gave Christine a hard time the other day, but she wasn't far off the mark about this little community. Pie Town is kind of a rough place, especially on folks who weren't born and raised here, people without family ties here. We're not all that friendly to strangers."

"You think that? Really?" Malene sounded surprised. "I thought we were a very welcoming place."

"Are we talking about the same town?" Roger asked.

"If we're talking about this one we are," came the reply.

"What about the Peterson sisters?" Roger asked, referring to the proprietors of the bakery.

"They finally got tired of everybody being so haughty toward them and moved over to Quemoda."

Malene hadn't heard this theory. "I thought they left because they could make more money over there," she said.

"They left because they couldn't get anyone to buy their pies!" Roger replied.

"I never thought about it." Malene took a sip of her drink. "Guess I'm not much of a pie person."

"What about that young couple who moved here a few years ago, tried to farm? The wife was starting a preschool."

"Well, nobody liked them because they were uppity, thought we didn't know anything about growing crops and raising children. She kept wanting to hold classes on breast-feeding and how to sterilize bottles and toys." She rolled her eyes. "Ridiculous."

Roger shook his head. "And then there was the guy trying to start a tractor business and that couple wanting to open a furniture store." He leaned back, stretching his arms above his head. "They all left within a couple of years of getting here. Let's face it, Malene, our record on hospitality ain't too great."

"Well, Father George is the new priest. We'll do right by him, I'm sure."

Roger shrugged. "I hope so. And I hope we'll treat the girl okay too, but I got my doubts."

Just then the phone rang. Malene lifted her hands to show that she was too messy to pick up the receiver. "Can you get that?" she asked Roger.

He got up from the table and picked up the phone on the third ring.

"Hello," he answered. There was nothing. "Hello," he called out again. And that was when he heard her voice.

"Daddy?"

"Angel?" Roger responded. He glanced over at Malene, who had turned quickly to him.

"Um, hey," Angel answered. "What are you doing there?" she asked.

"Having supper," Roger replied. "You okay?" he asked. He could feel his ex-wife's eyes on him.

"Yeah, I'm fine. I called to wish Alex a happy birthday," the young woman explained. She hesitated. "You having the party later today?"

"Yesterday," he answered. "Over at the school. It was real nice." He kept watching Malene to see if she wanted the phone.

"Oh God, that's right, it was yesterday," she said, and then she mumbled something Roger couldn't make out.

"You play ball?" she asked, clear enough for her dad to understand her.

"Alex hit a home run," he replied. He heard a sigh or an exhale, he wasn't sure. "You okay, Angel?" he asked again.

“Me? Oh sure,” she replied.

Roger thought she sounded drunk or high. Her words were a bit slurred, but it was also a bad connection. He figured she must be on a cell phone. Her voice kept coming in and out. “Are you still in Taos?” he asked, hoping to find out she was settled, had made herself a home.

“Nah, I left there almost a year ago. I’m in Denver now.”

“Denver,” he repeated. He blew out a breath. “I didn’t think Colorado worked out too well for you last time,” he commented. Suddenly the thought of his daughter being arrested and serving jail time flashed across his mind. Unlike in New Mexico, his status as an officer of the law had done nothing to help Angel get out of a jail sentence in the neighboring state.

“That was a long time ago, Dad,” she said. “I’m, you know, doing fine.” That was all she said.

“You want to speak to your mother?” Roger asked. He watched as Malene picked up a dish towel and started to dry her hands. She was reaching for the phone.

“Nah, I can’t really talk long. I’m borrowing a friend’s phone. Can I speak to Alex?” she asked.

Roger slid the receiver away from his mouth. “She wants to speak to Alex,” he explained to Malene, knowing the request would not be easy to hear.

Malene quickly understood that her daughter didn't want to talk to her. She thought about taking the phone anyway. Angel had called her house, after all. But then she thought better of it. They would probably only argue. She turned away from Roger and headed down the hall.

Roger could hear her tell Alex that he had a phone call. He heard the sounds of the boy's chair moving in his direction. "Well, it's good to hear your voice, Angel," he said as a way to say good-bye. And then he handed the phone to Alex.

Malene walked around her grandson and back to the counter to finish slicing the tomatoes. Roger and Malene didn't look at each other as they listened to the side of the conversation they could hear.

"Hello," Alex called out and then waited.

"Mom!" he exclaimed. "I knew you'd call."

There was a pause as he listened to what she said. His eyes lit up, and he had a huge grin on his face.

"No, it's okay. I understand," he said to her.

Both Malene and Roger knew Angel was apologizing about why she hadn't come home and why she hadn't sent a gift or a card and why she was a day late. They were used to these conversations, used to her always having to explain herself, the boy always excusing her. Malene stared down at her task at hand, while

Roger moved back to the table, took his seat, and watched Alex as he talked on the phone.

"Yeah, and I got a guitar from Grandma and Granddad, a computer game from Papa Oris. I got lots of books and cards and a couple of nice shirts." He stopped. He nodded his head. "Yeah, okay, it's okay." He waited. "I'll talk to you again sometime," he called out. And then, "Good-bye to you too. I love you, Mom."

He handed the receiver to Roger. "She couldn't talk because her friend told her to hang up."

Roger stood up and took the receiver from Alex and then placed it back on the holder attached to the wall.

"That was nice of her to call, wasn't it?" The boy smiled.

Roger and Malene both looked at their grandson and then at each other. They were thinking the same thing. Alex was so pure, so innocent, unable to be or stay angry at anybody, even his mother who abandoned him. They both took in a breath and nodded to the boy.

"It was very nice of her to call." Roger spoke for the two of them.

Malene turned back to finish slicing the tomatoes. She had nothing to add.

Part III

EIGHTEEN

I cannot help myself, I am sad for the boy. I see the way he lingers in his glances across the faces of those he loves, across the landscape of the mountain and the silent distant plains. I hear the shallow way he breathes. I watch how he struggles to pretend nothing has changed, everything is fine, and he is not weakened. But I feel his strength ebb, his sleep deepen. I know because of my own steps of sickness that carried me up to the portals of heaven. He knows too, but he fights it. "I have so much to do," he tells me. I smile and nod. "So did I," I explain.

"Is that why you're here?" he asked, surprising me, since I am always near. "Is that why you've been here? To carry me?"

I shake my head, but I am not completely truthful. I have come for him, but not just in death. I came for his birth too. I try to rationalize, but he only smiles. "It's okay," he finally says. "I'm just glad it's you."

He closes his eyes to sleep, to dream, to plan. I rest upon the delicate air between us. I float above but not beyond his call. His breath is tight and labored and shallow, his face flushed, his head bathed in sweat, and I fear he could slip away even now. I hesitate. I am not sure what I am to do.

It's not as if there were no warnings about this relationship. I was told how difficult this pairing would be, but I could see no other way. As soon as I knew, as soon as his comings and goings were revealed, it had to be. I was his. He was mine. I promised that I could conquer any temptation to change the course of life. His life. I promised them I would not interfere. I would let the days unfold in the right timing, the right way. But now I understand the counsel.

Now, the cautious undertaking, the lack of assurance, the slow, endless making of a decision, the hesitant way I was granted my wish, I understand. And before I can listen to what my thoughts, and their counsel, are reminding me of, I leave the room to find help. I decide. The time cannot be now.

NINETEEN

"I don't understand how you knew something was wrong," Malene said to her father as he drove the Buick, following close behind the ambulance.

"I can't explain it," he said, watching the road, driving faster than he should have been. He shook his head. "It was a dream. Woke me up and I just knew."

Malene looked away from Oris and stared out the windshield. "Mom," she said, her voice hardly above a whisper.

Oris didn't respond. He kept watching the road ahead of him and the ambulance, trying to keep up. "Put your seat belt on," he said.

Malene buckled the belt around her. "It looks like pneumonia again." She rested her elbow on the armrest and dropped her head in her hand. "His little lungs are so scarred. I just don't know." She shook her head. "This came on so fast. He was doing great at his birthday party. He's felt good for this whole week. I saw no signs that he was getting sick. I even thought his legs were getting stronger and that he was so much better. He was planning to start back to school with everybody else. We were going shopping to buy some new clothes with his birthday money. How did this happen? How did I miss it?"

"He'll be fine," Oris assured his daughter. He reached over and patted her on the leg. "He's a fighter, and he knows this battlefield as well as he knows the roads of Pie Town. He'll be fine," Oris repeated, trying to convince himself as much as Malene. "Alice wouldn't have come to me and told me if she wasn't planning to save him," he added.

"But that's what has me worried," Malene said. "She's never been to you before. She's never been to anyone but Alex before now. Something's different this time because she did come to you."

Oris didn't comment. He found the fact that his dead wife had visited him to be disconcerting as well, and it wasn't because he was disbelieving or afraid of visits from people who had moved beyond. He was afraid for the same reason his daughter was. Alice had never visited anyone but the little boy. Her coming to him instead was unexpected and seemed to render troublesome news. She had practically pushed her husband out of bed.

Both father and daughter knew that since he had been able to talk Alex claimed to have an angel watching over him. It was one of the first words he said, "Lady," pointing to the empty air above him. They thought he was talking about a nurse or his female doctor of whom he was especially fond. They waved it off and thought nothing of it. When he could put together sentences and make sense in a conversation, he had told Malene about the woman who came to him. He had explained that she was not a nurse or hospital worker, she was real and yet unseen by everyone but him.

He rarely spoke of her, but there had been enough times that Malene had finally pieced it together. She figured out who his lady was. Alex was being visited by Alice, his great-grandmother, her mother. For years she didn't speak of it to anyone, not even Roger. And then she had finally confided in her father one evening after he confronted Malene about Alex having a make-believe playmate. He was not sure it was normal for a child to be so sure of the presence of an invisible being.

"I knew it was her," Oris confessed. "I knew she came to the boy." He shook his head. "All this time, ever since you told me about his dreams, this woman, I knew. Ever since I understood he wasn't making up some playmate to take the place of his mother, ever since I knew not to be worried about what he saw, who he saw, I knew it was her. And I was happy and pissed off at the same time, because I wanted her for myself. I wanted her to come to me. All this time." He wiped his eyes. He had been up for hours and he was tired. "Now I wish she hadn't."

Malene reached her hand over and squeezed her father's arm. "You said it yourself," she noted. "He'll be fine. He always is."

They drove in silence for a while, making their way the 160 miles to Albuquerque, where they knew Alex would be treated in a pediatric intensive care unit. After all the years and hospital stays, they knew practically everyone who worked on that unit. They had even called the head nurse for the night shift once the paramedics arrived, letting her know that they were on their way.

"Roger getting one of the boys to come and pick him up later?" Oris asked.

His ex-son-in-law was riding in the ambulance with the boy. Malene had decided to let him go ahead while she rode with her father. She shrugged. In their brief conversation, the two of them hadn't gotten that far in their plans.

Roger had driven to Malene's house before the ambulance and after Oris. He was wearing his uniform because he thought it somehow granted a bit of authority when they arrived at hospitals, and they wanted all the extra attention or authority they could use. He'd also be ready to hurry back to Catron County to handle any emergency. As usual, he had brought along a small bag of toiletries. He kept one in his car at all times. He had become accustomed to the hospital runs and the overnight stays with his grandson.

Malene had called him as soon as she got off the phone with Oris, while she was in the room with Alex. At first she had thought her father was crazy, waking her up in the middle of the night, telling her to go and check on the boy. At first she refused, but when he had said that he was on his way over there, she had gotten out of bed and gone into the room next to hers. Oris had been right. Alex was hot and his breath was labored. There was a rattle from his chest. She called 911 and then Roger. She tried to wake Alex up, tried to cool him down, but all she had managed to do was to take his temperature, 103 degrees, put a pillow behind his back to ease his breathing, and get herself ready for the trip. She would ask Frieda to bring some things when they got settled in a hospital room. She was only concerned about making sure that Alex was getting the medical attention he needed. She was only concerned that he was going to be okay.

They finally reached the end of the state highway and turned onto the interstate. "Now we can make some time," Oris commented. "I knew I would need this new car," he added.

Malene glanced over at her father. She seemed surprised. "That's the real reason you buy a new car so often, isn't it?"

Oris smiled slightly. He checked his rearview

mirror as he pulled off the ramp onto Highway 25, heading north.

"All this time I thought you were throwing your money away or trying to impress somebody. You buy new cars to transport Alex." She studied Oris. "Why didn't you say something?"

"Not just Alex," he responded. "I started buying new cars just after you were born." He opened the window a bit. It was stuffy in the car, and he was starting to get sleepy. "Catron County is a long ways from doctors and hospitals. All we've ever had was that little health clinic over in Socorro, and I never trusted that foreign doctor."

"I don't remember us having a new car all the time," Malene commented.

"That's because you were paying too much attention to those horses when you were little—and that boy up ahead you married when you got to be a teenager—to notice what your old man was driving. Besides, your mama always kept that old car of her mother's. That's the one you mostly rode in." He turned on his emergency blinkers, following close behind the ambulance.

"That old green Dodge," she remembered. "Yeah, that's right, you would never let me ride in your cars. What was up with that?" she asked.

"You were messy," Oris answered. "And your mother let you eat anything in the car."

Malene smiled. "She was a lot looser about the rules than you were."

"That's an understatement if I've ever heard one." He blew out a breath. "You and Lawrence were coddled from the time you were born until the time . . ." He paused. "Until she died."

Malene considered her father's comments. She knew he was right about her mother's easy ways, her pampering, loving, permissive ways. She had never laid a hand on either of her children, was always patient and gentle in nature, even doling out punishment in soft kind words. Malene had intended to be the same kind of mother, but it hadn't turned out that way. She had never been as even-tempered with Angel, and even though she had never hit her daughter, she had often been angry enough to do so. The pair had gotten into more than a few battles. Malene always wondered why she hadn't inherited her mother's maternal instincts.

"So what about the cars?" Malene asked, recalling their conversation.

"What about them?" Oris responded.

"Why did you think you needed a car after I was born?"

"Your mama had a hard birth with you. We almost lost both of you." He shook his head. "So much blood. The midwife came over in time, and she was good, but the delivery was way beyond her capabilities. She finally acknowledged that things weren't going right and called for an ambulance." Oris rolled the window back up. The temperature in the car had dropped, and he was now chilled. "I couldn't wait. They were sending somebody all the way over from Glenwood. And they were having a hard time because it was icy and freezing cold. So I heated up the old car I had at the time and decided to drive your mother to Albuquerque myself."

Malene listened intently. She had never heard the story of her birth.

"Damn Ford broke down thirty miles from Magdalena. Radiator hose busted. We waited for more than an hour before the snowplow finally came up the road. He radioed the ambulance our location, and they got her to the hospital just in time to pull you out feet first." He gripped the steering wheel. "I swore to God and the doctor on call and to your mama that I would never drive a car that could break down and keep us from doing what we needed to do or being where we needed to be. So I kept my promise." He grinned. "And I ain't never been stalled on the side of the road again. When Alex was born, it just seemed like even more of a necessity. You can even fit a wheelchair in the trunk, and he can lie in the backseat, and I can drive him safely to the doctor."

Malene leaned her head back against the seat. "All this time I just thought your buying a new car so often was because of vanity." She closed her eyes. "I should have known it was love."

Oris glanced over at his daughter. He could see how much she had grown to look like her mother. The thought of his dead wife and how much he still grieved over her made his chest start to tighten, and tears filled his eyes. He wiped them away and pressed on. They were still miles away from the hospital.

TWENTY

"He seemed so good at his birthday party." Bea was chatting with Danny, the deputy, who had stopped by for a cup of coffee and a biscuit. He had been the one to break the news about Alex to everybody in town.

He shook his head. "Pneumonia again," he said, taking a sip of coffee. "Roger said he was pretty bad off last night."

"I heard the ambulance and wondered who had called," Bea noted. She slid a pitcher of cream over toward the young deputy sitting at the counter. "I thought maybe it was somebody over at Carebridge," she said, referring to the nursing home.

"I know. We've gone a long time without Alex

being rushed down to Albuquerque." Danny poured some of the cream on his plate, dipped his biscuit in it, and took a bite.

"I was just so hopeful those bad days were over." Bea stuck her small pad of paper in the front pocket of her apron. "Poor Malene. She must be exhausted by now."

"Roger said that she and Oris rode together and he took the ambulance with Alex."

Bea nodded. She looked up and smiled at the couple entering the diner. She pointed them to a booth by the window.

Danny ate another bite of biscuit and suddenly noticed the girl in the back washing dishes. "You lose Hector?" He was referring to the dishwasher who usually worked during the breakfast shift.

Bea followed his eyes to Trina, who was having trouble loading dishes in the washer. "He went to visit his grandmother in Phoenix. She was having hip surgery. Francine decided she would drive him over because she wanted to visit some friends. I needed some help, and I knew she was available." She watched the girl and grabbed a couple of menus to take to her customers. "Let's hope she can take orders better than she can wash dishes." She turned back to Danny. "What did Roger tell you about Alex when you talked to him?"

The deputy chewed his bite of biscuit. "Just

said it was pneumonia and that he was in intensive care and that he was staying up there until he hears more. I don't know if he plans to come back with Oris or stay up there with Malene. I guess he'll call and let me know if he wants a ride home."

"So, since Roger's away, does that put you in charge?" Bea asked, smiling.

Danny grinned. "Does it give me a discount if I am?"

Bea refilled his coffee cup before walking away. "Not here," she replied. "No discounts of any kind at the diner." She moved away from behind the counter and headed in the direction of her newly arrived customers.

Danny finished his breakfast and kept watching Trina. He had heard about the new girl staying in the apartment behind Roger's place, but he hadn't met her. He saw her at the birthday party, but he had spent most of the night trying to talk to Christine and hadn't introduced himself to her. He had, however, watched her as she drove away from the Catholic church with Rob Chavez later that night.

Christine had finally agreed to let him drive her home, and he was pulling out of her driveway when he decided to patrol the area a bit. Christine's house was at the end of the same road as the church and rectory, and he saw the two young people as they pulled out from the church parking lot. He thought about following them, having a closer look at things, but decided later that it was none of his business. Besides, after he drove around the church and didn't see anything suspicious, he hadn't seen reason to stop them. He wondered if his little sister, Rob's girlfriend since they had been in junior high, knew about the late night drive her boyfriend was taking with the new girl in town, but he concluded that he'd better not step into that situation either. He just decided to file away the information in his mind in case he needed it later.

"Trina, can you come out here and bus a couple of tables?" Bea had called out to the girl from the dining room. There were at least four tables covered with dirty dishes.

Trina emerged with a cart and began stacking dishes. She had filled up the cart, wiped off the tables, and was walking back to the kitchen when she noticed Danny.

Danny studied the girl. She was pretty, he thought, couldn't be much older than eighteen or nineteen, but he wondered what she was doing with a high school boy, and with that high school boy in particular.

She went back into the kitchen and emptied the container, filled up the washer, and started unloading the clean dishes. She walked out of the kitchen with a tray of glasses and stacked them behind the counter near the drink station.

When she finished she moved over to Danny.

"Hey," she said, indicating his uniform. "You work with Roger, right?"

He nodded.

"You hear anything from him this morning?" she asked. "Is Alex okay?"

She knew the sheriff had been called over to Malene's because she had been sitting on the top of her steps when he came out to get in the car. She found she liked sitting on the landing late at night because she could see the stars so clearly. She had been worried all morning since hearing where he was going, but she hadn't found anybody who knew anything about Alex. She hadn't heard the conversation held earlier at the counter between Danny and Bea. She didn't know the latest news.

"He's in the ICU in Albuquerque. It was confirmed to be pneumonia."

"Damn it," she said, dropping the empty tray beneath her arm. "I hate that."

"You know Alex?" he asked. He wondered how she could have gotten close to the little boy.

She shrugged. "Not long," she replied. "But I know he's a great kid and been through more than most kids should have to go through."

Danny wiped his mouth. "Won't argue with you about that," he noted.

"I saw you at the party," Trina said, studying the young deputy.

"Danny," he introduced himself. "Danny White," he added, holding out his hand.

"Trina," she said, wiping her hand off to shake his. "You been working with Roger long?" she asked.

"Few years," he answered. "Finished school three years ago, and I went to a community college down south. Came back here and got this job."

"Roger seems nice," she commented.

"Best sheriff in Catron County," Danny said, grinning.

"I guess that probably means he's the only sheriff in the county," Trina responded. "I rent from him," she added.

Danny nodded. "I heard he rented out Angel's old place. You're new here?"

"Just a couple of weeks," she replied. "I like it," she added, glancing around the diner.

"You got family in Catron County?" he asked, wondering if she was kin to one of the ranchers who lived on the outskirts of town.

She shook her head. "No, just came here 'cause I liked the name," she responded. "Just sounds like a nice place to live. 'Pie Town.' How can you go wrong in a town named after a dessert?"

"Not all that glitters is gold." Bea appeared next to Trina, having overheard the conversation. "And not every pie is sweet."

"What are you saying, Bea?" Danny asked, teasing the older woman. "You don't think our fair village is the perfect American small town?"

Bea raised her eyebrows. "I've been serving breakfast and lunch to the residents of Pie Town for thirty years, first in the schools and now in this restaurant, Danny White. Let's just say I know more than just stories of apple pie and baseball. We're a hard place to settle."

Danny laughed. "Bea, now why would you want to go and cause concern for our newest arrival in Pie Town? You trying to run her off?"

"Ain't my business whether she stays or goes. I'm just trying to tell the truth about the place." Bea reached for a glass, filled it with ice, then poured some iced tea.

"Small town can shelter a person from a lot of craziness in the world, but it don't free you up from the meanness," Bea noted. "Seems to me it makes more sense for a young person to move to a big city where she's got more opportunities to better herself." She grabbed some napkins and placed them on the tray next to the drink. "A new person in a small town is always suspect, and the old people never want to change."

Trina watched her. "I've been to big cities," she commented softly. "Didn't care for them." She shrugged. "And I'm not so worried about being suspect because I haven't done anything wrong. But even if I do, I figure it will take more than a city to better myself." She smiled at Danny, who blushed.

"That why you're so chummy with the priest?" Fred had been listening to the conversation. He pushed a plate of food through the serving window and rang the bell even though Bea was still standing right there. "Order up," he called out.

"I'm not blind," Bea barked. She reached up and took the plate.

"Who? George?" Trina asked Fred. "You think I hooked up with a priest to ride his coattail to heaven?"

Fred shrugged, holding up his hands. "Wouldn't be the first time somebody tried to get close to God through one of his servants."

"Please," Trina said, shaking her head. "First of all, I don't need a coattail to find my way to God since he's pretty easy to get to from just about any hike up a mountain or walk along some creek. And second of all, I'm pretty sure George's skills are limited in trying to help somebody like me."

"You saying you beyond redemption, girl?" Fred asked.

Trina shook her head again. "I don't know what you're talking about. I just know Father George has a lot to learn about this world."

"Well, maybe while he's trying to teach you about the next world, you can teach him about this one." Fred winked at Danny and headed back to the grill to flip some pieces of bacon.

She rolled her eyes at the cook. "Everybody

thinks I have a crush on the priest because we drove into town together," Trina explained to the deputy.

Danny didn't respond. He hadn't heard any of the rumors about the two of them, but he had noticed how troubled the new priest seemed to be around the girl at Alex's birthday party. At first, he thought he was imagining it, but Malene had mentioned the same thing when she saw how Father George made it a point to move to the far side of the shelter away from Trina.

"And George is so not my type." She grinned. "I mean, even if he wasn't a priest, he's like my older brother or something. Besides, I think it's kind of cute how he looks so worried every time I'm around. I think I remind him of someone who made him anxious. I sort of enjoy having that power over him." She said the last sentence quietly, like it was a secret.

Danny thought about her comment and wondered if Christine, the girl he had been chasing for three years, only allowed him to hang around her because she thought the same thing about him.

"Hey," Trina suddenly exclaimed. "Are you going to Albuquerque anytime to visit Alex? Because if you are, maybe I could catch a ride with you. I don't have a car," she added, "but I can help pay for gas."

Danny thought for a minute. Several things

flew across his mind, including what having this new girl in his car might do to his chances of finally landing a date with Christine. Even though the girl of his dreams hadn't agreed to go anywhere with him, he was pretty sure she was softening toward him, since she let him take her home from the birthday party. She actually seemed interested in him, talked to him most of that night, but he also considered the idea that maybe it was time he looked in another direction. He thought about seeing Trina with Rob the night of the party and about how his little sister would feel if she knew about it. Getting to know Trina better might help with that situation as well. He took the last sip of his coffee. He was just about to answer Trina when the door opened and in walked Father George.

"Well, speak of the devil," she said with a big smile on her face. "Never mind," she added, looking back at Danny, "I know where I can get a ride," and she grabbed her rag and empty tray and headed over to the table closest to the door.

TWENTY-ONE

Father George was not pleased to be driving Trina to the hospital. It had turned into an all-day event. After receiving the phone call from Malene about Alex's hospitalization, he had planned to make a visit to Albuquerque to see him, but he had not intended to take anyone with him, especially not Trina. He stopped at the diner for a quick bite before heading out. When she approached him about the ride, he tried to think of a way to tell her no, but her argument for them to go together was persuasive, and in the end he could not refuse her. Besides, George was not quick on his feet. He needed time to think about things before making decisions, especially if some kind of deception was involved. And even though he thought that if he bent the truth a bit and told Trina that he couldn't drive her, it wouldn't be held against him as speaking dishonestly but rather seen as an effort to protect necessary boundaries, he just couldn't tell the girl no. He hadn't had the nerve to deny her request while others watched. He hadn't had the sense to just say he couldn't do it. Once again he was stuck with this bothersome young woman.

His hesitation about driving her didn't have anything to do with worry about attraction. Even though he felt anxious around her, it wasn't that he was concerned about staying true to his vow of celibacy. It wasn't that he believed it was wrong for a man and a woman to be alone in close quarters together, as some of the older priests did. He didn't want to drive her to Albuquerque or anywhere in Pie Town because he knew it just didn't look good. He knew that people talked and that scandal made them talk even more. And he knew that even the hint of a scandal for a new priest in his first assignment would stay with him throughout his entire career. No matter how much good he might do in service to his parishioners or how tirelessly he worked for the poor or how diligent he was in his commitment to God, he would be remembered for the whispers that followed him from place to place.

"It doesn't matter what you do, it's what the parishioners think you do." That was Father Leon's golden rule, and George had taken it to heart. He had already noticed the looks he got, the rumors he heard. Bernie King had even made a point to bring it up at church, asking the priest if Trina came to Confession. George believed that his choice to continue driving around this young displaced woman was going to eventually heap trouble on his head, but in spite of his grave concern about his reputation, it seemed that Trina always got what she wanted from him.

"Alex looks really sick, doesn't he?" Trina commented as she slid into the passenger's seat, preparing to head home. She shook her head and then pulled down the visor in front of her. It was late in the afternoon, and the sun was bright and shining right into her eyes. "I've never been to an intensive care unit. That place is scary." She pushed her hair behind her ears and turned to George, who was getting into the car. "Can we stop and get something to eat?" she asked. "I didn't have a chance to grab anything before we left and I'm starved."

Father George got behind the wheel and pulled the seat belt across his waist. He thought about telling Trina to buckle up, like he did the other time they had been in the car together, but decided against it. "I need to get back for six o'clock Mass," he responded.

"Oh." Trina pulled her legs and feet up on the seat and wrapped her arms around her knees.

George turned on the engine and put the car in reverse, and then headed to the exit.

"Malene is exhausted," she noted.

George nodded.

"I guess she hasn't slept all night," she added.

"That was a nice prayer you prayed," she said.

"Thank you," he replied.

"What did you put on his head?" she asked.

"Oil," he answered.

"It wasn't the Last Rites or anything like that, was it?"

Father George shook his head. "Just a prayer of anointment for the sick." He eased out into the road.

"Good," Trina responded. "I don't think I could take it if Alex dies."

George glanced over at her. "Well, maybe you need to prepare yourself for that in case it happens," he said. "His condition appears to be very serious."

She looked at the priest. "No," she said. "I will do no such thing. Alex is going to be fine. You heard Malene and Roger. He's come through pneumonia lots of times. He's strong. This is just a minor setback."

Father George drove carefully toward the interstate. "I just know the boy is very sick and we must be prepared for the worst."

"What? No," Trina said again. "That boy is not going to die, and you need to do whatever you do to make sure that doesn't happen." She sat up straight in her seat.

George merged into the southbound traffic. "Trina, I'm a priest, not a miracle worker. And maybe you're right and the boy will be fine, but I just think we need to—"

"I don't care what you think we need to do," she interrupted. "That child cannot die. And you need to make sure he doesn't."

George picked up speed and shook his head. "Why do you care so much about Alex? You just met him. And what on earth do you think I can do?" He looked in his rearview mirror, making sure he was not pulling in front of anyone.

"I care about him because he was the first person in this town to actually welcome me here. I like Alex. I like the thought of getting to know him, watching him grow up, and you shouldn't have to ask me a question like that. And as far as what you can do, why don't you pray, sprinkle some of that holy water on yourself, use some more of that oil, say some magic words you learned in priest school? I don't know. I just know there has to be some reason you do this kind of work. You have to have something up your sleeve that keeps an innocent boy from dying." She slumped down in the seat and stared straight ahead.

George started to laugh.

"This is not funny," Trina said.

"I'm not trying to be funny," he corrected. "I'm just trying to explain that priests don't have any magic powers to keep children from dying. If we did, don't you think there would be a whole lot more people at Mass on Sunday mornings?"

Trina didn't respond.

George looked over at the young woman. He could see that she was upset. He blew out a breath, trying to think of what else he could say. "I will say the rosary for Alex. I will pray all the designated prayers on his behalf." He paused. "But, Trina, in the end it isn't up to a priest whether a child lives or dies. Those decisions are in God's hands."

"Then Alex will be fine," Trina declared.

"Why do you say that?" he asked.

"If God is good, like you say He is, and it's up to God if a child lives or dies, then what is good will happen and Alex will live."

George rubbed his eyes. He was tired from the day's travel, the visit with the sick child, and Trina's nonstop chatter. "That sounds logical, but it doesn't work that way."

"Then tell me how it works," Trina wanted to know.

"I don't know how it works," he answered her.

"You don't know how it works? Then why are you in this business?"

George shrugged. "Because it was the only business I was good at," he replied, surprising himself with his answer. He had never said that to anybody. He didn't even realize he had thought such a thing.

"Well, you don't sound very good at it today," Trina noted.

George drove without responding, and the two of them sat in silence for what seemed to be a long time.

Finally George decided to return to their conversation. He thought that maybe he should offer some counsel to his passenger, that even though he didn't really like her, perhaps he owed her some kind of comfort. "Look, Trina, bad things just happen. Children sometimes become sick and die. It doesn't mean God isn't watching or doesn't care. These things just happen." He looked over at the young woman.

"These things just happen?" she repeated. "What is wrong with you?" She glared at George. "Don't you even care about Alex? I mean, I know we're new in that town, new to Alex and Roger and Malene, but still, anybody can see that they're good people. Why aren't you upset? Why isn't it important to you that everything is going to be okay?" She thought about what the priest had just said. "And 'these things just happen'? Is that what you plan to say to Roger and Malene? Because if it is, you might want to rethink your bedside manner, if that's what you call this kind of counseling."

"And what do you suggest I say? What do you think I should be feeling at a time like this?" George sounded angry.

"Oh, I don't know, how about, 'this is really fucked up'?"

"Okay, I do not need to hear that kind of language in my car!" he shouted.

"All right, how about, 'this is really messed

up'? Or maybe you could show just a little bit of disappointment or anger that this innocent boy is suffering." She studied George. "Aren't you even the least bit mad about this? I mean, he's your parishioner. He's in your care. Doesn't it piss you off that God doesn't hear your prayers?" She turned away, rolled down her window, and stuck out her arm. "Don't you want God to give you some reason for this? Don't you want to understand why this is happening?" She turned back to George. "Are you not human at all?"

George could feel his face flush. "I don't have to answer to you," he responded.

"Oh right, because I'm not Catholic. Because I'm a woman. Because you think I'm just a common slut."

"You don't know anything about me and what I feel or what I think about God."

"Well, please tell me, Father George. I'm dying to know what is going on inside you since the only emotion I ever experience from you is annoyance at me or fear that somebody is going to see you with me. Honestly, I'm not sure if you feel anything at all, since you seem to button all your other emotions behind that black shirt and stupid white collar."

"You don't know me," he said again.

"Right," Trina responded. "So let me know you. Tell me what you feel about a boy you think is going to die. Tell me what you say to God when you think those kinds of thoughts."

George didn't reply. He stared straight ahead.

"Just like I said," Trina noted.

"How many more times do you plan on breaking into the church to have sex with Robbie Chavez?" George asked. Trina appeared surprised at the question. "Guess you think I'm an idiot as well as a phony," he said.

Trina didn't answer.

"I could report you to the police for breaking into the church." He waited. "I know there has been more than one night you've been in there. I know you stole the communion wine and that you think nobody sees you or knows what you're doing in there with that guy."

Trina rolled her eyes and shook her head. "Go ahead, George. Turn me in. That will really help you look better in front of the church folk. You can say you've caught a fornicator and a heathen, even though I have not had sex with Robbie Chavez. That should really get you some bonus points. Maybe you could even lead them in burning me at the stake. You priests seem to have a history with that kind of thing, right?"

George didn't reply right away. He saw the turnoff for Highway 60 and Pie Town, and he signaled to exit the interstate. "You just need to shut up about the things you don't know anything about. You just need to mind your own business and not worry about me and my faith and worry instead about the trouble you're making for yourself in this town."

"Just let me out here," Trina said, sitting up in her seat and reaching for the door. "I'll find another ride the rest of the way."

George didn't slow down. "I am not letting you out seventy miles from Pie Town," he responded.

"Because God can't be trusted to take care of me?" she asked. "Or because you're worried I might tell somebody you let me walk home?"

"Because it's not safe and you're being immature." He picked up speed.

"George, you either let me out of this car or I swear I will open the door and jump." Trina reached for the handle.

Father George had had enough. He pulled over. "This is your decision," he said. "I am not responsible for what happens to you."

"Well, what a relief for you," Trina said as she opened the car door and stepped out. "Good thing I'm not asking you to be responsible for me because it sounds like that may be the real reason you're a priest after all. You don't have to be responsible for anything. Just let God take the blame. I'm sure that makes him real proud." She slammed the door and headed across the road.

Waiting a few seconds, George considered

ordering her to get back in the car or putting on his emergency lights and following her for the last seventy miles of the trip. He glanced down at the clock on the dashboard. It was four-thirty. He had an hour and a half before he had to say Mass.

Father George pulled back into his lane and sped past the girl on the other side of the road. He had not felt this angry in a long time. He drove west and never looked back.

TWENTY-TWO

"Hey, Lena," Roger whispered from the hospital door, calling out to his ex-wife, who was asleep in the chair beside Alex's bed.

She didn't respond.

"Malene," he whispered, and she blinked her eyes. "Hey, why don't you go home? I'm here for the long haul." Roger had just gotten to the hospital. It was the fifteenth day of Alex's stay in the intensive care unit. He stood at the door until Malene noticed him standing there.

She yawned and raised her arms above her head and stretched. She had only recently fallen asleep. "What time is it?" she asked.

Roger glanced at his watch. "Eight-thirty," he

answered. "I'm prepared to stay a couple of days. Why don't you go home and come back on the weekend?" He moved into the room and stood next to the little boy.

"He's doing much better," Malene told him. She slid her hand across the top of her head, trying to fix her hair. "And he sat up for most of the afternoon yesterday," she added.

Roger nodded. "Is his fever down?"

"It's been normal since yesterday evening when I called you," she replied. She stood up from the chair where she had been resting and began folding the blanket she had been using. "I think we're finally out of the woods."

Roger stepped into the room and moved over to his grandson. He stood by the bed and reached for Alex. An IV line was taped to the back of Alex's hand, and his arm was bruised from all the needlesticks. When Roger touched him, Alex opened his eyes, blinked a few times, and smiled.

"Well, look who's awake," Roger said.

"Hey, Sheriff," the boy said, his voice sounding soft and weak. "You coming to take me in?"

Roger smiled. "That depends. Have you broken the law?"

"I stole Grandma's heart," he replied. It was a familiar conversation for the two of them.

"Well, that may require jail time, trooper," Roger said.

Alex winced as he tried to sit up a bit in the bed.

"You hurting?" Roger asked.

Alex shook his head. "No, I feel a lot better," he replied.

Roger grinned. "Then maybe we'll get you home soon," he noted.

"That'd be nice," Alex responded.

He closed his eyes, and Roger stood next to the bed for a few minutes, watching as the boy slept. He finally walked around the bed, pulled out another chair from near the door, and sat next to where Malene had been sleeping. She had moved over to the mirror and was brushing her hair.

"You look terrible," Roger commented.

"Well, thank you," Malene said. "That's always nice to hear." She moved back over to her seat.

"You know what I mean," Roger said. "Go home. Take a shower in your own bathroom. Eat at your own table. Take a nap."

Malene considered the instruction.

"I left Danny in charge for the rest of the week. I brought my stuff. Go," he ordered. "The car is parked on the top level in the lot." He reached in his pocket, pulled out the set of keys, and placed them on the table between them.

Malene nodded. She blew out a breath. "He does seem better," she said. She glanced over to watch Alex as he slept. "I need to go by work and make sure they're handling things okay. I know I left them in a mess. We were already understaffed before I took off."

Roger stuck his hands back in his pockets. "I went by yesterday. Christine's pulling double shifts, and a couple of the nurses are working overtime. They're fine. They asked about you."

Malene reached over to the bedside table and grabbed a bottle of water. She took a swallow. "You seen Daddy?" she asked.

Roger nodded. "We had dinner together last night at the diner. He seems pretty worried. He wanted to come with me today, but he decided he would cook some stew and take it over to your house for you when you come home." Roger stretched out his legs in front of him. "He figures he'll drive you when you're ready to come back."

"So you told him you were sending me home," Malene commented. "This is already planned."

Roger grinned. "You need to go home. You've been here the entire two weeks, Lena."

Malene took another swallow of water. "I just couldn't leave him this time," she commented. "I wasn't sure he was going to pull through."

Roger glanced over at their grandson. "He looks good now," he noted.

Malene followed his eyes. "Finally," she responded. "But, Roger, this time was so much worse." She turned back to her ex-husband and shook her head. “I don’t know how many more times he can do this.”

“Well, the good thing is that today we don’t have to worry about that,” Roger said. “He came through this crisis, and that’s enough for now.”

Malene glanced up at the door as a nurse walked into the room. “Hello, Mr. B.,” she greeted the sheriff. “You here to relieve Malene?”

Roger stood up. “I’m trying to get her to go home,” he replied. “But you know what a hard-head she is.”

The nurse began checking Alex’s IV bags, the line in his vein. “She loves this boy” was all she said. Syringe in hand, she pushed the fluid into a portal in the IV line. “The doctor wants him to keep taking the antibiotic,” she explained. “But only for a couple more days. It looks like the infection is mostly gone.”

Alex opened his eyes and smiled and then fell back to sleep.

“She tell you about last night?” the nurse asked Roger.

Malene answered before Roger could reply. “Hadn’t gotten to that yet,” she said.

The nurse shook her head. “We’re still talking about it,” she said. She pulled out a pad of paper from her front pocket and made a note. “Alex is a special kid.” She grabbed the stethoscope from around her neck, placed the end on the boy’s chest, listened for a few seconds, then looked at his vitals blinking on the screen above his bed. She took the stethoscope out of her ears and wrapped it back around her neck. "Sounds good," she reported. "Finally normal."

"No rattles?" Malene asked.

The nurse shook her head. "Nope, sounds clear. I think the staff wants to do something special for Alex," she said.

Roger appeared confused. "Why?" he asked as he sat back down.

"I'll explain it to you later," Malene replied.

Having finished what she came in to do, the nurse gently patted Alex on the foot. "He saved that little girl's life." She shook her head as she watched her patient sleeping. "I still don't know how he knew," she said. "Children . . . I guess they're just more attuned to stuff than we adults." She sighed. "Okay, I'll be back after a while to change that IV and to give him a bath. I'm hoping we can take him out for a spin around the unit later." She smiled. "I know he'd like to visit some of the other patients."

Roger turned to his ex-wife to hear the story about what had happened the previous night.

Malene met his eyes. "Alex had a dream," she said. "He woke up about three in the morning and called for me. He told me to go and get the nurse." She glanced over at the boy. "I thought he was sick or needed something, and I kept telling him that I would get him what he needed, but he insisted that I go and get the nurse on call."

Roger waited. "Was something wrong?" he asked.

"Not with him," Malene answered. "He had a dream or a message. I don't know." She stopped.

"What?" Roger asked.

"He told the nurse that the little girl down the hall . . . the little girl who came in a couple of days ago from the car accident I told you about, remember?" she asked.

Roger nodded. He recalled hearing about the terrible crash that had killed both of the child's parents and her two siblings and almost killed her. The staff at the hospital had been trying to contact family members, but they lived out of the country and had not been located. Malene had called Roger to see if he knew any way to assist them. He had made some calls to other sheriff's offices and to a few contacts across the border into Mexico, but he had not found any additional information.

"He told the nurse that something was wrong and the little girl was in trouble," Malene reported. "We tried to talk Alex out of it, tell him that he was just having a dream. We thought maybe his fever had spiked again, but he finally got so adamant that she go down the hall that she did." Malene shook her head again.

"And?" Roger asked. He had moved onto the edge of his seat, waiting for the rest of the story.

"And somehow the electric cord to her alarms had come unplugged," Malene said. "When the nurse entered her room, the little girl had gone into cardiac arrest and wasn't breathing. They did a code blue and saved her." She took the last sip of her water.

"And Alex knew this?" Roger asked.

Malene nodded. "He knew it before it happened. It was crazy."

"Has he talked about it this morning?" Roger asked.

Malene shrugged. "He woke up at six and asked about her, but that's been it."

Roger looked over at his grandson. He knew Alex was a special boy, had some relationship with Malene's dead mother, was more sensitive than any child he had ever met, but Roger had never known anything like this to happen. He glanced back over to Malene. "And how is the little girl?" he asked.

"Critical, but alive," she replied. "And still has no family with her."

"I'm sure the local force will figure it out," Roger responded. "They'll track down the grandparents." He watched Alex sleeping, and the conversation paused between the two.

"What do you think this means?" Malene finally asked.

Roger shrugged. "It just means he's more special than we even knew."

Malene didn't respond. "I'm afraid it means he doesn't have much more time here," she said softly.

Roger turned to his ex-wife. "I don't think that's what it means at all," he said. "Why would that have to be what this means?"

"Mama," she answered.

"What about your mama?" he asked.

"You know that she had this extra way of knowing things just before she died," Malene replied. "She knew Angel was going to give us trouble. She knew we were getting divorced. She knew Lawrence was getting deployed." Malene shook her head. "It was just like this," she said. "And it was just a couple of months before she passed." A tear ran down her cheek.

Roger leaned over and wiped the tear from Malene's face. "It's not the same," he said. "She was sick and he's just . . . he's just a little boy."

"Still. . . ." It was all Malene could say.

"Still nothing," Roger noted. "It's not the same," he repeated. He turned back to look again at his grandson, who was resting more peacefully than Roger had seen him do in more than two weeks. "He's just special" was all he could think to say while Malene nodded, dropping her face away from him and trying to trust what Roger was trying so hard to make them both believe.

TWENTY-THREE

When Trina woke up after a nap on the Thursday a few days after Alex came home from the hospital, she knew for sure what she had been trying for weeks to cover up and make go away. She was pregnant. She had fallen asleep after a dinner of leftovers from the diner, curled up on the sofa, the television blaring news of movie stars and their decorating styles. She had worked the breakfast shift for Francine, home from Phoenix but sick with a virus. She had seen Roger before he left to go pick up groceries for Malene and Alex, handed him a card to give to the boy, a get-well card that promised, when he felt stronger, she would play computer games with him, or poker, whatever he liked, and she would feed him ice cream and brownies she got from Fred and Bea. She wanted to ride with the boy's grandfather over to visit, but once she realized that Roger was leaving right away for the store, she decided not to ask to tag along. She had promised Bea she would cover for Francine for both shifts.

She had been up since five o'clock in the morning, worked breakfast and lunch, helped Fred wash down all the appliances, mop the floors, and take inventory of what was in the walk-in freezer. When she got home she decided to clean her apartment, and finally, by the time the news came on and she had sat down for the first time that day, she was tired.

She lay still for a minute, realizing that she was different after this nap, that she felt unlike herself, and considered how it was that she now was unable to deny that something was vastly changed about her. She thought about how it was that she had managed to hide what was happening, what had happened, for the past several weeks, but that now that ability to hide and keep hidden what was going on no longer existed. She thought about how many weeks she had been this way, counted down the days since she had been in Pie Town and the days since she last had sex with Conroe, and figured she must be almost seven or eight weeks along.

Her period was late by more than a month, and she was usually regular and paid attention to that kind of thing, but up until that evening nap, she had tried to make herself believe that she'd missed a period just because of the leaving she had done, all the walking she did to get to Pie Town, and the stress of hearing the truth from Conroe, the truck driver she met in Amarillo and followed to Tucson.

She thought she loved him when he offered her a ride alongside him in his new rig, hauling cars from Texas to anywhere west. She thought that all of the bad things that seemed to follow her everywhere she went, all the harm and sorrow and smart city boys, had finally done all the damage they could do and she was free now. She thought that because his name was Conroe, the same name as the tiny little town where her mother had once been happy, he was somehow different from the other men she had met since leaving home and that he was honest when he said she was beautiful and that he didn't want to sleep with her as much as wake up beside her.

She fell for him hard and stayed next to him in that big rig, helping him deliver the fancy cars to car lots and rich people who didn't want to drive their vehicles across the country and the new vans and wagons to the border patrolmen. She believed him when he told her he hadn't settled down because he had been waiting all this time for her to walk across his path and that he didn't have to wear a condom because he knew when to pull out. She believed him when he said he was only twenty-four and that he had a little house in Abilene where she could live when she got tired of the travel. Everything he said she took as gospel, and it wasn't because she was naive or stupid or hadn't been played before.

Conroe Jasper was tall and quiet and had hands like her grandfather's, thick and hard-worked, and she wanted to believe a man could be honorable and interesting. But in the end, he was just like the others, and she had walked all the way from Tucson to the Salt River Canyon before she'd even thought to take a ride with anybody else. She'd never walked so far in her life, but once she found out Conroe was well beyond twenty-four years of age, actually more like thirty-five, married with twin boys, and that the little house in Abilene was really a backroom at his brother-in-law's place where he already had a wife and a family, she couldn't stop pressing forward.

She walked in the heat of the day and late into the night. She walked along the highway, avoiding the stares of the children from backseats of buses and the catcalls from men out their open windows, and finally out across the middle of the desert where coyotes and owls watched her curiously and the stars filled up the skies. She walked until she fainted from exhaustion and woke up in that small clapboard house, with an old Indian woman speaking words she did not understand.

She stayed until she got the sign of where to head next. She stayed until she heard the name Pie Town. Trina thought she might be pregnant but tried to pretend otherwise, even though the old Indian woman patted the girl's belly and nodded with a smile. Trina had hoped, tried to make herself believe, that the woman simply wanted to feed her breakfast, thought that she should eat. Now she understood that the old woman had known what she herself had not wanted to know. Trina lay in bed, wondering if Conroe was heading to San Diego to deliver BMWs or El Paso to hand over patrol cars, or if he was home, having already forgotten the girl he said was worth the wait.

Trina knew her options. She could have an abortion or give the baby up for adoption. She even heard she could sell the baby and make some nice cash if she could find that 1-800 number she had been given when she was sixteen and thought she might have gotten pregnant by Tommy Dexter. She worked afternoons at the garage with her grandfather and had driven his truck clear over to Dallas to take a pregnancy test, and there she met a girl in the waiting room of the clinic who told her about the agency and her plans to sell her baby before it was born. Trina had been lucky that time—the test came back negative—and had never risked that again, at least not until this last time.

"Maybe this isn't all bad," she said to herself, even though she did not believe that to be true. She blew out a long breath and closed her eyes. She had done the very thing she swore she would never do again. She had done exactly the same thing her mother had done. She'd had sex without protection, and she had believed a man who talked too sweet. And now she would probably end up in the same way she had started. Only this time, instead of being the baby, mishandled and starved, beaten by a man who hated anything lovely, she would be the woman, her mother, broken and old, used up and worn down way before her time.

Trina sat up on the sofa and glanced at the clock. It was after nine o'clock, and she wanted to talk to someone. She wished she were back in Amarillo and could talk to Dusty or Jolene or even Lester, the bartender at the club where she hung out a lot. She hadn't contacted any of her old roommates since she climbed up into the cab of Conroe's truck because she knew that both of them and Lester would say the same thing. "You should have known better than to trust anybody with boots that shiny, and a man with a beard is hiding something."

Dusty would say that Conroe was too good at being needy and too smooth with his clumsiness. She was always a good read of men, and she had warned Trina that there was just something too clean about this boy, something too covered over. She had even guessed that he was married and had urged Trina to check him out before going out on the first date. Dusty found his name in the phone book on the Internet and told Trina to call the number just to see who answered. Trina had told her no and thrown away the piece of paper that Dusty had handed her while they drank beers on the house at the bar, compliments of Lester.

Jolene had not been overbearing in her suspicions of Conroe, but she did not approve of Trina packing everything she owned in a suitcase and traveling with him. Jolene told her to leave at least a few things hanging in the closet so he could see them, make it clear that she was coming back and not throwing away everything to drive west with him.

Lester could have cared less. He shrugged when Trina told him she was heading out with Conroe and said it was her life, but he had told her to call if anything happened and if she needed any help. He had even slipped her twenty dollars, all in ones, the tips from one night at Tank's Cowboy Bar where he worked, and told her to hide the money for an emergency. He'd thrust the cash into her hands and shaken his head like he also knew that things wouldn't work out.

Trina longed to talk to any of her friends. She almost didn't care that they would say they told her so. She wished she had a cell phone and could dial the numbers of people who didn't care if she was impulsive or spent too much money on lipstick and would call her Trina Lou or Trinie or Sweetie the way they used to. She wished that she could call and tell them what had happened, how she had discovered that Conroe was married, how she walked outside of their motel room and heard his voice from below, heard him laughing and chatting, so animated and fatherly, so different than she had ever heard him. She had gone out to find him, to bring him back to bed and stay past checkout time, and she stood out on the walkway, listening to him as he talked just beneath her, thinking she was asleep and wouldn't hear.

She listened as he talked to children, listened as he talked to *his* children, heard him tell his sons that he would be home soon and that they were to take care of their mom until he could get back and be the man of the house. She listened, her fingers gripping the rails, her robe hanging open so that the guy next door, watching from the window, could see her breasts, while Conroe promised them gifts from his trip and his presence at their fall baseball games, and then even a few minutes later when he talked to his wife, saying to her that he missed her and that she was the reason he was able to keep going. He said he was almost done with his work in Iraq and knew that what he was doing was good for the country and would give them some much-needed income. He would be home soon, he promised, and he was hopeful that there would be no more long-hauls, no more work overseas.

Trina stood a floor above Conroe Jasper, two

months after leaving Amarillo and falling in love, and could not believe the words that drifted up from below her. When he finished his call and came back to the room with a paper bag with two sausage biscuits, the bottom stained with grease, Trina had started walking. She took some money, packed her things, and never went back to talk to him, and he never went looking. She had walked to Salt River Canyon and then on to Pie Town, and now she was pregnant and alone, and she just wished she had a friend or somebody to talk to.

Trina got up from her sofa, put on a pair of jeans and a T-shirt, brushed her hair, and decided to do the most unlikely thing she would ever think to do. She figured that where she was going somebody would be there to listen, if not to talk. She hoped that when she got to where she was going she would find a friend, or at least a listening ear. Trina, pregnant and lost and alone, put on her shoes, the ones the Indian woman had given her, the buckskin moccasins, and walked to church.

TWENTY-FOUR

Father George was restless and thought about going to bed early. He had given Mass and greeted the group as they gathered in the education classroom, the women making prayer shawls, before changing out of his robe and going back to the rectory. He had eaten the dinner prepared for him by the women of the church, pork enchiladas with rice and beans, a dish that he had not expected to enjoy since he preferred a blander diet but had discovered he had actually come to favor, and after making a few phone calls, he had started looking ahead at the next week's sermon text.

It was a gospel story, a healing miracle performed by Jesus. George had studied it in his New Testament class in seminary. In the story Jesus is approached by a Gentile, a Syrophoenician woman who wants healing for her daughter. Jesus explains that he is there for the Jewish people, quotes to her a Jewish proverb that says something like food should not be taken from children and given to the dogs. And then this woman, this nonperson who shouldn't even be speaking to a Jewish man, responds that even the dogs get crumbs from the table. And then, just like that, Jesus heals the woman's child. He breaks rules and traditions and gives his gift of healing, a miracle, to a Gentile.

George had never liked the story, was never comfortable with the action of Jesus or the interpretation of the story by scholars.

He got up from his desk and decided to make a pot of tea. He hoped that the chamomile that he bought at the grocery store on his last outing would calm him, soothe his mind. He turned on the faucet, filled up the kettle, and placed it on the stove, waiting for it to heat.

George had never understood the harsh words of Jesus to the woman and he also never understood the way it appeared as if Jesus changed his mind and met her request. He knew that some scholars claimed that Jesus said the proverb just to show his disciples their prejudice and how wrong they were to exclude others. "It was a teaching moment," his professor had said. But then one of the students, an older boy who eventually dropped out of seminary, raised his hand and asked the questions that had shocked everyone in the class: "What if she changed his mind? What if Jesus had a conversion experience because of what this woman said?"

At the time George thought the student was crazy, heretical, and, like everyone else, had not been surprised when months later he had left school. But the questions he had asked stayed with George. They practically haunted him. He wondered: was it possible that the Son of God could have a conversion experience? Could it be that Jesus had started out thinking one way about Gentiles and women, the way all Jewish men thought about them in the first century, and then suddenly changed his thinking?

He poured a cup of tea and shook the memories and thoughts from his mind. It was more than he wanted to think about that week. He would simply preach on the Old Testament text and just not deal with the gospel story. And with that decision he dismissed the other thoughts he was having and recalled instead the events of the day.

Most of that Thursday he had been out of the parish and rectory making pastoral visits. He'd gone to Carebridge and conducted Mass for the few Catholic patients who could attend and made visits to the rooms, offering Communion to those who could not. He had visited Fedora Snow because she wanted to talk about the upcoming fall services, the Nativity of the Blessed Virgin Mary's Feast Day held in early September, only a few weeks away, the St. Francis Day Blessing of the Animals scheduled for October, and the Pie Town community dinner that was always held in November.

She had asked for the visit because there were things she needed the priest to know, things like

Millie Watson should not be in charge of the Feast Day meal because she always made her stew too spicy and never had enough desserts. Fedora wanted Father George to ask someone else to be in charge of that event, and she also wanted him to know that she didn't think the animals should be on the front lawn of Holy Family Church for St. Francis Day. The November community dinner, she explained, needed only publicity and no discussion since she had been in charge of that gathering for years and saw no need for any change. The woman had droned on for over an hour, and by the end of the visit Father George, feeling bored and in need of a break, had decided to stop by the diner for lunch and to catch his breath after he left Fedora's house.

After hearing from Bea that Roger and Malene had brought Alex home from the hospital earlier in the week, he decided he would drop by Malene's house after he stopped to see Frank at the garage to give him a Bible and rosary beads for Raymond, his son, who was in boot camp. He thought about that encounter too, his first with the owner of the garage, a Navajo, the son of an active member of Holy Family.

Frank had been polite but not thrilled to see the priest or to receive the gifts for his son. George explained that Frank's mother had asked him to bring Raymond the Bible and rosary beads, and Frank had made a kind of huffing noise at that. "Mama still thinks she can make Catholics out of us," he said, and Father George felt his face flush. He dropped his hands at his sides, still clutching the small Bible and the long wooden beads. And then Frank studied the priest and asked, "What is it with your kind? Why does everyone need to believe as you believe? Is God so small that there is only one way to name Him? Only one way to get His attention?"

George had tried to explain that Catholics and all Christians believe that it is only through God's son that one can find salvation and have eternal life. Frank just shook his head, leaning back under the hood to work on the engine of the car in the garage bay. "And your God only had one son, not many children? Why would the Creator of all worlds and all heavens create only one son?" George didn't answer. "And this need for salvation?" Frank asked. "Are we being saved from ourselves or from this God who is described as not just a God of love but also vengeance?"

The questions had rattled George. In the end, he had not given answers, only stood looking embarrassed while the man opened valves and flushed a radiator. Frank stood up and wiped his hands on the rag hanging from his back pocket. He reached out to receive the Bible and beads.

"I'll give them to Raymond," he said to the priest, and George handed them over. "But your Church and your God have brought only sorrow to my people. Our only need for salvation is to be delivered from the likes of you and your predecessors."

Father George had left that encounter to go over to Malene's to see Alex. And that visit had been just as unsettling. The boy was weak and had lost quite a lot of weight while being hospitalized, but he was alert and engaging, and when he realized that Father George was standing at the door with his grandmother, he made it clear that he wanted to talk to the priest alone. Malene had raised her eyebrows in suspicion at the request but granted Alex his wish. She backed out and shut the door as George stood just inside the room.

George now sat at his desk, recalling his last conversation of the afternoon, the one with Alex.

"How are you, Father?" the boy had asked, motioning the priest to come closer, to sit in the chair by the bed.

"I'm great," George replied, trying not to show signs of his fatigue. "But the question is, how are you?"

Alex smiled. "I'm home," he answered. "And that's all that matters."

Father George had felt uncomfortable in the boy's room, sitting by his bed. His early visits at

Carebridge and then his talks with Fedora and Frank had made him realize that personal conversations with parishioners and visits to the sick, whether in hospitals or homes or nursing centers, exhausted him. It had become the least favorite part of his job. The preaching and consecrating of the elements, the study and personal time of prayer and reflection, those ministerial tasks were his forte. He realized he should have received more training, more experience, in the pastoral care aspect of his ministry.

"Thank you for visiting me at the hospital that day after I first got there," Alex had said. "And for bringing Trina."

Father George nodded. He had not wanted to think about that day. He had not spoken to the young woman since she got out of his car on Highway 60 and he drove away. He had seen her through the diner windows on occasion, passed her once on Main Street, but they had not talked since the argument.

"I was glad to see you both," Alex commented.

Father George nodded. He had no reply.

"She's not what you think," Alex said, his voice small and weak.

"What do you mean?" George asked, not understanding what the boy was saying.

"She's not bad or anything," Alex replied.

Father George didn't know how to respond. He dropped his face. He wondered why Alex would say such a thing to him, and he worried that his discontented feelings about the other new resident of Pie Town had become too transparent. He was going to explain, but then, perhaps because of his fatigue and the day's other conversations, he thought better of it.

"She's lost is all," Alex added. "But things will be right soon."

Father George looked back up at the boy and decided that Alex was not fully himself, that he was speaking from weakness, and maybe from medication. The priest nodded and smiled. "Yes, I think things will be right for both of you."

"And you," the boy said, focusing his eyes on the priest. "Things will finally be right for you too."

Father George had been about to ask Alex what he meant, but Oris came in just at that moment, interrupting the conversation. Oris pushed past the priest and knelt by the bed, pulling his great-grandson into his arms. George noticed the tears in the old man's eyes, understood the intimacy of the moment, and decided to make a quiet exit. He left without saying good-bye.

He sat at his desk and remembered the conversations of the day with Fedora and Frank and finally Alex. He remembered that he had been struck dumb by Frank's arguments against the Church, that he had felt lifeless after hearing Fedora's complaints and instructions, and that he had been confused by Alex's words. He had driven back to the rectory trying to make sense of what the three conversations had meant, and especially what Alex had said.

"What would finally be right with myself?" George asked. "What is so wrong that would be made right?" But before he could answer, he saw the lights coming up the road, a vehicle pulling into the church parking lot, and recognized right away the make and style of the small pickup truck.

TWENTY-FIVE

Rob Chavez had finished the first football practice of the season and needed more action. He was fired up, excited about the team workout, and thrilled that the school year was about to start. This was his year, he had told himself. This year, his senior year, was going to be the best yet. He had all the plays down solid. He was more accurate with his passing and faster when he ran. He was confident, and he was revved up after the early practice.

After most of the other players were gone, the coach had called Rob into his office and told him that the University of New Mexico recruiter had called him over the summer and that he planned to drive up to meet Rob, watch him play a game. The coach seemed confident that this could mean a scholarship for his star quarterback, and if that didn't work out, he was pretty sure that Rob could get a complete ride at New Mexico State if he wanted it. The young player's statistics were impressive on the high school level, and he had broken a number of records during his last season. Healthy, stronger, heavier, Rob was certain that this football season would be the year he dominated and the year when he would be given a scholarship and a chance to get out of his hick hometown. It had been a great evening.

He was still dating Katie White, had been all summer, even when there had been a couple of times he messed around with the new girl in town. He and Katie broke up for a week or so after she found out he was seeing somebody else, but they were back together, and he was pretty sure she hadn't figured out who the somebody else was. He was pretty sure no one knew about him and Trina.

Trina had gone pretty far with Rob in their few short get-togethers. There had been oral sex and a lot of heavy petting. He had stayed over at her apartment a couple of nights. She had declined intercourse, claiming she didn't want the experience with a virgin, nor did she want the reputation that would surely follow. She had taught him a few things, but finally cut things off when she thought Katie had figured out who she was and told him not to come over to her apartment anymore. He needed to focus on one relationship at a time, she told him, and she didn't want to be responsible for breaking another girl's heart.

Rob really put the pressure on Katie after that, and she continued to be resistant, but he was sure, with a little more pressure, and especially with football season starting and the return of his all-star status at school, he would get what he wanted from her. He was certain of it, and he was starting to feel like maybe this was the night.

There had been no plans to get together that week, especially not on a Thursday night, because of his practice and her volunteer work at the nursing home, but he needed to see her. He wanted to tell her about what the coach had said about a scholarship to UNM, and he wanted to move things along. He was tired of waiting. He wanted to have sex.

He drove past her house, slowing down and almost turning in before he noticed the squad car in the driveway. He sped up and passed the house, preferring not to visit when her brother was at home. Danny had made it clear to Rob the last time he saw him that he had a vested interest in Katie's well-being and that if Rob hurt his little sister in any way, there would be punishment served. Rob understood and did not want to press it with the lawman. Rob's brother had been arrested by Danny for possession of marijuana a couple of years earlier, and his brother happened to mention that Danny had a mean streak. Rob didn't want to see it. He hurried past the house and then turned back toward town.

Rob was about to go home, just forget about seeing Katie, when he saw Trina walking up the street. It surprised him to see her at such a late hour, and he wondered if she was going home from a date or heading out for one. He wondered if this could be his golden opportunity, if not with Katie, then at least with her. He slowed down as he neared her, rolling down the window on the passenger side so they could talk.

"Hey, beautiful," he said, grinning. "I was just thinking about you," he lied.

"Hi, Rob," she said, without looking in his direction. She kept walking.

"So, why's a hot girl like you walking by herself alone at night?" He put the car in reverse and drove very slowly, staying beside her.

"You need to keep moving, Rob," she said. "In the right direction."

"Come on, hop in." He kept trying.

"I'm fine," she countered.

"Don't you want a lift?" He remembered the first time she had gotten in his truck, and he could feel himself getting excited.

Trina kept walking. This was one time she wasn't interested in dealing with testosterone. She didn't reply.

Rob stayed right beside her. "What? You won't even speak to me?" he asked, trying to sound hurt. "I did what you asked. I've stayed away."

Trina cast a glance in his direction. "Thank you," she responded. "Now why don't you run over to your girlfriend's house and try to get into her pants?"

"Oh, come on, Trina, give a guy a break. Just get in. I'll take you wherever you want to go. I won't ask nothing from you. I just feel like giving a friend a lift." He eyed his rearview mirror, making sure no other traffic was coming his way. "We are still friends, aren't we?" He grinned.

"I thought I made it clear about us," she said.

"Perfectly clear," he noted. "I'm not ready to go home. I'm jacked up after football practice, and nobody is out, and it's a beautiful night to ride around. Just let me drive you where you're going."

Trina stopped, knowing it was a bad idea, but decided she would rather ride than walk.

"Rob's limousine at your service," he said.

"Oh, all right," she responded, opening the door

and jumping in. "But I'm not messing around with you. I'm tired," she said.

"No messing around," Rob said with a wink and put the car in drive and cut a U-turn. He drove right past Danny as the deputy was stopped at the corner without seeing him. He was way too excited about having Trina sitting next to him.

"Where shall it be?" Rob asked. "You want to drive up to the ridge or over to the cemetery or just ride around?"

"I was on my way to the church," she said.

"Even better," Rob said. He made the turn to head up in the direction of the Holy Family Catholic Church.

"I'm not going there for that again," Trina said, referring to the previous times they had been in the sanctuary together. "I'm going to talk to Father George," she explained.

"Why on earth do you want to talk to him?" Rob asked, having forgotten that the new priest was living in the rectory and didn't go to sleep as early as Father Joseph. He drove quickly.

"I don't know. I just think he might be able to help," she said.

"Why don't you give me a shot?" Rob asked, reaching over and touching Trina on the leg. "I think I can help you a lot better than he can." He slid his hand up her thigh while he headed up the road to the church.

Trina sighed, taking his hand and throwing it

back in his lap. "Are you going to take me there or not?" she asked.

"Baby, we can skip church and I can take you to heaven if you'd just let me," he replied, this time reaching up to grab her breast.

Trina yanked away his hand. "Rob, I am so not interested in this," she said.

"Oh, come on, baby." He reached over and pulled her hard, dragging her closer to him. They had gotten to the church, and he was heading into the parking lot. "Let's just have a little fun for old times' sake."

Trina, now practically sitting in the driver's seat, slammed her foot down on the brake, throwing them both forward and jamming Rob's face into the steering wheel.

"What is wrong with you?" he yelled, reaching up to touch his face and feeling blood now dripping from his bottom lip.

She felt for the gear stick and threw the engine into park, slid over to the passenger's side, and reached for the door handle. When she started to open the door, Rob pulled her back.

"What are you doing?" he asked. "Are you crazy or something?"

"Or something," she answered him. "Just let me out and you go home." She already had the door halfway opened, and she threw her elbow back hard, catching Rob in the chin.

Rob winced from the blow and then pushed

her hard out of the truck. “Fine, bitch. Get out.” And before she could close the door, he sped away.

The night was not going at all like he had hoped.

TWENTY-SIX

It was well after midnight when Bernie King was driving back from an estate sale down in Silver City. A ranch had foreclosed, and the bank was selling off all the equipment, the stock, and the land. He hadn’t planned to stay as long as he did, but he ran into an old buddy who had grown up in Pie Town and then moved to Carlsbad when he was a teenager. They found each other just before the auction started and decided to have dinner together afterward. They ended up talking well after the restaurant quit serving and stayed as long as the manager would let them, drinking coffee and reminiscing about old times. When the hour came to say goodnight, Bernie thought about getting a hotel room at the place where his buddy was staying, but finally decided he would drive home.

He didn’t buy much at the sale, a few odds and ends, wires and tools, a good-looking table saw. He hadn't really gone down there planning to buy anything. He just liked to see what other folks had, offer support in some small way to the family, and maybe find a bargain. Turned out, the family was long gone from their farm and from Silver City, and the only representative for the property owner was a man from the bank. Bernie could tell who he was because he was wearing a suit and because, after he walked over and whispered to the auctioneer a few times, he distanced himself during the rest of the sale from most of the ranchers standing around.

Like the other foreclosure sales Bernie had attended, this one was a fairly sad event, and the longtime rancher had almost decided this would be his last. It was just too hard to see a man's property picked over and measured so nonchalantly. It was hard to know that a person, a rancher like himself, had lost everything he had worked so hard to have. It just made him feel bad to bid on the details of a man's life, and he had been just about to leave before the thing started when he had run into his old pal. He stayed for the entire sale, ended up enjoying the auction, and even bought the saw, which he got for a very good price and knew he was certain to use.

Bernie rolled down the window to stay awake. He thought the fresh air would help. He was not used to being up so late, and he was sleepy. He glanced down at the clock on the dashboard and realized it was way past his bedtime. He thought about the next day and wondered if he could sleep an extra hour in the morning or if he would need to start early trying to make up for the day's work he had lost already.

He turned off Highway 32 onto Highway 60 and headed into Pie Town. He was glad he was almost home. He slowed down as he drove through the center of town, checking out all the storefronts and buildings. His was the only vehicle on the road. As he headed across to the other side of town, he looked at all the houses, naming the occupants to himself, and then dropped his speed again when he drove past Francine's house. He noticed a light on in the backroom and wondered if she stayed up that late every night. He wondered about the waitress, wondered if what he heard was true, that she was interested in seeing him.

Bernie had been in love only one time, and when he was rejected by Coleen Winters back when they were in high school, he had never made an attempt at love again. He threw himself into his work on the ranch, taking over when his parents died, and filled his days with managing the farm, repairing old fences, and tending to the cattle. He was lonesome only at suppertime, when he fancied the thought of a wife sitting near him, a few children around the table. But once he had put a television in the kitchen and started eating his dinner to the evening news, he found he actually preferred to live alone.

As he watched Francine's house grow smaller and smaller in his rearview mirror, he figured it was best to leave things as they were. He was too old, he told himself, to think about finding love. He had made a good life for himself, built up a nice bank account, and taken good care of his family's place. He had managed a solitary life this long, and he thought there was no reason to end what he had worked so hard to maintain. Besides, he enjoyed the friendship with Francine and thought sharing meals with her at the diner was probably as good a relationship as he could have.

He kept watching his mirror until he took the turn out of town that went past the Joyners' old place, with its row of dilapidated barns, the road that would finally lead him out beyond the Catholic church and home. He was yawning, blinking hard, and was just about to make the curve near the church when he thought he got a glimpse of a young woman, the same young woman he had met in the parking lot of the diner when the priest arrived and the same one who had filled in for Francine while she was visiting friends in Phoenix. He could see it was her, heading in the opposite direction, walking off of the road, in the fields, and moving in the direction of Pie Town.

Bernie stopped the truck and stuck his head out the window. He was going to yell out to her, offer her a ride back home since he certainly didn't think it was safe for her to be out there by herself, when something else caught his eye. He turned back to look out the windshield and suddenly noticed smoke, a plume hanging above the road a few hundred yards away. He put the car back in gear and inched around the curve to see where the smoke was coming from.

"Jesus Christ," he said, stopping again in the middle of the road. "The church is on fire!"

Bernie pulled his cell phone out of his front pocket, punched in 911, and let them know where he was and what was happening, and then he called Roger to make sure the sheriff was aware of the fire. When he hung up from his calls, he suddenly remembered what had captured his attention before he had seen the burning church. He turned back around to search for the girl. He looked across the fields and down the road for Trina. He even put the truck in reverse and backed around the curve, looking everywhere, but could not find her. Suddenly, Bernie thought of Father George. He put the engine back in drive and headed toward the burning building. He stopped in front of the church, jumped out of his truck, and ran toward the rectory, hoping that the priest was in his bed and had not ventured into the sanctuary for some late night prayer.

PART IV

TWENTY-SEVEN

The boy has moved closer to me. He sees me in a new way now, knows me in a deeper sense. He already has knowledge well beyond what I had when my body was in his state. He is smart that way. I suppose he always has been. I have heard the old ones mention that being born with a physical body so frail, so slow to thrive, stimulates the manifestations of other experiences. Perhaps they know best.

I remain near. I have heeded the warnings and not stepped in like before. I have not eased the pain in his legs or opened the constricted airways to help him breathe better. I have not brought home those who wander. I have not entered the dreams of others. I do not slow down the rate of his heartbeat or pry open the weary eyes of those who give him care. I let them sleep. At least for now. I let him bid his farewells in his own way, and I do not interrupt. I cannot promise my resolve, however, will last.

Ah, I had such hope for this town, this family, this boy. I had such confidence in the foundation of this place, the brown earth, the velvet sky, the plains and mountains. I believed in the landscape of those who live here, the hearts of those who love more than they fear. I had such longing for life to flourish in this place, for mercy to stand unguarded and compassion to walk upright and proud. I hoped for goodness to thrive, for all that is lovely to bloom and grow, for truth to be held up by everyone.

But now fire has ravished hope. Ashes are all that remain, and I am forbidden to bring to life that which is dead.

He makes his own way now, and all I can wish is that somehow he can do in these last faint whispers of his small, unlived life what cannot be done from beyond.

TWENTY-EIGHT

Roger stood at the steps leading to the front door of his tenant's apartment. It was late in the afternoon, a few days after the fire, and he knew he had waited as long as he could to make this official visit. He never cared much for this kind of conversation to begin with, but he especially didn't want to have this particular one because Alex, still frail and weak from his illness, had begged him to wait and just let Trina come to him.

Roger still wasn't sure why Alex had been so upset about his plan to ask the girl a few questions. He had tried to explain that he wasn't accusing Trina of starting the fire. He just had heard that she was seen around the time of the fire near the church and wanted to ask what she knew.

Alex, however, had insisted that the town was blaming their newest resident, and that for the sheriff to go visit her and ask her point-blank about the night of the fire was to take sides with those spreading the rumors. Roger had not even intended for Alex to know that he was planning to talk to Trina, but the boy had overheard his grandparents' conversation after Roger stopped by to check on Malene and Alex and to bring them a few things he had bought from the grocery store. Some items were on sale, and as he usually did, he had stocked up on foods that he knew were favorites of his ex-wife and his grandson.

The two of them were going through the bags when Alex got out of bed and into his chair and wheeled himself into the kitchen. It was then that Roger was telling Malene the latest from the fire investigation. Alex already knew as much as everyone else, maybe a bit more, since he had been awake when the sirens started and before the fire engine roared through town and down his street. He had called out to Malene and made her get up from bed and call Roger to make sure nothing had happened to the sheriff or to Trina or to anyone they loved. Roger had promised the boy that he would report what he knew when he knew it, and he had stuck to his word. He stopped by Malene's on his way home from the fire and told them everything.

Roger had explained that the church was a total loss. The fire and smoke had destroyed most of the building, and what wasn't burned was damaged from the water. There was not much left but a couple of pews, the sign in the front yard, and the marble altar, a gift from the diocese when the church was first built. The good news was that Father George was not in the sanctuary at the time of the fire. He was asleep, and the rectory was spared.

Bernie and the priest did what they could to keep the fire contained. When Father George attempted to run into the sanctuary and save the hand-sewn paraments and the sanctuary Bible, the consecrated elements, and a few of his vestments, Bernie stopped him, explaining that the church was too old, it was burning too fast, and the fire was just too hot. Even though the pastor's office wasn't burning at the time and the priest fought with the rancher to get in there, when a beam in the ceiling fell Bernie decided that it was just too dangerous to go in. Father George could finally only watch as all of his books and notes, his ordination gifts and remembrances, his handwoven stoles and custom-made robes, his sermon files and his certificates—all that was sacred and meaningful to him—were lost to the flames.

Once the firefighters had put out the fire and the smoke had cleared, Roger walked with George through the ruins, where they found a few things. A chalice and plate given to him, George explained, by the priest in his hometown, a long silver cross blessed by the pope that he wore on Sundays, a few photographs in frames he had kept on his desk, and a crucifix someone had given him from a mission trip in Mexico. That was all that was spared, and as he walked and searched he clutched these few belongings to his chest. Father George was so clearly distraught by what had happened that Roger left him to himself. No one else dared tried to comfort him with promises of replacements or anything to do with the business of insurance. They figured it was best to leave him alone as he continued sifting through the ashes, trying to find the things he had lost.

By the end of the following day, it was clear to the sheriff and the members of the Catron County Fire Department that the fire was started by a couple of candles left burning too close to the altar cloths that had been folded and placed on the altar after being cleaned by members of the Altar Guild. The fire, it was determined, started around 1:00 A.M. and was finally put out, the last flames extinguished, at 6:15 A.M. The sun was just beginning to rise as the first responders were leaving the scene and as the townspeople drove up the hill and around the curve to see the damage from what was already being called the Holy Family Fire.

There was other news about the night of the fire, news that was commonly known and shared by Roger with Alex and Malene. Mass had been held at five o'clock that evening. A meeting of the prayer shawl group had been held from 6:00 to 7:30 P.M., and the last member to leave, Cora West, shut the back door of the church at

7:45 P.M. She left only after turning out all of the lights and checking all the doors, making sure they were closed and locked. She could not recall whether any windows were left opened but was confident that no one had entered through an unlocked door and that there were no candles burning when she made her exit.

Later, when the captain of the fire department was finally able to locate and speak to the priest, Father George confirmed that he had left the sanctuary after Mass, blowing out the altar candles, and had not returned to the church anytime that evening. He had been in the rectory, he reported, for the rest of the evening, working at his desk and talking on the phone. He did not know of any other meetings being held in the church after the prayer shawl group. The fire captain told Roger that he wanted to press for more information, but he chose not to ask any further questions. It was clear that Father George was deeply affected by the fire and his own personal losses.

What also became clear—to the captain, a thirty-year veteran fireman from Fence Lake, to the sheriff, and to everyone else who heard the news about the Holy Family Fire—was that Bernie King had discovered the fire and called it in and that someone had been in the church after Mass and the meetings, lit candles, and left them burning. Beyond that known and accepted bit of information, there were only speculations, and there were quite a few of them.

When Roger heard the two reports about Trina being in the vicinity, one from Danny White, his deputy, who saw the girl in the truck with Rob Chavez heading in that direction around 9:30 P.M., and the other from Bernie, who was sure it was Trina he saw walking in the fields away from the church around 1:00 A.M., he explained to Malene, thinking that Alex was not listening, he made a plan to visit his tenant later that afternoon. That was when Alex had wheeled himself into the kitchen and begged his grandfather not to ask the girl questions, not to treat her as a suspect or even as a person of interest, a phrase he had learned from the years of hearing about Roger's work.

Roger had tried to assure Alex that the visit would not be an investigation and that he was not making any assumptions about Trina's whereabouts at the time of the fire. He was only following up on a few stories that were going around, he tried to explain, and he promised he would not try to intimidate or scare Trina and that he would treat her the same way he would treat anyone else he thought might have information about the fire.

Roger stood at the bottom of the steps to Trina's apartment and remembered the conversation he'd had with his grandson.

"I've asked everyone the same questions," Roger said to Alex. "I'm not accusing anybody. I'm just trying to find out the facts, see if anyone knows something that can help us figure out what happened. I'm sure whoever started it didn't mean to leave candles burning. I'm sure it was an accident, and I'm just trying to learn the facts."

Alex shook his head. "Everybody already thinks she did it," he said. His face was flushed, and Roger was worried that the boy was getting too upset.

"Who thinks she did it?" Roger asked, unsure of what his grandson knew.

"Danny does," he answered.

"How do you know that?" Roger asked.

"I heard him talking to Christine when I went with Grandma to work. He saw Trina in the truck with Rob Chavez, and he thinks they went to the church together to make out." Alex had his right hand balled into a fist.

"Well, first of all, Danny should not be talking to anybody else about what he thinks about a case." Roger glanced over at Malene, who shrugged. She didn't know about this conversation. "And secondly, Danny doesn't know if Trina started the fire."

"He thinks she did it," Alex said, shaking his head. "And so does Mr. King and Ms. Francine."

This news surprised Roger. "What makes you

say that?" he asked, wondering how his grandson had so much information.

"Papa and I went to the diner, and they talked about it. Mr. King says he saw her walking in a field about the time he saw the fire, and Ms. Francine made that kind of clucking noise she makes when she talks about people in trouble." The boy looked as if he was about to cry. "It only takes a couple of people telling stuff and folks believe the worst." He turned to Roger. "You can't let them say these bad things."

Roger glanced away. He wished he could stop this kind of gossip, but he knew that the law, unfortunately, couldn't stop folks from talking. He was about to explain this when Alex spoke again.

"It's the same thing they did to Mama," he said, and both Malene and Roger turned quickly to the boy.

They didn't respond.

"I know the things they said about her," he explained. "You thought I never heard, but I did. I know they thought she was bad for having me and not having a husband. And I know they still think she's bad, and I know you got divorced because somehow all the bad things that people said made you quit believing in each other." Alex leaned back in his chair. It was clear that he was exhausted.

Roger dropped his head, recalling that Malene

had tried to comfort their grandson, that she was finally able to get him back to bed, and Roger himself had promised him that he wouldn't let the things that people were saying influence him in his thoughts about or actions toward Trina. Alex had finally fallen asleep, but not before he shook his head and whispered, "They're going to run her off."

The sheriff was just about to turn around and go back to his house, choosing not to make the visit, to put off the conversation he knew he had to have, when Trina opened the front door and glanced down.

"Hey, Roger," she said, smiling, not at all alarmed to see him there. "You coming up?"

TWENTY-NINE

"I need to talk to Rob." Katie stood outside the boys' locker room just after school and just before football practice.

"He's getting dressed," the equipment manager explained and was about to shut the door in the girl's face.

Katie caught the door before it closed. "No, you need to tell him that I have to talk to him."

The manager, Billy Owens, a freshman, had

just started his job with the football team, and he tended to waffle in his decision-making. He knew that the quarterback would not be pleased to have his girlfriend call him out of the locker room before practice, and that if the other players found out they would give him a hard time, but he also knew that Katie was best friends with Nichole Barrett, and Nichole Barrett's younger sister was Iris, the girl he had had a crush on since fifth grade.

He knew he risked being reprimanded by Rob if he did what she asked, but he also knew this could be beneficial when it came to the girl of his dreams. Maybe, he thought, if I do this for Katie, she'll remember and mention it to Iris. He paused, looking at the girl, then looking behind him in the locker room. He figured he could tell Rob and not let the other players know. He made up his mind.

"All right, wait right here," Billy said.

Katie backed away from the door and leaned against the wall. She knew Rob wouldn't be pleased to see her, would probably even yell at her for calling him out of practice, but she needed to tell him what she had just overheard. She needed reassurance that nothing had changed, that their stories were still reliable, and that no one knew what really happened the night of the fire. Katie felt her neck start to itch, and she knew it was turning red. She always broke out in hives when she got nervous. She glanced around to see if anyone was watching and took a deep breath.

Finally the door opened. "What do you want?" Rob asked, surprised to see her. Apparently, the manager had not told him who wanted to see him, only that someone had asked for him in the hallway. "I told you not to come here." He looked up and down the hall, making sure they were alone.

"I know, I'm sorry," she said. She reached up to scratch her neck and then reached out to take Rob's hands.

He yanked his hands away. "I said, what do you want?" he asked again, sounding perturbed.

Katie stepped back. "I heard Debbie Crawford telling some girls that she knew your truck was at the church the night of the fire," she said. She pulled her hair around to the front, trying to hide her neck.

"Everybody knows my truck was at the church that night," he said, looking angry. "I told the police I took Trina there. They know that," he said again. "Everybody knows that."

"I know," Katie said. "I'm just . . ." She shook her head. "I just think somebody's going to find out," she whispered, glancing around.

Rob stepped toward her and grabbed her by the arm. "I told you, nobody is going to find out as long as you keep your mouth shut," he said.

"Everybody thinks she did it, so just shut up about it."

Katie looked down. "I'm, I'm just scared," she said.

Rob sighed and grabbed her other arm, pulling her into him to reassure her. He whispered in her ear. "Nobody knows we were there," he said, "and that's the way it will stay. Nobody saw us there. Nobody can prove we were there. We're the only ones who know. But," and he pulled away and stared her straight in the eyes, placing both hands on her face, "if you keep whining like this, somebody is going to get suspicious. So stop it. It's fine."

"Everything all right out here?" Coach Simpson had rounded the corner and was making his way to the locker room. "Chavez, you planning to practice football or get a room?"

"Sorry, Coach," Rob replied, dropping his hands and stepping back into the locker room. He didn't even say good-bye, just left Katie standing right where she was while the coach watched.

"Young lady," Coach Simpson said with a nod as he followed his star quarterback.

Katie stood at the door as it closed in front of her, feeling stupid for being there. She had expected that kind of reaction from Rob. He never wanted her around when he was practicing football or playing football, except in the stands with other fans. He didn't even want her around when he was talking football with his friends. He claimed he cared about her more than anything, even sports, but once school started, it was obvious that she was not his first love.

She stood there, scratching her neck, and waited. She wanted to knock on the door again and call him back out and explain that people were still talking and that some of her friends had asked her about Rob and Trina and even though he had said nothing had happened between the two of them, even though he claimed he had only met her during the summer and had spoken to her a few times and that he had seen her walking and offered her a ride that night, she just needed a little more reassurance from him. She couldn't seem to stop worrying about Rob and that girl and the night of the fire. She had thought she was fine, and she hadn't felt nervous for weeks, but ever since school started she was anxious that someone would find out about what had really happened that night at Holy Family Church.

Weeks had passed and she regretted everything about that night. She regretted letting Rob in the house with his bloody lip and believing his pitiful story about getting hit at practice, she regretted sneaking out after her parents had gone to bed, and mostly she regretted agreeing with him to let him take her to the church. The entire night had been a mistake, and she wished she could take it all back, wished she had never answered the door, and wished most of all that she had never left the house.

Rob had been all hands when he stopped by, and she worried that her parents would come down to the basement and catch them. When she kept telling him to hush and to stop, that he was going to wake her mom and dad, he had pulled his keys out of his pocket and told her that he had a great place for them to go. Katie had not wanted to leave the house, but he was so persistent, and she had felt bad for him because of his lip, and deep down she worried that she had made him wait too long. He just seemed so needy. She worried that if she didn't go with him and didn't have sex with him, she would lose him. And Katie did not want to start school any other way than as Rob Chavez's girlfriend.

Once they had parked his truck down the road from the church and walked through a field to the back door, she was feeling less anxious about it, even a bit excited. He had promised her this would be the most special night of her life, and it was in lots of ways. When they got there, Rob had been so tender with her. He lit candles and spread a blanket on the floor. He had told her that she was the most beautiful girl he had ever seen and that having sex would make their love even more special. He had promised her that his last year in school would be their best and that she would be a part of his new life when he went to college, while she finished her senior year. He told her that he loved her and was sure he wanted to marry her. He said all the things she wanted to hear, and all the things he said were very special. That part, the part before he took off her clothes and slid her next to him, that part was everything that she had hoped it would be.

The last part, the act itself, was not so special for Katie and wasn't nearly as good an experience as it apparently was for Rob. He was clumsy and too aggressive. He grabbed and pulled and bit and pushed himself inside her before she was ready. It was painful and not as easy as he had promised. By the time school started they'd had sex five or six more times, and it didn't hurt as much as it did that first time, but it was still not anything she enjoyed.

He did, at least, have condoms and used them every time, including that first night, so she didn't have to worry about getting pregnant. But there were certainly other things to worry about. The biggest worry, of course, being the fact that when they left the church that night, sometime after midnight, Rob had folded up the blanket, blown out the candles he had put on the floor, and hurried them out the back door, hiding the key above the ledge where he had found it and forgetting about the candles left burning on the table.

When Katie later heard the news—the report that

the fireman made to the sheriff and her brother, the one Danny shared with their parents a few nights after the incident, the report concluding that the fire had been started by burning candles on the altar—she had gotten up from the dinner table and run straight to the bathroom to vomit.

When Katie called and told Rob what she had heard, he convinced her that the story he had already told Danny and the sheriff was the perfect story. He explained it to her the same way he explained it to them. He had given Trina a ride to the church that night about an hour before he got to Katie's house. He had dropped her off in the parking lot and left her there.

He promised Katie that everyone thought the new girl living in Roger's apartment had been the last one at the church that night and that she was not denying she had been there. "It is," he said convincingly, "a perfect story. No one thinks anything other than that." He persuaded her that, for her own benefit, she needed to keep her mouth closed. And she had done what he asked. She hadn't even told Nichole that she was no longer a virgin.

Once school started and people were still talking about how the Monsignor in Gallup had decided not to rebuild the church in Pie Town and the Catholic residents would have to attend Mass over in Omega or Quemado, how Trina had set the fire on purpose because she was angry at the priest, and how Father George was asking to be reassigned because the fire had taken everything from him and he didn't want to be in a place that reminded him of such loss, Katie had begun to doubt Rob's assurances that no one would find out about them being at the church and leaving the candles burning and that Trina would be held responsible for the fire but not charged with any crime.

She had begun to doubt not only what her boyfriend told her about the fire and about no one finding out, but also what he said about her being his one true love and how he could only love her. She had begun to wonder about all that he said about that night, about getting injured at football practice and giving that girl a ride and wanting to have sex only because he wanted to be as close to Katie as he could be. She had started to doubt everything about that night, about their relationship, and about Rob Chavez.

Katie knew she wouldn't be able to talk to Rob again until he came to her house that night. She turned down the hall, walked outside, and watched as the football team headed out the back door of the locker room and onto the field. She thought she saw Rob look in her direction, and she smiled and lifted up her hand to wave. If he saw her, he never acknowledged her, and she dropped her hand, sliding her fingers, scratching, all the way down her neck.

THIRTY

Father George Morris had not slept in weeks. In fact, if he counted back to the last time he'd had a full night's rest, he would have to go all the way back to the night before the fire. That night he had slept deeply and soundly, waking even a little later than dawn, his usual hour for morning prayers.

Now every night was a struggle. He lay in bed. He tossed and turned. He prayed. He said the rosary. He got up and read scripture. He went back to bed. He tossed and turned some more. He figured he was getting a couple of hours of sleep sometime between the praying and the tossing, but in the mornings he felt as if he had been in some great, long, and losing battle.

He looked up at the calendar still hanging on the wall in front of his desk. The day was circled in red ink. Moving day. Leaving day. He was heading out later that afternoon for California, to a seminary in Berkeley to work in the administrative office as assistant to the president. It was a good job, and he was lucky to get it. And leaving parish ministry and taking an administrative position, getting out of the intimate work of being in the lives of people entrusted to his care just seemed a better fit. The Monsignor in New Mexico had made the arrangements, and Father George was thankful.

He had heard about the opening and made queries. In the end, they had all agreed that it would be a good match. He had great computer skills and excellent organizational qualities, liked order, and was task-oriented, everything the president needed in an assistant. It had been decided in only a matter of weeks, and even though everyone saw the new job as a chance for the poor parish priest who had lost everything in a fire to start over, no one spoke of it in that way. The diocese was being refigured in the western part of the state anyway, and a priest would no longer be serving the parish in Pie Town. It was a good placement at the seminary, a good move for the Gallup diocese and a good match for Father George Morris.

If anybody in Pie Town was upset about his leaving, no one said so. If any of the parishioners were sorry to see him go, it was never brought to his attention. The Altar Guild had planned a nice reception at the parish in Omega on his last Sunday. The members of the three churches had raised some money to help him buy replacement books, and the prayer shawl group had sewn a few new vestments. But no one stopped by the rectory to try to change his mind. No one hung around after Mass to try to understand his reasons for leaving. Accepting what the fire had left them and honoring the decision handed down to them from the diocese that no church would be built in its place, no one seemed concerned that the church would not be rebuilt and that Father George Morris was moving on.

He yanked the calendar off the wall and stuck it in a box sitting by the desk. "It's for the best," he told himself and opened the desk drawers to see what else he had left to pack. He shuffled through a few papers, pulled out some ink pens and a pair of scissors, dropped them into the box. He shut that drawer and pulled out the one beneath it, thinking about his short tenure in Pie Town, thinking about the few sermons he had preached in his time there, the few people he had actually gotten to know. His time in his first parish had been short and not very successful. He would mostly remember being the priest in place the night the church burned down, and that was how Pie Town would remember him as well. He sat down at the desk. He was tired from the packing.

After weeks of living next to ashes, next to the place where the church had been established over one hundred years before, next to the tiny chapel built by the townspeople, he had not spoken to anyone about the night of the fire. If Trina had used him as an alibi, if she had told anyone about the time she had been around the church, starting in the parking lot and concluding in the rectory, about what she was doing the entire time she was there and what time she left, he hadn't heard it. The town had somehow gotten wind of the news and assumed that she set the fire, unintentionally of course, so no charges would be filed and no payment demanded from the young woman. There were rumors that she did it on purpose. A few said that she was in the sanctuary with a boy for reasons other than religion, some said that she did it out of meanness or spite, while only one or two suggested that she was there to pray. Everybody accepted that Trina was the cause of the fire, but they differed on her motives. As for Father George, he had not seen or talked to her since that night.

The sheriff had stopped by the rectory a few days after the cause of the fire had been determined, but he hadn't asked about the priest's interaction with Trina. He asked Father George only about the meetings or gatherings the priest had known to be going on at the church building, when he had left the sanctuary, whether he went back into the building after services, and if he had seen Rob Chavez's truck in the parking lot. The only question Roger had asked about Trina was whether or not the priest had noticed her getting out of the truck.

When Roger had showed up at the front door, Father George had been prepared to tell the sheriff everything, even though he had not wanted to explain the details of that night. But when Roger never specifically asked him about his activities that evening and about what had occurred at the rectory, he had not volunteered the truth. And once everyone began to treat him as if he had been victimized because of the losses he suffered, staying clear of him, not pressuring him for information, he just didn't see any sense in telling what he knew. Besides, he had told himself time and time again, he didn't know what Trina had done when she left the rectory. She could have gone into the sanctuary, lit a candle, and left it burning. He didn't know, and he didn't see any reason to tell anyone about her visit and about their lengthy and intimate conversation, about how, before she left, she had covered him with a blanket and removed his shoes because he had fallen asleep on the sofa.

Besides, she had not called him for assistance. Apparently, she had not told anyone that she was with him that evening. No one had asked him to verify any story that she had given. So he had just decided not to hand over more information than was required. If she needed him, he convinced himself, she would have called and asked. He would assist only if she needed it. Because the truth of the matter was that it would not bode well for the priest if it was discovered that he had been alone in the rectory with a young woman, especially that young woman, well after appropriate meeting hours and late into the night. The two of them had talked a long time, and he had fallen asleep, and he didn't know what time she left. That story would not be good for his reputation.

And yet, ever since the fire, ever since the night Trina jumped out of that pickup truck, Rob skidding off, almost knocking her over in the parking lot, George watching from the window and then going out to check on her, bringing her into the rectory, washing off her scrapes and giving her a cup of tea, talking for hours, ever since that night he had been consumed with the idea that he was reliving another night, another series of events that followed that night, and a decision he'd made that would haunt him every single day of his life.

He opened another drawer in the desk. He noticed the contents: a calculator, a small book of the Psalms, some loose paper clips, staples, a few bookmarks. There was nothing he wanted to keep. He closed the drawer and opened the next one. He leaned down and pulled out the few files he had kept in this drawer, stuffing them into the box. A piece of paper slipped out, falling to the floor, and he reached down to pick it up. It was a folded receipt that had been filed in his papers from his seminary days. He opened it and saw that it was hardly significant, a receipt for lunch, and he was about to throw it away when he noticed the date, April 16, a month before his graduation and ordination. He knew immediately that it was hardly an insignificant day.

April 16 was the day Lisa Myers tried to visit him at the seminary, the day she left campus and went to her appointment at the abortion clinic to end her pregnancy, the day he had heard five or six times that morning that a girl was looking for him, calling the phone on his dorm floor, asking a couple of students, a professor, a secretary, about his whereabouts, the day he hid from her, in the library, in a classroom, in chapel, and finally in the cafeteria, where he obviously bought a salad and a chocolate chip cookie, a can of soda, paid $4.53, and the day he received, just as he was finishing his meal, a note written by Lisa and delivered by a fellow student, saying that she was gone and that the deed was to be done.

George balled up the receipt and threw it in a trash can at his feet, shaking his head. "These two things are not related," he told himself. "Lisa Myers was only trying to get money from me, she was not seeking my assistance as much as she was trying to ruin me." He slumped in his chair and dropped his head in his hands, remembering that day in April, remembering how he hid from her all morning, how he had repeatedly phoned her before that day and told her not to visit him, that he didn't want to see her and that if she was pregnant, then she needed to take care of matters herself. He had convinced himself that he was not the father of her child, that he barely even remembered that night in Cincinnati, and that he was not responsible for his drunken behavior. He was almost through with his education and his time of discernment, he had always intended to be a priest, and nothing was going to stand in the way of making that happen. The pregnant Lisa Myers was not his problem.

George closed his eyes, recalling how shocked he had been when she phoned him the first time. He didn't remember giving her his phone number, or even his name. And yet, she had stolen his wallet. She knew everything there was to know about how to track him down. He thought about that night with his friends, the night they left him, the night he was planning only to walk back to the hotel and go to bed.

She had stopped him just as he left the restaurant, asked him for directions, which he didn't know, and then, as he was walking away, called him back. He had turned and followed her. For some reason he still didn't recall, she had said something funny, something interesting that caught his attention, and he had gone with her somewhere and they had drunk more and he was sick and she was laughing, going through his wallet, and then, well, then . . . then he had sex with her, fell asleep, woke up alone, and found his way back to the hotel just as his roommates were about to call the police. He had lost his money, his identification, and his virginity. And then, a couple of months later, right out of the blue, she had called to say she was pregnant with his child.

Young George Morris, about to graduate, about to be ordained and called to his first parish, about to see his dream become a reality, had told her that he didn't know who she was, that she had called the wrong guy, and that she shouldn't call him again. When she called the third time, he finally admitted that he was the one she'd been with that night in Cincinnati, but he insisted that the events of that night had been her doing, that she had planned it all and seduced him to steal his wallet, that Lisa Myers, whoever she was, could be locked up for her theft, and that if she was really pregnant, then she was going to have to handle her own problems. That's how he'd said it. "Handle your own problems." And then she showed up on April 16, and then she was gone, for good. He never confirmed the abortion or found out why she had driven all the way to the seminary to see him. He had finished school and his requirements, received his call to Pie Town, New Mexico, and left the rest of that night in Cincinnati, that final semester in seminary, and that day, April 16, behind him.

That night with Trina, pregnant and asking for his advice, the two of them talking for two or three hours, sipping tea and actually conversing like friends, him even telling her about Lisa and then explaining that she could have the child and manage, or she could give the baby up for adoption. That night was completely different, the two pregnancies were completely different. And in both cases, although he'd engaged in very different conversations and there would probably be different outcomes, he had done nothing wrong. He was sure of it.

Father George thought about Trina, wondered how she was doing, whether she'd decided to keep the baby, and whether anyone else knew. He doubted that she would stay in Pie Town, because he had already heard how some of the townsfolk talked about her, how some of the kids at church called her "fire-starter." Bernie King had told everyone that she was wild, running in the fields that night, and that she probably started the fire intentionally. Father George guessed that Trina would eventually decide, as he had, that this town was not hers, not her home, and that she would hitchhike back to Texas, where he hoped she had some family and support.

He shut the desk drawer, bent down, and picked up the box. He taped it shut, then stood up, placing it next to the other boxes near the door.

He looked at his watch. He planned to drive to Gallup, meet with the Monsignor, and then catch a bus to San Francisco, then over to Berkeley later in the week. He would start his new job in a few days. This would all be behind him soon enough.

Pie Town and pregnant Trina, losing everything in a fire at his first parish, the crazy townspeople who never really liked him, the rattlesnakes, the skunks, the desert heat, it would soon all be behind him. "I will soon be able to start a new life," he said out loud. He leaned against the wall, looking at the boxes, and shook his head. He did not want to admit it, but he clearly realized that this was not the first time he had said those words to himself.

THIRTY-ONE

The nurse had come and gone. She had called the doctor and ordered morphine, in hopes that the medication would ease the pain in Alex's legs, lessen his anxiety, and help him rest. Malene peeked in his room, after walking the nurse out and saying good-bye, and watched him sleep. It had been a long and restless night.

With the decline in his health, his body worn

out from repeated infections, the birth defect with its never-ending ramifications, and the recent bout of pneumonia, Alex was losing his battles. At first, when his fever spiked again, the first night home from the hospital, the night of the fire, the boy had refused to let his grandmother call an ambulance. Adamant that he did not want to leave Pie Town, he took the Tylenol, let her bathe him in alcohol, and ate chips of ice, and finally the fever went down. The next day, feeling somewhat stronger, eating a little something and keeping it down, and with his temperature back to normal, the boy had spoken seriously and decisively to his grandparents.

He explained that he didn't want to go back to the hospital again, and with an understanding well beyond his eleven years, he stated that he knew that his body was tired and would not be able to fight much longer. He wanted, he carefully and genuinely explained, to stay at home.

Malene had fought the boy, resisted his arguments for days, even stormed out of the room the first time he mentioned it. Roger hadn't fared much better. He hadn't argued with Alex or refused to let him finish what he wanted to say, but he was certainly not willing to go along with his grandson's decision. Finally, after three days of hearing him say the same thing again and again, they gave in and said they would talk to the pediatrician in Albuquerque about his wishes. They all agreed to follow whatever plan of treatment she recommended and to take whatever advice she offered.

They never told Alex, but they fully expected the health care professional to side with them and to give them ideas on how to keep Alex willing and focused on getting better, how to get him to agree to go back to the hospital. They left Pie Town and drove to Albuquerque convinced that the doctor, a pediatrician whose life oath was to do no harm to children and to offer them quality of life as well as quantity of life, would agree with their sentiments and offer them strategy and alliance to counter their grandson's wishes.

After they had arrived at Presbyterian Hospital and had a long talk with the doctor, who had cared for Alex since his birth, after she had gone over the boy's history, his last hospitalization, the findings and X-rays showing scar tissue as thick as smoke in the little boy's lungs, after she detailed the steps they would need to take as his condition worsened, the therapy and medications, the required surgeries, and after hearing about the little boy's clear and independent decision not to fight for his life, the doctor, shocking the grandparents, had sided with Alex. They argued with her too, threatened to get another opinion, to take him to another hospital, but in the end they abided by their word. And just as they had told their grandson, Roger and Malene kept their promise. Alex would stay at home, with no more hospitalizations or surgeries, no more heroic efforts to save his life, and, after having made that decision, had been a hospice patient for a little over a month.

Malene's house had been full of people coming and going for those three weeks. Her father stayed most days, just sitting by Alex's bed, watching over him, counting his breaths when he slept, reading him the latest issue of *Farm Life* when he was awake. Oris showed up at breakfast and didn't leave until the sun was firmly set. Trina came over most evenings, played cards when Alex felt like it, watched movies she had rented when he didn't. Fred and Bea kept Malene's refrigerator full of Alex's favorites, and others from the community dropped in from time to time, some staying a while, sitting with Oris or Trina, laughing at jokes, offering prayers, others dropping off casseroles or comic books, standing awkwardly at Alex's bedroom door, uncertain of what to say or how close to get.

The day after Alex's initial assessment with the hospice nurse and social worker, Roger had gone home, packed his suitcase, and moved in with Malene. There had been no conversation between him and his ex-wife, no discussion of boundaries or what it meant for him to be there.

They just both understood that he was not going to be far away from Malene or Alex. There was no question about where Roger Benavidez was staying.

Without telling anyone, Roger had driven to Colorado and all over Denver trying to find Angel. He had made phone calls to every sheriff's office in New Mexico and the neighboring state, searched on the Internet for websites or chat rooms where she might show up, called rehab facilities and social service agencies, begging for information about his daughter. In all that time, he had not found any trace of her. Malene knew he was searching, but she never asked what he had found. She understood that when Roger knew anything, had any news, he would tell her. Beyond that, hearing about his futile search only unsettled her.

Alex never asked about his mother and seemed unbothered that she was not there. He seemed to have made his peace with Angel and her absence from his life long before his condition worsened. He never mentioned a desire to see her or say good-bye to her. Once, when the nurse was given a report on Alex's anxiety and heard about his sleeplessness, she had asked the boy and his grandmother if he was anxious because he did not have his mother with him. Alex had smiled and answered, "She's fine. I'm not worried about her. Some people just need to find their own way." Malene had shrugged upon hearing his response. "He seems to know himself and his mother pretty well," she had explained.

When he was asked about his worries and fears, he had only talked about the town and Father George and Trina and the fire, claiming that some people, some towns, needed help, needed to be pushed along. Not realizing how serious a matter this was to the young boy, Roger, Malene, and the hospice staff all patted him on his legs or on the top of his head and spoke in chorus, saying, "It'll be okay," or, "That's too much for you to worry about." But it did worry the boy, and it was all he really wanted to talk about.

Trina would listen to his concerns, tell him what she knew and how she felt, but the door to his room was always closed during those conversations, and no one ever knew what the girl accused of starting the fire told him. Once Alex learned that Father George was packed up and leaving town, he seemed to ask fewer questions, and his restlessness turned into a kind of quiet, albeit unhappy, acceptance.

Malene closed his bedroom door and walked into the kitchen. The nurse had left a brochure on the table, "When Your Loved One Is Dying," and she picked it up, without opening it, and slid it under some papers by the phone. She was not at all interested in reading it at the moment. She sat at the table, glad for a few minutes of solitude, glad her father had driven over to the rectory, though he had not explained why, glad Fred and Bea had already dropped off the week's meals, glad Trina was working at the diner and that the social worker wasn't due for another couple of hours. She was even glad Roger was working, still sorting through paperwork about the fire and still trying to decide if charges would be filed. She wanted a few minutes alone. She had taken a leave from work, and she had not spent more than a couple of hours away from the house. She went outside and sat on the porch a few times each day, and she walked in the mornings up and down the street while Roger fed Alex his breakfast or the nursing assistant gave him his bath, but she never left, and she never had any time to herself.

Ordinarily, she would have driven over or walked to the church to pray. But after the fire, that was not an option. Father George had offered her the parish in Omega and Quemado, but they were too far from her house, and they were not her own. She had declined that offer.

She poured herself a cup of coffee, the pot still hot, and took a sip. She closed her eyes and thought of her mother, wondered if she was still visiting Alex.

"Mom, you here?" she asked and then waited.

There was no sound except the ticking of the kitchen clock, no presence felt except that of those who had been in the house earlier, no notion that anyone else was in the room.

Malene kept talking anyway. "I figure this is your doing. I figure you gave him this idea that it's so perfect wherever you are, so peaceful and wonderful, that he decided to go with you." She took another sip of her coffee.

She shook her head. "I don't like it," she said. "Not one bit." She felt the tears gather in the corners of her eyes. "I didn't like it when you left and this . . ." she stopped. "This is worse than I ever imagined."

She wiped her eyes. "He's just a boy, Mama, just a little boy." She slid her hair behind her ears and rested her head in her hands. "Can't you do anything? Don't you have any power wherever you are to change the course of things, or at least change his mind?"

She waited, but there was no answer. She thought she heard a flutter or something in the den, but then she realized the window was open and it was just a slight autumn breeze coming in. She knew her mother wouldn't answer, but that was who she prayed to, that was who she called upon, had been calling upon since Alex was born and Angel left. When she tried to draw up some image of God in her mind, she always started with a picture of her mother. Mama was the one who answered, who gave comfort and strength, who brought peace. Or didn't. Malene didn't really think of her mother as God, but she certainly thought of her as the way to get there.

"I'm sorry," she said, hoping her mother was listening. "I know you wouldn't want this. I know you've done whatever you can." And she reached for the coffee cup and held it in both hands, warming her fingers and thinking about Alex and the nurse and morphine and his impending death. She thought about Roger and his quiet grief, how he wept only when he thought no one could hear him, alone and behind locked doors. She thought about her dad and the way he refused to see this as the end, how he kept buying magazines and bringing over photo albums, talking incessantly, reading articles, so uncomfortable when it was silent.

She thought about the new girl, Trina, and the strange bond forged between her and Alex. She thought about the fire and how it seemed to take the last bit of drive out of her grandson, and she thought about Father George and how clumsy and awkward and wordless he had been in his last visit. She had even asked Roger about that conversation, which they had both witnessed, asked if he had questioned the priest fully about the fire, said that he seemed guilty or distracted or something and she didn't want him around Alex acting so strange. She thought about Christine and Danny, Fred and Bea, Francine and Bernie, even Fedora Snow, who had come over and changed Alex's sheets while he was being bathed, just wanting to do something useful. The dying of this child, Malene knew, was more destructive than fire, more damaging than smoke and water. Alex, taking his last breaths and giving up, was the end of everything that was cherished and revered and honored in Pie Town. As far as Malene knew, when Alex died, they might as well roll up the sidewalks and take down the signs. The community would be dead.

Malene heard a car pull up and figured her time of solitude had come to an end. She took her last sip of coffee, got up from the table, and put her cup in the sink. When she glanced toward the front windows, she could see someone walking up the steps to her porch. She slid her hands down the front of her blouse and pants in an attempt to straighten up her appearance and headed to the door. She expected to see some friend or well-meaning neighbor and was already planning her speech that Alex had just fallen asleep and could not be disturbed. She opened the door and could not believe her eyes.

"Hello, Mom."

Malene felt her mouth open but could not form any word of greeting or response. Angel had come home.

THIRTY-TWO

"How long has she been in there?" Roger was home for lunch and a visit with Alex.

Malene shook her head. "About an hour, I guess." She glanced up at the clock on the stove, trying to remember exactly what time their daughter had arrived.

"Well, how did she look?"

"Same as always. Just like you. Her hair is a little longer and she's lost more weight, but she still looks like you. Dark and handsome." Malene attempted to smile.

"What did she say when she got here?" He had only had time to walk in the house and start heading down the hall before he was stopped by his ex-wife. She had waved him into the kitchen and told him that Angel was in the room with Alex. He sat down at the table in shock when he heard.

Malene shrugged. " 'Hello, Mom,' and then she asked if she could see him. That was it. I was as shocked as you are and didn't ask her any questions. I just escorted her to his room and opened the door. He was awake and lit up like a Christmas tree when she walked in behind me. That was it. I just left the room after that."

Roger leaned back in his chair. He couldn't believe that Angel was there, in that house, with her son. He didn't know how she had found out, since he'd never had any confirmation that she'd received any of his messages or gotten the news about Alex. He folded his arms across his lap. It didn't matter now, he realized. She was home.

"Do you think she's going to stay?" Malene was asking. She sat down at the table next to Roger.

He shook his head and raised his eyebrows. "Your guess is as good as mine," he answered. He lifted an arm and rested his chin in his hand. He still couldn't believe it. Angel was home.

"Well, she should stay," Malene said.

Roger eyed his ex-wife. "Angel has never been one who went by the *shoulds* in this life."

Malene nodded. "You're right. But I mean, she came. She's here. You'd think that means she's staying."

"You'd think," Roger responded, unconvinced.

"You're right," Malene noted, understanding what Roger was saying. "She won't stay. But still . . ."

"She came," Roger interrupted.

Malene nodded.

The two of them waited in silence at the table, listening for any noise that might come from their grandson's bedroom, leaning back, straining to hear. All they could make out was the light sound of conversation, an occasional laugh.

"You want a sandwich?" Malene asked, realizing they'd never hear anything from that far away.

Roger nodded. "I can fix it," he replied.

Malene shook her head. "Nah, I got it." She stood up from the table and walked over to the refrigerator. "Ham?" she asked.

"Fine," he answered. He shook his head again. "I just can't believe it," he said.

"I know," Malene responded. She started making the sandwiches. "It's a miracle," she added.

"Maybe," Roger responded.

Malene finished making their lunch and placed the sandwiches on napkins. She got two glasses out of the sink and poured them both some iced tea. She sat down with their lunch and bowed her head. Roger did the same.

"Amen," she said softly, and Roger lifted his head on cue.

"So, what's going on at work?" she asked, taking a bite of sandwich.

Roger shrugged. "Closing up the case on the fire," he answered.

"You saying it was Trina?" Malene asked.

Roger shook his head. His mouth was full.

Malene waited.

"Officially, it's been ruled an accident without any names attached," he said.

"How about unofficially?" Malene asked. She and Roger had not talked too much about the fire. Their conversations since Alex had become a hospice patient were mostly about Alex.

"Unofficially?" Roger asked. "Well, unofficially, everybody assumes Trina was the last one in the church building."

"But you don't?" Malene asked.

"I don't know what to think," he finally said. "She won't say much, just that she was there and that it doesn't really matter what she says because folks have already made up their minds that she did it."

"Well, she's right about that," Malene responded. "Except, it does seem like if she didn't do it, she'd tell you."

"Maybe," Roger said. "But maybe there's more to it than just saying she didn't do it."

Malene was curious. "Like what?" she asked.

"I just got a funny feeling that there's more that went on that night up there at Holy Family than what we've been told," he answered.

"Well, I sure think Father George knows something. He's acted odd ever since," Malene noted. "Maybe you could go talk to him again, ask him some more questions."

Roger shook his head. "Well, that's not going to happen. Father George left this morning for Gallup and then will be on his way to California."

"Oh," Malene responded. "Well, I guess Daddy missed him then."

Roger's face was a question mark.

"Daddy said he was going over to the rectory, didn't say why."

"Well, yeah, he probably missed Father George," Roger responded. "I saw him drive past the station about nine o'clock. Looked like he was heading out for good."

"What about Rob Chavez?" Malene asked. She knew the boy's truck had been seen at the church the night of the fire.

"Well, see, that's something else that bothers me," Roger replied. He ate the last bite of his sandwich.

"I think there's more to that story too," he said.

"Like what?"

"Like, he was there longer than he's saying or he came back. There's just something about his story that's too neat, too perfect. Did you know that he came by the station to tell me and Danny that he was there before we ever went to question him?" He shook his head again. "Just feels too neat," he repeated.

Malene nodded. "Does Trina say anything about him?" Like everyone else, she knew that Rob and Trina had been seen together before. Even Alex knew that much.

"Just that she wasn't there with him. She confirms his story that he dropped her off and then left." Roger patted his stomach. "Good sandwich," he noted.

"Thanks," Malene responded. "Then why do you think he's got more to say than what he's saying?" she asked.

"Just a hunch," Roger replied. "He and his girlfriend, Katie, act very odd when I've run into them."

Malene raised her eyebrows. She hadn't heard any of this news before, and it was interesting to her. "Maybe there was a private prayer meeting at Holy Family," she said, smiling.

"Well, whatever happened that night, I don't think it was a prayer meeting," Roger said.

"A mystery!" Malene said, sounding excited.

"And one that won't ever be solved," Roger replied. "Because, as of eleven-thirty this morning, the case is closed."

"For the books," Malene noted. "But not for that poor girl everybody's blaming. Did you hear that somebody keeps leaving boxes of matches at her front door?"

Roger nodded. "Some kid's idea of a prank."

"Well, she didn't seem to think it was very funny when she told me about it earlier in the week," Malene said. She stood up and began wiping off the table. "I think she's really feeling the hostility from people around here. I think you were right when you said our town has no hospitality."

Roger knew what his ex-wife meant. He had noticed how folks were treating Trina, how they whispered about her when they thought she wasn't listening. She had been working a few hours at the diner every day, and he had seen the stares and heard the talk when she left the main dining room and went back to the kitchen. He confronted the behavior when he could, explaining that there was no evidence that she had started the fire and that, the last time he read the Constitution, folks were innocent until proven guilty. He had said as much to Bernie and Francine, a few of the high school kids sitting at the counter making snide remarks one day, and even to Danny when he made some comment about the girl's guilt. But Roger's ideas about justice were unheeded and overlooked. The people of Pie Town had made up their minds about the fire and who started it, and blaming Trina just seemed a good reason for people to stay mad. And even though most of them attended Holy Family Church and most of them had gotten to know Father George, no one in a long time had really cared about the parish. They went to Mass, but church was not a place that people in Pie Town cherished. The diner was more of a community center than the church, and Roger couldn't understand why everybody seemed so angry at Trina that the church was gone.

He had asked Trina how she was faring since the fire, and he could see that the young woman was shaken by the way people were treating her. He figured that just like the priest, she would soon be leaving Pie Town too.

"She's pregnant, you know," Malene said, jolting Roger away from his thoughts.

Roger nodded. He had guessed as much. The young woman's tight T-shirts were even tighter, and there was definitely a bump where there wasn't one before. He figured that was another reason the people in Pie Town had chosen her as the object of their derision. An unmarried pregnant girl, especially a stranger, could be quite the target in a small town. He suddenly thought about Angel and how the three of them had dealt with the disapproval from neighbors, the long stares, the whispers, the guarded sympathy.

"Any idea of who the father is?" Malene asked. She knew Roger and the girl had enjoyed a number of conversations since she moved into the apartment behind his house.

Roger shook his head. "She hasn't talked to me about it," he answered.

Malene nodded. "Well, let's just hope she does a better job of raising a child than . . ." She stopped when she saw Roger looking behind her, his face suddenly pale.

"Who?" The voice came from behind Malene. "Let's hope that the new girl does a better job raising a child than . . . me?" It was Angel. She had made her way into the kitchen before Malene had heard her coming. She stood in the doorway, tall and thin, her long hair pulled back in a ponytail.

"Angel," Roger said, sounding as if he was going to try to smooth things over.

"It's okay, Dad," Angel responded, holding up her hand. "It's the truth. I have been a terrible mom," she said in a matter-of-fact way. "I was just lucky you were both ready and willing to step in and take my place."

Malene turned around and faced her daughter, who was standing at the door.

Angel shrugged. "Besides, Alex forgives me, and that's really all I could ask for." She looked beyond her parents at the clock. "My ride's meeting me in an hour at the diner," she said. "So I'm going to walk around town a bit. Alex asked me to do him a favor," she added, and then turned and left.

They both listened as the front door opened and closed.

Malene glanced at Roger, who got up from the table and followed their daughter onto the porch. She didn't move.

THIRTY-THREE

Oris glanced down at the clock on his dashboard. It was almost one o'clock in the afternoon, and he was still twenty miles from Gallup. He had driven over to the rectory after breakfast, the events of the previous night still playing over and over in his mind, only to discover that the priest was gone. When he called the parish number he had listened to Father George's message explaining that he would be in Gallup for a few days and then driving to California to start his new work as an administrative assistant in a seminary. He had explained that a priest from Vietnam would be arriving soon to lead the three Catholic churches in Catron County, and then he recited a few numbers that could be dialed in case of emergency.

Oris had driven back to town and had his oil changed and his tires rotated at Frank's garage before he left town. "Vietnam," he had told Frank. "Are there no American priests anymore that the diocese has to start sending preachers from Vietnam?" And then he had launched into his tirade about nobody speaking the original American language anymore, English, and Frank had started talking in Navajo, calling it the original American language, making Oris mad. He shut up after that, but he was still upset. He had needed to see Father George, and the man had up and left that morning.

Oris hadn't planned to drive to Gallup, felt like he had done what he should do by driving out to the church, but after waiting on his car he couldn't shake that irritating feeling that he wasn't done, that he couldn't give up. By lunchtime he had convinced himself that he had to chase down the priest, so he had gassed up and followed the leading of his heart.

He headed west on Highway 60, stopping at the cemetery for some clarification, and then drove north on Highway 36 over to Fence Lake. There he turned onto Highway 602, which took him through the Zuni Reservation before finally heading up toward Gallup. He was taking his time, not speeding because he was still being cautious with the Buick, but now he was starting to get hungry and wished he had stopped at the diner and eaten lunch before leaving town.

"Nobody's going to believe me," he said out loud. "Especially not that priest." Oris couldn't even believe it himself.

"What am I supposed to say to him anyway?" he asked. "My dead wife told me to come and get you and bring you back to Pie Town?" He shook his head and gripped the steering wheel. "Yep, that's reason to change your plans, change the plans of the diocese of the Catholic Church, and come back to a place that never even accepted you to begin with."

Oris sighed. "I never cared for the guy anyway," he said. "There's just something not right about the boy. Everybody could see it when he drove into town that first day with a girl sided up next to him." He narrowed his eyes and kept talking. "I tell you, something ain't right about him. He's hiding something. He doesn't even own a decent pair of boots."

He turned up the volume on the radio and listened to the old country tunes playing on his favorite station. Willie Nelson was singing. "You used to love this music, remember?" Oris was talking to his late wife. Alice enjoyed the old ballads. "Loved the cowboy music."

He glanced over at the seat next to him. It was almost as if she were sitting right beside him. He smiled. He liked the thought of her visiting him, even though he understood she wasn't flesh and blood. She wasn't alive. He liked the thought that she finally broke through his dreams and his longings and showed herself to him. He had missed her so much.

He knew it was her as soon as the dream started, knew it was her coming to him just like she had come when Alex got sick. It felt exactly the same, the room filling up with her, his dreams and his sleeping mind so clearly focused on her, so clearly focused on something beautiful and pure, his heart so sure of what she was saying.

The first time she had come to tell him to get to Malene, and he had done it, and it was right. And this time it was to speak to that priest, the one he didn't care for and the one who had left town. But it didn't matter what she asked, he was going to oblige her. Oris would do anything for Alice, alive or dead, but especially since she was dead. He'd do anything to keep her around, to have her close by. He would continue to obey her every wish if he could hold on to the idea that she wouldn't leave him.

After the first night, the night she woke him to tell him to take care of Alex, he had started waiting for her. He figured that if she came once, found a way to reach across the divide between life and death, heaven and earth, and get to him, she would find him again. So he lit candles and built a little altar, calling her to him, started making a place for her at the dinner table, on the sofa in front of the television, even in their bed. He fixed supper for her, buying extra tortillas from the diner, pouring two glasses of milk, setting places for them both. He washed the extra set of towels, placing them by the sink in the bathroom, and even cleaned out a drawer in the nightstand in case there were things she wanted to put there. He bought a hairbrush and the rose-scented hand lotion she used to love to wear, her favorite candies, the butterscotch ones with the soft centers, and reading glasses, and he set them all around the house to make her feel comfortable, make her feel at home, make her never want to leave.

No one else knew what Oris was doing. Since he stayed all day at his daughter's house, watching over his great-grandson, and since Roger and Malene were preoccupied with Alex, they didn't seem to notice his curious new ways. Malene never suspected that Oris was waiting for Alice, making space for her, holding on to the belief that she'd come again. He pulled his curtains late in the afternoons so his nosy neighbor Fedora Snow wouldn't see him and tell everybody what she saw. He even kept it from Millie Watson, his oldest friend, the neighbor who knew everything about Oris, including what he looked like without pants.

He drove along and recalled the night a few days before when Millie showed up at his door about suppertime. He had answered and stood in the doorway, trying to block her view.

"Oris," she asked, peeking around him, "you got company?" She had seen enough of his sneaking around to go and ask the man directly. She cared about him enough to confront him. She worried about Oris, even if she didn't tell him, and she knew he was up to something, she just didn't know what.

He denied it, even though she finally was able to use her cane and maneuver herself around her neighbor. When she saw two places set at the table, she raised her eyebrows at Oris, looking like she had caught him in a lie, which she had, and then she just shook her head and walked away. “Whoever she is, I hope she don’t mind her dinner burning.”

And Oris had run back to the stove, realizing he had left the burner on high and scorched the potatoes. He wondered about Millie, whether she’d say anything to anybody, but he knew he didn’t really care. They could say he was entertaining a woman or had a girlfriend or even that he was losing his mind, he didn’t care. Alice had visited, and that meant she would come again.

Still, he didn’t understand this dream. He didn’t understand what Alice was trying to make him see when it came to Father George. What did that man have to do with his family? he wondered. What could that young priest do that would comfort his dead wife?

Oris considered Father George, how strangely he had been acting since the fire, how he had visited Alex when Oris was there and couldn’t stand still, wouldn’t look the boy in the eyes, didn’t pray. Oris had asked the priest if something was wrong, if he needed help of some kind, but the man had just shaken his head and mumbled something about it all working out.

Alex had noticed it too. When he asked to speak to the priest alone, Oris had left the room. Father George came out a few minutes later looking even more disturbed, as if the boy had said something that spooked him. When Oris asked his great-grandson if everything was okay, the boy had just shaken his head and said that things were not right at all and that he didn't know how to fix them.

And now Alice was telling Oris that he was supposed to stop the priest from running out of town and bring him back. The only problem was that Oris didn't understand what he was bringing him back to. Or who. There didn't seem to be anybody who really needed him when he was working or missed him now that he was gone.

Father George stumbled his way through Mass most weeks. He had no real gifts of ministry that Oris could see. He was as awkward with people as he was reading scripture. His prayers were memorized and hardly heartfelt. He couldn't sing, didn't lead with much authority. Frankly, Oris didn't see why the man was in the ministry to begin with. He didn't seem much like a priest or even a man of faith. And Oris certainly didn't understand why Father George was needed in Pie Town.

He glanced at himself in the rearview mirror and stared. He was surprised because he saw what he knew Alice saw. He saw how he had participated in the priest's departure. He hadn't given George a fair shake. The truth was, nobody in Pie Town had.

Oris had teased Father George about rattlesnakes and yelled at him about his driving. Bernie King had given him a hard time about the skunks and told him he'd never find friends in Pie Town. Fedora Snow worried him to death with church politics, and everybody raised eyebrows about his relationship with that new girl. The town had done a poor job of offering the young man any sense of hospitality, any kind of decent reception upon his arrival or even during his first few weeks, so that if he was hiding something, needing a friend or a confidant, he had certainly been persuaded that he wouldn't find it in Pie Town.

Oris felt a little guilty. He knew he could have done a better job of welcoming the priest. He knew he had been hard on the man. He had attended only one service. He hadn't even gone up to the church after the fire to see if the priest needed any clothes or wanted help trying to replace what had been lost. Oris had even thought, as did a few others in town, that Father George might have had something to do with the fire, something to do with Trina, the one everybody believed started the fire.

He rolled down the window a bit to get some fresh air and wondered if the priest knew the girl was pregnant. An old man, Oris was usually one who missed those kinds of things, but he hadn't missed that one. She came waddling up to his table at the diner, shirt pulled tight across her little bulge of a belly, and even made a comment about how she was surprised that she didn't get sick being around so much food, how the baby was making her hungry all the time instead. That's how she said it, "The baby is making me hungry." Oris had not responded. He was so shocked that the girl was talking so openly about a woman's way, about an unmarried woman's way, he had not known how to comment. Nobody else in the diner had spoken a word either. They were still mad at her for burning down the church, they sure weren't going to congratulate her for giving birth to a baby born out of wedlock.

"Is that who needs the priest?" Oris asked out loud, still not sure. "That girl?" he added.

He turned to look beside him. "It ain't his, is it?" he asked, and then had to smile because he could feel his dead wife punch him in the ribs.

"Well, even if that baby is his, I can tell you that he doesn't want anything to do with that girl. That's been obvious since they drove into town together. He's scared of her for some reason. There's either a history there or she reminds him of somebody else. So I doubt I can get him to come back to take care of her. You better give me something more to work with than that."

Oris thought about the night before and how Alice had spoken to him, pulled him out of sleep and sent him on what was feeling like a wild goose chase, how he had received clarity about who he was supposed to go and find, just not what he was supposed to say when he found him.

It happened just before the break of dawn, when he had been dreaming about a pool of clear blue water, the sun bright and full, the sky cloudless. It was the most beautiful body of water he had ever seen, and he wanted to dive into it, let the blueness cover him, swim beneath its unblemished surface. He dipped his toes into it, and it was cool and refreshing, and he was just taking off his shirt, pulling off his pants to jump in, when she had called him. As clear as anytime she had ever called out his name. "Oris, Oris, wake up," she said. "Wake up and get Father George."

Oris woke up and never saw her, never felt her touch, only was clear in his senses that she had been present, that she had given him the dream of blueness, he knew that. And she was telling her husband to get up and find the priest. He had waited the entire morning for more instructions, a detailed direction, some sensible motive, for her to join him for breakfast, but there had been no other contact, no other information. At a table set for two, he had eaten his morning meal alone. But for some reason Oris did not understand, some unknown and otherworldly reason, Father George Morris was going to have to come back to Pie Town.

Oris noticed the road sign just as he drove past it. He was four miles from Gallup.

THIRTY-FOUR

Trina folded her clothes and stuffed them in a duffel bag she'd gotten from Hector, the dishwasher at the diner. She sat down on the sofa, pulled off her shoes, and rubbed her swollen feet. She had just returned from work, a lunch shift on a Saturday, and she was tired. Her ride, Frank Twinhorse, was driving down to Texas to go to his son Raymond's boot camp graduation ceremony, and she knew that he would be there to pick her up in a couple of hours.

Trina glanced around her apartment, still deciding what she was taking and what she was leaving. In her few months living there, she had accumulated quite a few things, and she was having a difficult time letting some of her stuff go. It wasn't like her to be sentimental about pictures and knickknacks, coffee mugs and books, but as she glanced around she realized that she had started to make herself a home there in that garage apartment. Noticing the way she had decorated, she was surprised to realize that she had built a little nest for herself.

Since leaving home at sixteen, Trina had never been one to stay too long in a place, had never attached herself to a house, so feeling this way about an apartment—a couple of rooms and the things she had bought at yard sales and thrift shops—was not anything she had ever really experienced before. It never dawned on her that she had made a home for herself in Pie Town and that she would feel a little sad to leave it.

The truth was that Trina didn't usually make herself at home in the places she stayed, but she was also usually not one ever to be run off. When she was six and all the other children ganged up against her one afternoon at the playground, claiming she was half-breed, part Indian and part white trash, unfit to come near them, she had simply pushed them aside and taken her place on the swing set and refused to leave. They all stood around her, boys and girls, yelling at her, spitting on her, throwing clods of dirt, but she was unflappable, keeping them at bay because she kept swinging, higher and higher, threatening anyone to come too close or they'd be pummeled by her feet, up and back, up and back. One boy tried to catch the swing as she pressed past him, but when she noticed what he was doing, she kicked backward hard and fast, catching him in the throat and knocking him down. And even then, even with the other kids saying she had killed Ricky Daughtry, she kept swinging. They rolled the boy away from her, and he eventually caught his breath and got up. Finally, Ricky leading the pack, they all walked off, leaving her alone, leaving her to her swing and her resolve never to be pushed away from a place she had chosen to be.

Over and over that kind of thing would happen to Trina. Classmates, especially the girls, teachers, coaches, pastors, parents, every season there was somebody telling her she didn't belong somewhere. And she refused to bow down or cower like a dog with its tail stuck between its legs and leave. It wasn't pride or some desire to be included that taught her to stand her ground; she usually left those unwelcoming groups eventually. It was something else, something her mother had passed along to her daughter before losing herself to the bottle and the addiction she wrapped herself in.

It was some notion that Trina learned before she even knew she was learning survival skills. It was the instinct she was given that she was always going to have to fight, going to have to make a place for herself. She knew before she could walk and talk that her life was going to be a battle, and she never entered a place, joined a gathering, walked into a classroom, or ran onto a soccer field expecting to be received. So that when she was bullied or rejected, she didn't run off and pout or get her feelings hurt, she just assumed that was the price for being a part of a group. She accepted that bad behavior and unwelcoming gestures were just a part of the initiation rites of any party or company. She wasn't turned off or turned away by how the other kids acted toward her. So, while others called her obstinate or mulish, she just thought she was playing by the rules that somebody put in place long before she had anything to say about it, and the only time she was ever surprised or taken aback was when she was accepted, when she was welcomed.

Trina had built her life on a set of beliefs that said she was different but deserving, social but wary, friendly but decidedly not in need of friends. She had made her way through childhood and adolescence, middle school and a year of high school, Parkway Baptist Assembly and two Presbyterian churches, parties, Girl Scouts, soccer teams, after-school activities, and even a stint on student council—after being told she would have to be elected and ultimately she was—fighting to be included, refusing to be pushed out. And she stayed counted as a member in good standing of those groups until she was bored or restless.

She left when the others had given up trying to

bully her or dismiss her or overlook her. It was only when she had defeated their hostility and won some kind of acceptance, though always with a measure of resistance, that she decided to quit, to walk away and leave. Trina prided herself on never, ever being told when to leave. Until now. Until Pie Town, this place she thought had received her, this place she had thought she would call home.

She glanced over at the small table she had covered with a brightly colored tablecloth. Bea had given it to her when Trina commented on how much she liked it. It was a sample for the diner, one that Bea had not chosen. So instead of packaging it up and mailing it back to the restaurant supply store, she gave it to Trina. And Trina, never having owned a tablecloth, never having had her own table, washed it with dish soap and made sure it was dry before spreading it over the old table in the apartment, then added a small vase of flowers and a set of salt and pepper shakers. She loved that table with its bright colors dancing across the top. She got up from the sofa and sat down at the table, smoothing down the cloth and following the floral design with her finger, a gesture of good-bye.

She wasn't sure if it was being pregnant that had somehow made her sentimental about her decorations, a tablecloth and knickknacks, and if it was also the reason she had become sensitive for the first time to how she was being treated. She didn't know if she was already experiencing some kind of maternal drive to protect somebody else and create a homelike atmosphere, or if she was just tired of not being received.

Maybe, she thought, having finally experienced friendship in her life, the real sense of family she enjoyed in Amarillo with Dusty and Jolene and Lester, she was spoiled now, needy in some way she had never known. Once she got a taste of full acceptance, genuine love, sincere hospitality, and a place she looked forward to coming to after a day's work, maybe it had broken her, forced a crack in that hard thick wall around her heart. She wasn't sure where the feeling came from or how it happened, but Pie Town had hurt her.

Trina got up from the table and removed the salt and pepper shakers, setting them on the back of the stove, pulled off the tablecloth, and folded it, having decided that she would find room for it in her duffel bag. She laid it on the table and looked around at the other stuff she wanted to take with her. She walked over to the three built-in shelves by the old television that was in the apartment when she arrived. She picked up the picture of her with Alex at his birthday party, but took it out of the small frame she had bought from the thrift store in Quemado when she went shopping with Malene. She took the tiny ceramic horse Hector had brought her from Phoenix, a thank-you gift for working his shifts, wrapped it in a piece of newspaper, and placed it in a zippered compartment of the bag. She removed the picture of the Rio Grande River that Roger had brought her from his house to hang on the empty west wall and then put it back, realizing she would have no way to carry it.

She flipped through the pages of a few books, old pocket-size Tony Hillerman mysteries she had been reading, a Bible that, like the television, had been there when she moved in, a phone book, and was returning the last paperback to the shelf when a piece of paper slipped out and fell to her feet. She picked it up and walked back to the sofa. As soon as she saw it she realized what it was. That piece of paper had been the final push for her to get out of town.

The day she found the paper stuck in the screen door had not been an unusual day. She was helping Fred and Bea clean the diner, working a few hours after the lunch shift, so that they would pass the upcoming state inspection. Hector and Francine had gone home. Even though more than a few customers had asked them about their newest employee and what role she had played in the fire at the church, and even though Francine had complained that a pregnant waitress got better tips than an old barren one, Fred and Bea had not asked Trina about her involvement in the fire, nor had they mentioned her pregnancy.

They had participated in the whispers behind her back, made their own speculations about what she was doing at the church late at night and who the father was, but they had primarily stayed out of the town gossip. In fact, they had given Trina more hours of work, not because they could afford her and needed the extra help, but because they felt sorry for the young woman they had come to like.

Trina had hardly noticed the harassment from the folks in Pie Town. She didn't even flinch when Bernie brought up the fact that he had seen her in the field the night of the fire and asked her in front of more than a few people what she was doing out there. She had answered him honestly and without hesitation. "I went to the church to pray," she had replied loud enough for everyone to hear. "The last time I heard, that was not a crime. And when I found that the church doors were locked, I prayed in the field, talked to God right out in the moonlight. He seemed okay with that, even if you aren't." And then she had taken his empty dishes from the table in front of him, dropped them in the container she was using to bus the tables, smiled, and walked back to the kitchen.

She had confronted a group of high school kids sitting at the counter one afternoon. They had stopped at the diner for sodas and ice cream but then couldn't let an opportunity to harass the new girl pass them by. Two of them were friends with Rob's girlfriend Katie; Trina had already run into them once downtown and endured their attacks. One of the girls, plump and angry, pushed her ice cream across the counter back to Trina, complaining that she didn't want her sundae made by a pregnant fire-starter. The other girls had giggled, hiding their faces behind their hands, and Trina, standing behind the counter directly in front of the girl, took the sundae and ate it herself. Then she patted her belly and said, "It might be a good thing for you to lay off the ice cream. Otherwise people might start to think you're in the same boat as me."

That had made the girl so mad that she got up and left her friends sitting there, face-to-face with Trina and without nearly the same amount of bravado and meanness. They paid their bill and left.

Trina had found the boxes of matches on her landing, told Malene about that, and had even caught a couple of teenagers planning to leave a can of gasoline at her front door. She had heard them creep up the steps, and she opened the door as soon as she knew they were there. One of them jumped off the landing, and the other slipped and fell, tumbling down the stairs and taking quite a beating. Even though all of these incidents had troubled Trina a bit, it was that piece of paper, finding it stuck inside her door, watching the young woman she had never seen before walking down the street putting fliers in all the doors of all the houses around her, that was the final straw.

Trina opened it and read:

Come to the church.
Come see what the fire has done.
Sunday, 10:30 A.M.

She folded the paper and held it.

When she found it and read it the first time, she hadn't understood what it meant. She thought that maybe it was some kind of community-organizing prompt. She thought maybe somebody was hoping to have a church service. She even considered that Father George was trying to rally the town for Mass. But then she remembered that the priest was leaving town, and when she asked Fred and Bea about the flier and they explained that they hadn't heard who was responsible, only that everyone had gotten one, Trina suddenly understood that this was her demise. The people of Pie Town were finally being organized to bring her down. It was a lynching party, she was sure of it. And even though she didn't know who the woman was leaving the fliers, gathering the townsfolk together, Trina figured she was some messenger from the Catholic church, some member of Rob Chavez's family, or some relative of his girlfriend. Trina didn't really know who was behind this idea to run her out or have her arrested or cause her some harm, but she knew that it was about to happen and that the people of Pie Town would easily turn into a mob and come for her.

Trina was not so much concerned for herself, since she knew what she was capable of handling. But she was concerned for Roger, the sheriff who had given her a place to stay and never taken a rent check from her, who had stood up for her after the fire, telling people she was not responsible and to leave her alone. She was concerned for Fred and Bea, the couple who had given her work and not bothered her about her pregnancy and who had already experienced a decline in business since the fire. She was concerned about Malene and Alex and that the townspeople might distance themselves from them when they needed their friends the most. And she was concerned about the baby. She didn't know how she would be received in Amarillo—she hadn't been able to contact Jolene or the others—but she thought it couldn't be worse than what she was facing in Pie Town. So Trina had quit her job at the diner and written two letters she planned to give to Roger and Alex. She was leaving, pushed out, bullied, forced to exit before she was ready.

She put the paper in her duffel bag, a sort of

sick memento to remind her not to get attached to another new town, and wiped her eyes. She was trying to zip up the top of the bag when she heard the knock on the door.

"Frank, I'm not quite ready," she yelled as she left the sofa.

Trina kept her hand on the door handle when she saw who was standing there.

"Hello," the girl said. "I know you don't want to see me, but I just need to talk."

Trina stepped back and opened the door. "I'm getting ready to leave in an hour," she said. "So say what you need to say and get out."

Katie White walked in and Trina closed the door.

THIRTY-FIVE

Roger and Malene had decided as soon as they heard about the fliers that they would not attend the Sunday morning meeting. They thought the same thing that Trina thought when she saw one —that it was some attempt to rally the masses.

When Roger received a copy of the flier from his deputy, he was unable to verify who had made them, so he began questioning lots of people to find out who was behind the mass distribution. When no one would take responsibility, he made it clear to everyone that he refused to show up at a town meeting that was not authorized and properly organized. He refused to attend an unlawful assembly and be forced to answer questions he didn't have to answer from people he thought had no right to ask.

On Friday, before leaving the station, he assigned Danny to handle security detail at the meeting and told him to call if things got out of hand. "Otherwise," he told his deputy, "don't call me. And stay out of the discussion. Don't get involved," he instructed.

Having decided not to attend a meeting being called for what seemed to them like vengeful and unhelpful reasons, Malene and Roger also decided not to mention it to Alex.

The boy was already so concerned about the town, about what would happen to a village without a church, about what would happen to Trina and to Father George. He wanted to talk about it to everyone, wanted the priest and Trina to work something out together, wanted his grandfather to use his authority as sheriff and order the diocese to build a new church. Alex would work himself up into a terrible frenzy, and it would take hours to calm him down.

After the fliers were distributed, Malene and Roger met Alex's visitors at the front door and instructed them not to tell him about the meeting. They didn't want their grandson to learn about what they considered to be a witch hunt.

"If he asks about the church or Father George, just say you don't know anything," they would explain. "Do not engage Alex in conversation about what is happening or what has happened in this community. It is much too troublesome for him."

Roger had stopped by to visit Trina early Saturday morning, not having had an opportunity before then to talk to her. He walked up the stairs in hopes that she hadn't been spooked by the flier, only to discover that she was gone. The apartment door was unlocked, the place clean and mostly empty, and as he glanced around he found two letters on the table. He sat down, noticed her packed duffel bag near the door, and read the letter addressed to him, realizing then that she was soon to be gone for good. He left the letters there, deciding that he would return to the apartment later.

When he went back to Malene's to tell her what he had found, they decided that when Alex was a little stronger, maybe in a couple of days, they would explain that Trina had moved back to Texas to be with her family because of her pregnancy and then give him the letter addressed to him, which neither of them had read and hoped would not upset him.

And so, on that Sunday morning when everybody else was marching to church, Malene and Roger sat at the table, drinking coffee, working the crossword puzzle from the newspaper together, Malene calling out clues and Roger guessing the answers, and hoping the phone wouldn't ring. They were talking about Oris, his trip to Gallup, and how neither of them knew what he was doing or why he had already spent two nights there. Malene decided he must be buying a new car.

When Alex, having crawled out of bed and slid into his chair, wheeled himself into the kitchen, they both jumped from the table in shock. They had not seen the boy out of bed for days. He sat in his chair in the doorway to the kitchen and made the announcement, "We have to go to church."

At first, Malene thought the boy was delirious and thought they were supposed to be at Mass. "No, baby, we don't have a church anymore. We can't go to worship today."

"We have to go to church," Alex repeated. "It's Sunday, and there's a meeting. We have to be there."

"How do you know about that?" Roger asked, turning to catch a glimpse of Malene, wondering if she had an explanation.

"I made the fliers," he confessed. "I made them when Mom was here."

"What?" Malene exclaimed.

"It was my idea to do a flier. We need to come together. We need the church. We need Holy Family. It needs us."

And then, just like that, Roger and Malene understood. They understood that the meeting was what he and Angel had been discussing in private when she had last visited and that she had been the one who made the flier, then copied and delivered them all across town. They recalled that before she left the house after her visit she had made the comment that she had some errand to run for Alex, but neither of them had paid any attention. Roger had taken her to the station to use the computer and copier without ever questioning what she was doing. He thought she was contacting old friends on the Internet or making something for the boy. He was busy and never noticed how many copies she ran.

When she left, explaining that her ride was supposed to meet her at the diner, Roger had tried to talk her into staying but then gave up after seeing the look on her face, knowing his pleas were useless. He walked back to his desk, understanding that his daughter had come to town, seen her son, and done what she thought she needed to do. He was not going to make her stay, and all he thought about was how he was going to explain her departure to Malene and Alex. He never considered that she was making fliers for her son to organize the community. And now he realized that she had left the station and walked or driven around town to every house, every car, every establishment, without being seen or recognized, and delivered Alex's fliers.

"Why?" Malene asked. "Why do you want the town to come together?"

"Don't you see this is why I can't be in the hospital?" He shook his head. "Somebody has to tell people."

"Tell people what?" Roger asked. He had gotten up and moved over to Alex, kneeling in front of his grandson.

"Tell them that we need Holy Family. We need the church," he repeated. His face was flushed, and Malene began to worry that he was feverish.

"Baby, the diocese will decide that. We don't get to say whether or not they have a church here. Look, we can go to one of the other places if you want Mass." She knelt next to Roger, placed the back of her hand on the boy's forehead. He was warm but didn't seem to have a fever.

"No," Alex exclaimed. "The diocese isn't the one to make that decision. We have to make it. We have to show it is important. And it is important. Pie Town has to have this church. Father George has to stay." He pounded his fist on the arm of his wheelchair. "I have to tell them!"

"Okay," Roger said, backing away. "Okay, just calm down. Let me change clothes, and I'll get your coat, and we'll drive over in the squad car." He turned to Malene and shrugged. "It's what he wants," he said.

She nodded. "Let me get dressed and I'll go too." Then she looked back at Alex. "You want to go in your pajamas?"

Alex glanced down. Clearly, he hadn't thought about what he was wearing. "Maybe I'll put on a pair of jeans," he said and then smiled. "I'm sorry," he added. "I know how you worry about me, but this is something I really need to do. This place is going to need this church in order to be a home for people. Pie Town is going to need Holy Family."

Malene nodded. "Okay, fine. I understand. But how about after you put on your jeans, you have some juice and a piece of toast before we go?"

Alex noticed the clock. It was not quite ten o'clock. He nodded, realizing he had time. He took a few deep breaths and seemed to relax. Malene got up and began fixing him some breakfast while Roger wheeled the boy back to his room and helped him get dressed.

"Doesn't he look good this morning?" Roger said to Malene when they returned to the kitchen.

"You mean Grandma looks good this morning," Alex replied and smiled. "I saw how you two were gawking at each other at the table." He added, "It's sort of disgusting."

Roger grinned and tousled Alex's hair. "Well,

now that you mention it, she certainly does look good, and it is not at all disgusting."

Alex rolled his eyes. "You two need to stop pretending you don't want to be together and just get married again," he said.

Roger glanced over at Malene, who quickly turned away. "Well, look who suddenly feels strong enough not just to get out of bed but also to start meddling," he said.

"Here," Malene said, putting a glass of juice in front of her grandson. "Why don't you drink something and quit talking? You're going to need your strength to tell everybody else what to do."

"Right," Alex responded with a big grin.

"We'll be right back," Malene said after buttering the toast and putting it on a plate on the table next to the juice.

"And then we can go?" the boy asked.

"And then we can go," Roger answered.

"Hey," Alex said, and his grandparents turned back to listen. "I love you. It's hard, I know. Everything, it's hard, and well, anyway, I love you."

"We love you too," they said in unison.

Roger and Malene walked out together and stood in her bedroom.

"I don't think this is a good idea," Malene whispered, looking in the closet, trying to find something to wear. "Suppose everyone's mad and besides, what's he going to say that will change anything?"

Roger shook his head. He went into the guest room across the hall to put on his uniform before going back to talk to Malene.

"We'll just let him say what he wants to say and then we'll leave," Roger promised. "Besides, it seems like he feels a little stronger. He does look better, and maybe this will help."

"Help who?" she asked.

"Him, the town, I don't know, everybody. Seems like everything is falling apart. Maybe he has the answers we don't."

Malene stepped out of her gown and robe and began putting on a pair of pants and a top. "I don't know, Roger. I think he's asking too much of himself, expecting too much of this town. You said it yourself: we don't have a good record of hospitality, of doing the right thing when it comes to new folks." She suddenly noticed that her ex-husband was watching. "What?" she asked, buttoning her blouse.

"He's right, you know, you really do look good," he replied. "I forgot how much I love to see you get dressed."

"Or undressed," she said with a smirk. "Okay, focus," she said to herself as well as to Roger. "We'll just drive him over, help him out of the car, put him in his chair, and let him make his plea. And then we're coming home. It's chilly out there, and I don't want him catching a cold."

"I'll get his coat and a blanket," Roger said as he turned to walk away.

Malene stood in front of the mirror, looking at herself smiling, thinking about Roger, his comment, Alex's observation. She thought about her ex-husband, how nice it felt to have him there, how right it seemed for the two of them to be together. She thought about her grandson and the meeting and wondered what Alex could possibly say to bring the community together.

She thought about how upset he was going to be when he found out that a new priest had already been assigned, that Father George had been given another placement, and worst of all, that Trina was gone. She worried about what might happen when he found out his new friend had been run out of town and when the people at the meeting didn't respond the way he wanted.

Still, Roger was right and she knew it. Alex was stronger, acting more like himself. And if anybody could say anything to make people listen, it was Alex. She just didn't know what the boy had planned to say and what would be the reaction. She worried that any negative reaction would cause another setback.

"It will only be a few minutes," Malene said to herself. She reached for a hairbrush on the dresser and started to brush her hair. The curtain over the window fluttered, and just as she glanced behind her, noticed the movement, and felt the slightest breeze drift across her, she suddenly thought of her mother, sensed her presence in the room as if she was passing through, and then heard the crash.

THIRTY-SIX

Even though Trina had heard Katie's confession and knew that the girl was planning to tell the rest of the town that she had started the fire, her decision was the same. She was still leaving Pie Town. The trip had been delayed because Raymond's graduation had been postponed. More than two-thirds of his class had come down with the flu, and instead of forcing sick soldiers to march in an afternoon sun and then pass on the very contagious virus to family and visiting army officers, they had put the ceremony off by a few days. Frank had called Trina just as Katie was walking out the door to tell her they wouldn't be leaving until Sunday morning.

Trina was disappointed but still determined to go to Amarillo. Just after ten o'clock on Sunday morning, as the townspeople were gathering at the site of the burned church, Trina threw her bag in the backseat of Frank's car, climbed into the passenger's side, and closed the door. "Let's get out of here," she said.

Frank put the car in reverse and backed out of her driveway. "Nice morning," he said, and they both glanced up at the sky.

As they headed out of town, they noticed a few people walking on the road, moving in the direction of Holy Family Church. Neither of them spoke of the meeting.

"Did you get breakfast?" Frank asked.

Trina nodded. "I went out awhile yesterday, took a walk, and stopped at the diner and bought some doughnuts."

"That's a healthy way to start the day," Frank responded. "I have some fruit in the cooler." He reached down and opened the ice chest that sat on the floor between the two of them.

Trina shook her head. "No, I'm good right now," she said. "Maybe later."

Frank nodded. He checked the gauges on the car and adjusted the mileage counter. "So, how was your talk with Katie?" he asked. She had told him about the visit when he called to tell her that the trip was to be delayed.

"Fine. She was just trying to ease her conscience, I guess." She sighed. "She and Rob started the fire."

Frank nodded. "I figured as much," he said.

Trina turned to the driver. "Why did you figure as much?" she asked. "I thought everyone in this town thought I started that fire, including you."

Frank stared straight ahead as he drove. "You never asked me what I thought," he replied. "In fact, you never struck me as a girl who cared too much about what others thought."

Trina considered what he said. It was true, she hadn't asked him. Actually, she hadn't asked anyone what they thought. And it was true, she hadn't really cared. She knew what she had done and not done, and what people thought hadn't concerned her. Not until she had seen the notice stuck in her door. Not until she thought the town was meeting to condemn her, meeting to condemn Roger and anybody who stood up for her.

"Is she planning to tell the group at church?" Frank asked.

Trina shrugged again. "I don't know."

The two didn't speak for a while. Trina watched as they headed farther out of town.

"So, if Katie is going to clear your name, why aren't you staying?" Frank still did not look in Trina's direction. He was carefully watching the road.

"My leaving isn't about having my name cleared," she replied.

"No?" Frank said.

"No," Trina answered.

"Then what is your leaving about?" he asked.

Trina glanced over at the driver. "I just don't belong there," she replied softly.

Frank then turned and studied Trina. "Well, you're the first white person to admit that," he said and smiled.

"Yeah," she said, "that's probably about right. Those ranchers around there, they all act like they were the first ones to drive a plow in the fields or walk a horse up Escondido Mountain."

Frank laughed. "You learned a lot in your short time in Catron County."

"You don't have to be here long to recognize arrogance," she responded.

Frank reached in the cooler and pulled out an apple. He rubbed it on the front of his jacket and took a bite.

"Yeah, I guess white folks have done a lot of taking over of other people's homes," she said as she looked out the window. "My granddad used to say human beings were going to have a lot of explaining to do to God on Judgment Day and white folks would be in his office the longest. He was Choctaw."

Frank took another bite from the apple. He responded only with a smile.

"What about you?" Trina asked.

Frank waited, finished chewing, and then asked, "What about me?"

"Why do you stay there?" she asked. "I mean, I know it's your home and you have more of a right to stay than anybody, but what did anybody in that town ever do for you? Why would you want to put your business in a place that talks so bad about you?" Trina had heard the racist comments about the Indians when she worked at the diner. She had even heard some things said directly about Frank and his family. Apparently, the homesteaders held long-standing grudges against the Navajo people from the area.

Frank shook his head, thinking about the question. "People will say anything about somebody else just to keep from dealing with their own pain," he said. "Truth is, we all want to blame somebody for our troubles, and it's never too difficult to find an enemy." He glanced over at Trina and winked. "And that's not just the white folks. We Indians knew how to do that before the Texans moved out here."

Trina nodded. "So you think I should stay in Pie Town? Set my big ole pregnant belly in everyone's face and make my claim here too?"

Frank finished his snack, rolled down the window, and threw out the apple core. "I'm not saying what you should do. I'm just saying you have as much of a right to live where you want to live as anybody else." He rolled the window back up. "You're going to be a mother, and you need to make a home for your child. You shouldn't let anybody make that decision for you. If you want to live in Pie Town, then you should live there."

Trina took in a deep breath and thought about

what Frank had said. She remembered how it was for her when she had first come to Pie Town. She thought about the dream and the name of the town on her tongue when she awoke. She thought about the old woman who had nursed her back to health, fed her, given her shoes, how the name had come to her like a blessing. Trina thought about how it was when she arrived, meeting Roger and Alex, how it was to find out she was pregnant there.

She thought about the conversation she had with Father George, the one they had the night of the fire, the one when she told him she was pregnant, and the one when he told her about that girl he met when he was in seminary, the conversation that somehow opened them both up in a way that felt deep and honest and real. She remembered the ease that settled between them, filled them up, the tender way he held her hand. And then by the next morning when the church was nothing but ashes, all that truth was gone, the tenderness vanished, and everything she thought she had with the priest was lost, burned up, and disappeared. She thought about how he would look at her after that, like he was afraid of her, afraid of what she knew and might tell. She thought about the note she found and how she had ultimately chosen to leave and go back to Texas, try to start over again in a state that she knew but didn't love.

“Did you tell Alex?” Frank asked. He knew how much the boy worshiped Trina.

Trina shook her head. “I wrote him a letter. He’s too sick. I don’t think he’s really concerned about me and my whereabouts.”

“We both know that’s not true,” Frank said.

Trina didn’t respond. She crossed her feet at the ankles and blew out a long breath.

“Angel ever find you?” he asked.

“Who?” she asked. She didn’t remember Alex’s mother’s name.

“Angel Benavidez,” Frank answered.

Trina glanced up at Frank. “What do you mean?”

“She was putting up those fliers for Alex.”

Trina sat up a bit in her seat. “Alex was behind the fliers?”

Frank nodded. “I thought you knew,” he said.

“No, I thought that somebody was trying to organize a meeting about me, to run me out of town.” She remembered the woman she saw distributing the fliers, the one she didn’t know.

“So that’s why you’re leaving?” Frank persisted.

Trina didn’t answer. “Why did Alex want a meeting?” she finally asked.

“To tell everyone you weren’t guilty, I suppose.” Frank seemed concerned. He pulled off the road and put the engine in park. “You never heard any of this before now?” he asked, sounding very surprised. “You never saw Angel?”

Trina kept shaking her head. "Why would Angel want to see me?"

"I don't know the answer to that," Frank replied. "I just know that she came by the garage and asked me if I knew who you were, that Alex had mentioned you to her, and that she wanted to meet you. I told her where you lived. I thought she was going to see you before she left town."

"No, I never met Angel." Trina leaned against the door.

Frank stared straight ahead. They both seemed to be stunned by what they were finding out.

Finally, it was Frank who broke the silence. He turned to Trina and could see her working through the information. "You want to go back?" he asked. "You want to ride this thing out?"

She waited and then sat up. "I don't know," she said. And then she drew in a breath as if the decision was being made as she spoke. "No, I've already said good-bye. I think this is best."

Frank hesitated, looked as if he was going to say something else, and then seemed to think better of it. He turned to face the road. He put the car into drive and pulled back onto the highway. The two of them did not speak of Pie Town again.

THIRTY-SEVEN

They all walked or drove up the winding road that Sunday morning. Just as if they were going to a church service. Just as if it was a typical Sunday morning in Pie Town, just as if it was only the Catholics going to midmorning Mass, hoping for redemption or inspiration or something to get them through another week. They walked in file, Protestants and nonbelievers, old-timers and the newly baptized, all of them making their way to a church that no longer existed.

The late autumn winds had started blowing, and the sand cranes circled high above the heads of those moving along the road and making their way into the parking lot next to a charred and ruined piece of land, while the snow geese called out, announcing their arrival. The birds, native to Canada and the Pacific Northwest, were already arriving at Socorro, a few miles east of Pie Town, having made their way south, another sort of migration of salvation.

Although many of them had their own reasons for going to the called meeting, most of them were going just out of curiosity. They had all gotten the flier, stuck in doors and under mats, on the sides of mailboxes and on windshields. Nobody knew who had created the mailing or who had delivered them, since no one had taken responsibility for making the handbills and distributing them. But everybody in town had gotten one, and everybody in town, Catholic and otherwise, was curious enough to go out to the burned-down church and see who was calling a meeting and what was going to be reported.

Everybody from Pie Town was there except a few who never participated in any public gathering: the Indians living on the edge of town, Frank Twinhorse, having already left for Texas, his son Raymond, the old people at Carebridge, a few teenagers who had intended to go but overslept, the sheriff and his family, and the new girl who lived in the apartment behind him.

Danny White figured he should be the first one to arrive. He knew he was going to be the only person of authority in attendance, and he wanted to get there first to establish his presence to anyone planning to make trouble. He also thought that getting there early would give him a look at who else arrived before the crowds and help him figure out who had planned the assembly.

He left his house early, around eight o'clock, drove around town to do standard surveillance, and stopped at his parents' house for a cup of coffee and his mother's sweet rolls. He and his parents talked for a while, read the paper together, and then the couple went back to their bedroom to get ready before church. Checking his watch, Danny got in his squad car and drove to the church. He had not seen his little sister at breakfast, but he hadn't expected to. She was a teenager, and it was Sunday morning. Danny just assumed she was asleep.

Thinking she was still in her bed at home was only part of the reason he didn't recognize her standing alone in the center of the charred lot, the area that used to be the front of the sanctuary, the area marked as most sacred. He also didn't realize it was her at first because she looked so lost and helpless. He never remembered seeing Katie look so broken, so small.

He pulled up and got out of the car. He turned behind him and could see the line of people coming up the road, slowly moving in their direction.

"What are you doing, Katie?" he asked, heading toward his sister, suddenly concerned that something was not right.

"This is it," she answered. She had dropped down and was touching the ground. "This is where it happened."

"Where what happened?" Danny asked, reaching down to lift her up. "What are you doing here? You're chilled." And he took off his jacket and threw it around her shoulders. "How long have you been here?" he asked, looking around to see if anyone else was there.

He noticed that the rectory was empty, the doors and windows closed and covered. He knew that Father George had left and that the new priest wasn't due for a few weeks and might not live in the rectory in Pie Town anyway. A truck pulled into the lot, and Danny turned to see who it was.

"I need to tell you something," Katie replied. "I need for you to know the truth."

A door slammed. It was Bernie King. Of course, Danny thought, this meeting was his doing. He hadn't shut up about the fire since he first discovered it. He turned back to his sister. "What are you talking about?" he asked, thinking he needed to get his sister away from there, thinking she was acting a little crazy. And then he looked at her more closely, noticed that she had been crying for a long time, saw the deep red marks on her neck from scratching her nervous hives, and suddenly thought that something had happened to her. "Katie, are you hurt? Did somebody hurt you?"

The girl shook her head. "I just need for them to know."

More cars pulled into the driveway and parked. People were getting out and starting to walk toward the deputy and his sister. Just then, Danny turned around and saw Rob Chavez coming in their direction.

"Katie," the boy yelled out. "Katie, shut up!" And he started running toward them.

When Rob got to Danny, the deputy turned to his sister, and when he saw the look of fear in her eyes as she cowered behind him, he snapped. He thought that whatever had happened to Katie—and something had certainly happened to Katie—happened at the hands of her boyfriend. He spun around and threw a punch at Rob, knocking him off his feet.

"What the hell did you do to her?" Danny asked, grabbing Rob by his collar and yanking him up for another blow.

"I didn't do anything to her!" he yelled, trying to pull away. "I just need to talk to her!"

Danny reached back and slammed his fist into the boy's face. A crowd was starting to gather. Katie was screaming at her brother to stop, trying to pull him off, and Rob was trying to cover himself. Danny was going after him again, yanking him off the ground and throwing more punches. "Did you hurt my sister?" he shouted, punching him harder and harder until he was finally restrained by Bernie and a few other men.

"What the hell is going on?" Bernie asked. "Danny, get ahold of yourself!" He pulled the deputy away.

Katie ran over to Rob and knelt down by him, trying to see how badly he was hurt, trying to wipe away the blood, crying, telling him she was sorry. And he pushed her away and began walking to his truck.

"Get back here, you little son of a bitch," Danny yelled out to Rob, trying to free himself from the men holding on to him. "Come back here and get what you got coming! I swear, I am going to kill . . ." He didn't finish because somebody was yelling that Roger was calling on the radio in the squad car, telling his deputy that he needed help at Malene's.

"It must be Alex," Bea called out. She and Fred had walked from the diner. They had hoped to bring the crowd the reassuring news that Trina had left town and so they could leave well enough alone and move on with their lives.

Upon hearing Alex's name, the crowd followed Danny to his car, leaving Katie alone as she dropped to the ground and wept, crying for the crowd to listen, crying to be understood. The people of Pie Town gathered around the squad car as if that was the reason they had all been summoned to the church parking lot in the first place and waited for the news.

"Sheriff, it's Deputy White, over," Danny reported, his tone short and clipped, the anger still obvious. "What's the problem?" he asked, wanting to get back to taking care of Rob Chavez.

As everyone held their breath, they heard the news they'd hoped they would never hear.

"It's Alex, Danny. He's gone."

THIRTY-EIGHT

Father George had his instructions. He was to go to Northern California for an extended personal retreat before starting his new assignment. The Monsignor thought the priest needed some time alone to consider his situation, find healing for the stress he was under that was a likely result of the trauma of the fire. It was common practice for priests to go to a monastery and receive spiritual direction from one of the monks, have time for rest and prayer before the next placement. Everyone agreed it was the best thing for him.

George had disagreed at first, claiming he didn't need the retreat, explaining that he wanted to go ahead to his new assignment. And then Oris had shown up in Gallup at the diocesan house. Late in the afternoon, just before prayers, just before the reading of the Psalms and the silent supper, he stood at the chapel and waited. The old man had asked to speak to George, and once alone with him tried to talk him into returning to Pie Town.

The visit, the talk, had unsettled the young priest. Oris told him he had been sent to bring him back, and when George had questioned him about who had sent him, thinking the parish had called a meeting, that maybe they were making the same request to the Monsignor, Oris spoke of angels, a woman he once loved, and messages from heaven. Clearly, the old man was having some sort of breakdown. George listened for a while but then politely explained he couldn't go back to Pie Town, that he didn't belong there, the fire had made that clear. And after saying no to Oris, declining his invitation to return and his plea to go back and try to make things right for the old man's hometown, try to rebuild the church and the community, he had decided the retreat was probably in his best interest. He decided he wanted to get out of New Mexico, out of Catron County, and far away from Pie Town. As soon as he had gotten permission, he had taken a cab to the bus station and was waiting for the westbound bus.

"You going to Oklahoma?"

Father George glanced up. A girl stood next to him.

He shook his head.

"You got room for me to sit?"

He nodded and then moved his duffel bag from the bench, giving her room. He was wearing a windbreaker wrapped tightly around him so that his clergy collar did not show.

"I'm going to Oklahoma. I'm going to move in with my sister," the girl explained.

He smiled.

"Well, she's not really my sister. She was married to my brother and she told me to think of her as my sister. That was about six years ago. I was only thirteen. My brother was killed last spring. He was in Iraq."

Father George looked away. He didn't want to think about it but the girl reminded him of Trina, her size, the way she dressed, the way she talked, her bright, open eyes.

"I was in a women's shelter here," she noted. "Saint Mary's," she added. "You heard of it?"

Father George shook his head.

"It's nice. A woman from North Carolina runs it. Sister Charlotte," she said.

Father George nodded.

"My boyfriend beat me up. That's why I was there." She leaned back against the bench. "He's in jail."

Father George placed his hands in his lap, his shoulders drooped.

"I'm going to Oklahoma City because Laura says she has room for me and that I can stay and get my GED. She didn't get married again." The girl turned to study George. "Are you from Oklahoma?"

He shook his head.

"You going to visit somebody in Oklahoma?"

He shook his head again.

"Is there something wrong with you? I mean, why don't you talk?"

Father George glanced away. “Just enjoying listening to you,” he replied.

“Oh well, that’s different. Most everybody tells me I talk too much. Randy . . .” She paused. “That was my boyfriend,” she explained. “He said I was like a damn leaky faucet, drip drip, drip . . . he’d say.” She shrugged. “I don’t know. I just like to talk.” She turned to George. “Are you in college?”

He shook his head.

“You been to college?”

“Yes,” he answered.

“You come home?” she asked.

George studied the girl. “What do you mean?”

“Did you come home to Gallup?”

He shook his head. “No, I’ve been working and now I’m going to California to rest.”

“That’s home then? California?”

George shook his head again. “No, that is also not my home.”

She nodded. “I understand. I don’t really have a home either,” she said. “My dad was in the navy, we moved a lot. And then my mom left him and we moved back to Albuquerque and then when I turned sixteen she told me I had to get out of the house.” The girl yawned and then covered her mouth. “Randy and I lived in a motel downtown for about six months, but before that I don’t think I had the same address for more than a couple of weeks.” She laughed. “Funny, isn’t it?”

George waited. "What?" he asked.

"Just funny that neither of us has a place to call home and now we're getting on a bus, going somewhere else that isn't home."

There was a pause.

"Randy always promised me he'd make me a home. Must have said it a hundred times." She shook her head like she was trying to rid herself of unwanted thoughts. "But you should never trust a man who has to make a promise." She turned to George. "Naomi, at the shelter, told me that. This was her third time in there. She kept going back to her husband even though she knew he would kill her. She said he always promises he won't do it again." She shuddered. "Well, at least I wouldn't believe that promise!"

George thought about what the girl had said. He thought about her comment about home and he wondered when the last time was he had felt at home. Moving around so often as a child, going away to seminary. The truth was that the only time he really did feel at home was when he was at church, but even that had been a long time ago. And then he thought about what she said about promises, and suddenly remembered the conversation he had with Trina the night of the fire, something he had said.

She had just explained that she was pregnant, and after she said it she held out her hand and he had taken it. He couldn't remember before that night the last time he had held a woman's hand. And it startled him to feel how small it was, how easily and simply it fit in his.

"If I have this baby," she had said, "I need to have a home. I need this baby to have a home."

He had made a pot of tea and after telling her about the girl from seminary, the one he had gotten pregnant, the one who had an abortion, he reached out for her hand and he told her that he would help her make a home. No, he didn't just tell her, he promised her. "I promise that I will help you and your baby have a home here in Pie Town." That's what he said, the exact words.

George rubbed his eyes. That conversation, that vow, felt like it happened so long ago. He knew he had meant it when he said it, believed it when he promised her, but then after the fire, after the accusations and the realization that everybody thought Trina had done it, after the first interview with Roger and the fire chief and the questions that were never asked, the ease with which his silence fell, he just couldn't go back, just couldn't tell the truth. He could not keep his promise.

"You okay?" The girl had been watching him. "You sort of look like you saw a ghost or something."

George faced the road ahead of them. A bus was coming in their direction. "I think this is the one to San Francisco," he said. "The one to

Oklahoma City comes in about an hour." And as he stood up to leave, he bent down to pick up his duffel bag and his jacket fell open, his collar suddenly becoming visible to the girl.

"Hey, you're a priest," she said as he turned away.

And he stopped and zipped up the jacket, covering himself, and headed to the bus.

THIRTY-NINE

There was no consolation for the people of Pie Town on the Sunday they were to assemble at the burned-out church, the Sunday Alex died. No organizing, no clarity, no hope. Katie White had finally gotten everyone to listen to her as she explained that she and Rob Chavez had been at Holy Family the night of the fire, that it had been the two of them who left the candle burning on the altar. She screamed it out after everyone had heard Roger's announcement about Alex, screamed out the entire thing, how Rob had dropped Trina off but then had later gone and gotten her and how they had snuck into the church without ever alerting the priest and had snuck out the same way.

She shouted her confession, ran from person

to person, looking for absolution, but no one responded, no one really cared. They only looked at her, looked through her, as if she was a babbling idiot. In the wake of Alex's death her confession mattered little.

For the next week Roger and Malene walked around like ghosts. Ever since the hospice nurse called the time of death at 10:30 A.M. on Sunday morning, and after the funeral home personnel drove over and removed Alex's body, the grandparents had wandered from place to place as if they were waiting to be swallowed up by the earth.

Neighbors and friends came to sit and hold vigil, and they came armed with food. They brought casseroles and homemade tortillas, pitchers of iced tea and bottles of wine. They made biscochitos and baked cakes, had bowls of chile stew and plates of tamales. They made sausage from their hogs, chorizo, slaughtered for the season, and searched for the fattest and most tender chicken breasts to grill in open pits like their ancestors used to do. In sorrow and in sympathy, they brought the very best they had.

Malene accepted each gift, each offering of friendship, each token of helplessness, but she ate only what was fed to her, only what was spooned to her from Roger's hand. She was like a child, sitting at the table, hands in her lap, leaning toward her ex-husband, chewing and chewing.

And even though she ate sopaipillas, empanadas, and fresh posole, she never tasted a thing. Food became only something she had to swallow like medicine. She didn't speak to anyone, wouldn't brush her hair, and had to be forced out of bed by her father. She could not even cry.

Roger was no better. He stayed with his ex-wife, moved into the master bedroom with her, the two of them curled around each other every night, arms and legs wrapped around pieces of their broken hearts. He received visitors, talked the small measured talk that goes on in houses where death has struck. He watered the plants around the house, long since wilted, took out the trash, mopped the floors, changed their sheets, even went through closets throwing out old clothes, but he had closed and locked the door to Alex's room. He could only walk by it, stand there with his hand on the knob, unable to enter.

The funeral was held at the chapel at the funeral home in Red Hill. More of a memorial service really, since the body was not present, having been donated to science at the boy's wishes, the funeral was brief and ordered. Everybody from Pie Town was there, and many had to be turned away because the seats were full and the line of those standing was three deep and stretched around the room and outside under the large stained-glass windows. A few of the townspeople spoke about the boy, about how he had meant something special for them, some secret act of tenderness, about his quiet and kind ways. A resident of Carebridge, driven to the chapel by ambulance and carried up the stairs by an attendant, explained how Alex was their favorite visitor at the nursing home, how he read them stories or taught them new card games, how he never complained when he had to stay late because his grandmother couldn't get off duty, and how his laugh was like the sunshine.

A few of the teachers from his school spoke of his commitment to his work even when he was sick and unable to attend classes. The choir from the middle school sang. And the principal read a poem Alex had written about the rain in the desert, hope in darkness. The Monsignor sent a priest from the Gallup church to pray, recite scripture, and share a letter of condolence from the diocese office explaining that Father George wanted to attend the funeral but had left for a silent retreat and was out of state.

The service was dignified and fitting and everyone but the boy's mother, Angel, was there. No one had been able to reach her after she had been given the news of Alex's death. It didn't seem to matter to her parents. Like everything else, Roger and Malene seemed unconcerned that Alex's mother was not present. They sat quietly during the funeral. They nodded and smiled through the stories, received the gifts made of memories from others, embraced the town's grief, but neither of them, even one hour after they left Red Hill, could report a single thing that had happened. Their loss covered them like a sickness.

Oris was just as bad. Ever since he returned from Gallup, having heard the news in a phone call from Malene and unable to convince Father George to come back or the diocese to build another church in Pie Town, he spent most of the days and a large part of the nights sitting at the cemetery, staring at his wife's grave, stunned by his failure and his disappointment. Millie tried to comfort him. She brought him the latest issues of farming magazines she stole from the medical clinic and hung around until he would finally ask her to leave. Mary Romero brought him coffee and cake to have while she sat nearby at her husband's grave, studying Oris for hours, trying to get him to leave when she left. Even Fedora Snow met him in his driveway one day and invited him to supper later, trying to make amends.

The town and Alex's family were lost to their grief, lost to the cold clutch of sorrow, lost to the notion that anything would ever be right again. Winter, with its cruel bursts of ice and rain, its long barren nights of frozen darkness, had descended upon Catron County, upon Pie Town, but finally, even as they took a slight comfort in seeing that the condition of their hearts matched the condition of the sky, something changed.

Sometime just after midnight on the day of Alex's memorial service, when everyone else was asleep, tucked into beds in their tiny cells at the monastery in Northern California, where Father George was in private retreat before starting his new job, the young priest received a message from God.

He was praying, as he had been for days and nights, begging for relief or forgiveness or anything to ease the pain in his mind, bolster his lagging faith, and undo the knot that was lodged deep in his chest. He was tired and just as he was about to fall asleep, kneeling at the altar, Father George suddenly felt lightheaded, a flutter in his chest, and an overwhelming sense of warmth. All around him, within him, there was warmth. And while held in this pool of heat, delighted and at ease, he heard a voice.

At first, he didn't believe he was hearing it. He thought he was weak from fasting, imagining things, voices or spirits, or that one of the other priests was playing a joke on him, but then the voice, a woman's, came again. The words sharp, clear: *"In that place lies your vindication. In that place is the source of your salvation."*

And just like that, the pool of warmth became a pool of light. A perfect golden light that surrounded him and filled him, and in that moment he knew. He knew what Oris had tried to tell him before he left New Mexico, how the widower had been sent by this angel, his angel. He realized the forgiveness that had come and yet, in the split second of mercy, he also understood that he had not been relieved of the promise he had made to Trina. In that moment of compassion also came the penance.

He left before morning, the sky still dark and studded with stars. He walked and hitched rides from San Francisco to Gallup to see the Monsignor at the diocese, catching rides from two truckers and a vanload of Mormons, and in absolute clarity of what he was to do.

Once he was allowed to see his superior, he told him everything. He told the entire story of how he had gotten drunk and impregnated a girl and later refused to assist or help her. He explained his silence about Trina being with him the night of the fire in Pie Town, how he had not stood in defense of a girl who had been wrongly accused. He told of his promise and his failure to keep it. All of this he told without hesitation or defense, and then he waited for his judgment.

It didn't take long. The older man dropped his head and then lifted it again. Absolution came from the Monsignor, instruction for counseling and a designated time of probation, and then the Monsignor paused. He turned to the young priest standing before him and said, "I assume this conversion experience that has led you to confession has also led you to an understanding of service."

Father George raised his shoulders, lifted his face, and replied. "Pie Town," he said. "I am being sent back to Pie Town."

Father George explained about Oris's visit earlier when he had been in Gallup, and about the unexpected voice that came to him while praying. He told him about the pool of light, the sweet experience of relief. He said he knew he had to return to the place he had abandoned, the people he had left behind.

As the Monsignor listened he suddenly remembered his own visit from the old man from Pie Town, how he had begged the Church to rebuild after the fire, to give his town another sanctuary. "We cannot rebuild the church," he had explained to the man and then again to Father George. "There are no funds. If you do this thing, you will have no assistance from us here."

And Father George had smiled and nodded. The news did not discourage him.

After listening to Father George's request, engaging in his own time of prayer and discernment, talking to the young man's spiritual director from his seminary, as well as his hometown priest, the Monsignor agreed and sent the young priest back to his original post.

Upon hearing the news, Father George had

turned to leave the office, the joy spread wide across his face, when the Monsignor stopped him. He reached behind his desk and pulled out a large box, explaining that the old man from Pie Town had asked that Father George be given its contents. "I forgot that I had this. After you left, I had planned to mail it," he explained. "But since you're here . . ." And he handed the box to George. "I can't imagine what it is."

And George opened one end and peeked inside. He smiled and closed the box without displaying what he had seen. He bowed and left the diocese and his superior.

Father George, freed and focused in a way he had not been in a very long time, found the old station wagon parked in a lot behind the offices, drove out of town, stopping only to gas up, make a call, and then a visit to an out-of-the-way stop in Amarillo.

It had taken him a while to track her down, but he recalled enough of her story, their conversations, that he remembered the name of the bar she frequented. From the bartender he found the place she was staying. In the end, it hadn't taken much to convince her to join him. It seemed, in fact, to George that she had been waiting for him to call, that she had been expecting him, expecting the best of him. And when he drove into town, she was standing outside the bar, her suitcase packed, a knowing smile across her face.

"Took you long enough," she said as she threw the suitcase in the backseat.

"I'm a little slow," he answered. And he opened the passenger-side door while she got inside.

The two of them, therefore, arrived in Pie Town and the parking lot to the diner in the exact same way, but in an entirely different spirit than they had first appeared almost six months prior.

When he opened the door and stepped out of the car, Trina was already standing beside him, delighted with herself and her growing belly, confident and rested, stretching as if she had finally gotten home, as if she had already been received. When the priest emerged from the car, the first thing everyone noticed was his feet.

Without knowing that Oris Whitsett had chased down the priest in Gallup, been refused and then later gone shopping and bought the man a gift, the people of Pie Town just assumed that somewhere along the way from Northern California to Pie Town, New Mexico, somewhere along his journey from distant and unattached bidder of the Church to confessed and redeemed sinner, somewhere from lost to found, blind to seeing, broken to mended, Father George Morris had found a good pair of boots.

Part V

FORTY

I am as light as a feather now that he is with me. I go places I never before had interest in or desire to visit. We dance upon moons and sail across low clouds. I never knew I was so lonesome for company. He is as young now as he was then, a child wanting to stretch and go farther than yesterday, try a new dive, see a sunset from another pinnacle. He is my joy.

Of course, his first desire is to go home, to finish what had begun, to see come to pass what was birthed in his frail, beating heart. We have been granted permission, and I have told him my tales, recorded the events he missed and what has already fallen into place. He smiles, seeming as if he somehow knows more than even I, and I smile in response because maybe he does.

We come with the wind because humans always find hope in the change of wind. It is the breath of God, after all, and it is meant to remind them that there is more to this world than just themselves.

We come with strangers, once unwelcome and now necessary, once ridiculed and now desired, once held at arm's length and now pulled desperately into hearts. And we laugh at the absurdity of it all. These are the two who will bring hope back to this place of despair. These two, pushed out and pushed away, and the one still preparing to come, these are the ones who will put the world back on its axis. These two, not angels, not those with special powers or sleight of hand, but these two, broken and healed, lost and found, these two bring the gifts from heaven.

God is a God of humor and mystery. And though it seems long and often unpredictable, we enjoy the ride.

FORTY-ONE

"It sure is something," Trina said as she stood with George across the road from the new church. "You did it. You got this town to build Holy Family." She shook her head. "I never thought I'd see it."

George turned to Trina in surprise. "What? I thought you believed in this idea. You were the one who told me to go for it."

Trina grinned. "I believed in it and I wanted you to succeed. I just never thought you'd get everybody together and do it." She rubbed her full belly and blew out a breath. The walk around the new church had exhausted her.

"It is a miracle." George looked again across the road and remembered how he had tried when he returned to town to convince the community to build a new church. He knew the grief over losing Alex had affected everyone, and he knew there was a pall that hung over the town and everybody in it. And even though he understood the loss and the slow, hard way it settled on Pie Town, he thought he could get at least some of the people interested in the church.

He talked about it until he was blue in the face, held meetings at the school, at the diner, out in the park. He talked and talked and talked about the importance of a church, how Pie Town needed a place of sanctuary. He visited people in their homes, visited them at work, doing everything he knew how to do to raise money and interest until finally he was just about to give up.

He looked up at the sky, thankful for the arrival of spring, thankful for all that happened in the previous months in Pie Town.

"She came to you again, didn't she? That was your miracle." Oris was standing behind them, leaning against his car. He had driven Trina over to see the church since she had been on bed rest for most of the previous month when the finishing work had been completed. "I knew it was her. I told you she was still here."

"Yes, you did, Oris," George responded. "But I don't think it was her this time. It didn't sound like her. The voice sounded different."

"Who came to see you?" Trina asked, not having heard the stories about Alice. "And what did she tell you that made everybody listen?"

George thought about that morning he had awakened early and decided to take a hike. It was the morning after his last called town meeting, the one that only Oris had attended. He was discouraged and burdened and he left the parsonage and headed east and south, finally making his way to Alegros Mountain, the highest peak near Pie Town. He hiked all the way to the top and stood, looking over Catron County, over Mangas Creek and the San Agustin Plains. He peered out across the vastness of the earth, the mountains and the valleys, the land of high desert, dry washes, and hard, scrubby pines. And as he saw the miles and miles stretched and stretching around him, he finally began to see how small his little church actually would be and began to consider how insignificant his work, his call, his place was.

He stood looking out all around him realizing what was becoming his failure, his unfulfilled dream, and asked the question out loud, "What shall I do?" He waited and after hearing nothing, he called out again, "You sent me back, called me back, but nobody listens to me. I don't know what else to say to these people."

And in the silence of the morning, just as he was turning to walk down the mountain with no answer, no direction, he saw a hawk circle above his head, its wings outstretched, floating on the early morning breeze, alone and sailing, and he heard the voice speak to him, quietly and easily, like the voice of a child. "There is nothing more to say, only that to do."

And with the words fresh upon his heart, that was what he did. He quit talking and starting building. He started building a ministry and he started building a church. He pulled his face out of notes or books or even scripture when he preached and he spoke only from the heart and only what he held to be true. He visited the townspeople and sat with them, sometimes for hours, talking only about ball games and lighter subjects, without mention of building projects. He smiled more easily, even laughing from time to time, and it had even been reported that he had been seen weeping openly on more than one occasion.

He comforted Malene and Roger, not by trying to push them away from their grief and sorrow by making them think about a new church. Rather, he would just show up, go with them to the grocery store, or take Malene to the beauty salon. He'd help Roger with some of the calls made to the sheriff by families in need or crisis, and assist Malene at the nursing home. Father George even found Angel and arranged a meeting for her with Roger and Malene, riding with them over to her new home in Colorado.

He became present and available to Trina, driving her to the clinic for her appointments, organizing the women in the church to help her buy some clothes, getting her the necessary medical attention when she started having trouble, making sure she was staying in bed, getting her books about having a healthy delivery, and even speaking to Frank Twinhorse on her behalf, not that she needed it, to get her a job at the garage after the baby was born, working as an apprentice and waiting for Raymond to come home since they had been writing letters to each other every day since his deployment.

Over the weeks, Father George and Frank actually became friends, Frank taking the priest to the most sacred place in the county, over to Salt Lake, where the Indians, the Zuni, Hopi, Apache, and Navajo, had been making pilgrimages for centuries and telling him stories of the Navajo way, the story of creation, of Spiderwoman, and how the earth and its inhabitants are all intricately related. The priest had even asked Frank to find a shaman to bless the ground before he laid the foundation, a kind of permission asked of and granted from the people who first lived and farmed the land. And it was after that blessing that George started to build.

"Oris's angel," George finally answered Trina. "Her name is Alice and she was the one who got me back here and the one who helped me find you." He stuck a toothpick in his mouth.

Trina looked at the priest. "I didn't think you believed in angels," she recalled.

"I didn't believe in a lot of things," he responded. "What can I say? I'm a different man." He winked at Trina. "I got boots."

"Still . . ." Oris said. "It took more than an angel to build this church. It was a lot of folks to get this thing done." He grinned at George. "No disrespect, Father, but you are useless with a hammer."

George laughed. "Well, thank God Bernie came around when he did. I was about ready to quit that day he finally got out of his truck and walked across the street and helped me stake out the foundation."

Oris nodded. "That was a good couple of weeks after he had been watching you. He'd come up to the diner and give us a report every day at lunch about your progress." Oris changed his voice to sound like Bernie's. " 'That stupid priest is hammering the stakes in backward,' he'd say. 'He's tying the strings loose and at the wrong ends.' " Oris laughed. "And then, we'd all finish eating and drive out here and watch you make a fool out of yourself."

"Yeah, I was meaning to thank you for your support during that time." George reached behind him and gave Oris a punch on the shoulder.

"Well, we eventually all pitched in," he responded, rubbing his arm. "Sooner or later everybody did their part." The old man smiled.

The three of them stood looking at the new church, recalling the efforts of everyone in town, the way they came, a few at first, more later. They thought about all the work that had been done by the people of Pie Town that winter, the men who laid the foundation and hoisted the frame, the women who nailed in the beams and mixed the stucco, the children who carried tools and picked up trash. They knew that the rebuilding of Holy Family Church became important to all of the citizens of Pie Town. It became the endeavor that brought them together, sealed them in their commitment and their refusal to see the construction fail. It became their place, their church, their sanctuary, and day after day, night after night, shifts came and went, until by the time of completion, the finishing of every wall and floorboard and altar railing, every person, even those uninterested in the outcome, had, in one way or another, without being preached to or harassed, without explanation of what was supposed to happen or request for assistance or membership, participated in its success.

"It sure is something," Trina said again, rubbing her belly and shaking her head.

"It certainly is," Oris noted. "We have ourselves a church."

"More than that," George added. "We have ourselves a home."

FORTY-TWO

When the time came it wasn't clear which service would be the first held in the new building. Just like everything else regarding the facility, the design, the furniture, the fixtures, the colors, this decision was made by consensus. A meeting was held and all voices were heard.

Some thought the church should have its own special gathering, held only in honor of the completion of the building, a dedication event, complete with high-ranking priests and dignitaries from the state. Others thought the first event should be a Sunday Mass, the perfect demonstration of the building's purpose.

Once these ideas were shared, along with a few others, and it seemed like everyone was starting to take sides, it was Trina, the newest resident of Pie Town, the apprentice to Frank at the garage and girlfriend of his son, befriended by Katie White and doted on by Fred and Bea, who made the one suggestion that stopped the bickering and caused everyone to agree that her idea was the right way to start up Holy Family Church again.

Roger and Malene were to be remarried, and Alexandria Georgia, daughter of Trina, goddaughter of the Benavidez couple, would be baptized. It would be a service of beginnings, a service of promises and hope, and a celebration of love.

There would be no invitations extended to those known by titles or elected duty. The diocese was informed but not expected. The newspapers were given a public announcement, but nobody in Pie Town wanted to see anybody other than those who had actually participated in the church's creation and completion. In fact, the only famous person in attendance was the owner of a restaurant in Santa Fe, Cowgirl BBQ, who was asked to be the guest judge of the town's first annual pie contest, a main attraction event to be held at the festival following the service.

When the day came, all of the townspeople, arriving in procession, forming a line of hope and community, agreed that it was a perfect day for a wedding and baptism. Clear sky, warm air, the smell of lavender lightly drifting with the breeze, the desert ground coming alive with blooming willows, black-eyed Susans, and full golden bushes of Chiamisa, family and friends reciting prayers, laughing and eating and dancing and embracing the goodness, the bounty of life, it was all that was needed for a day of celebration and blessedness.

Father George was in particularly good spirits, donning a floral shirt and white linen pants, his boots replaced by a pair of teal hiking sandals. He made sure the windows were open during the service and spoke of the land upon which they stood, the land of dreams of homesteaders, and the generosity of the indigenous people, those who arrived there first. He spoke a prayer in Navajo, read scripture in Spanish, and quoted a poem by Emily Dickinson.

He asked Roger and Malene to speak from their hearts of their love, and everyone cheered when they said they had never really stopped loving each other and this was more a reunion than a wedding. And everyone wept when they called out the name of their beloved, dearly departed Alex, who had brought them back together and brought them back to love. They made their promises to each other to love and respect, to honor and cherish, and then they made their promises to Trina and her baby girl, naming their dreams for a child so full of hope, who had come at a time of such great need for them and the others. They vowed their love to each other and to the God who had walked with them through the dark valley, holding their hands and pulling them back to each other. And after they had said all that they wanted to say, Father George placed rings on their fingers and pronounced them husband and wife.

Then he called the people to the front of the church and filled a baptism font with cool water collected from spring rains by all those gathered and brought to the service in pitchers, plastic cups, and glass jars. He said a prayer over the water, thanking God for that gift of life in which they found refreshment, and he baptized little Alexandria Georgia in the name of love and with the hopes and prayers of the whole town. With the sacrament completed, he walked down the aisle, holding the baby in his arms, while grand-mothers and children, old men and teenagers, reached out to touch her fingers and tenderly lay their hands upon her head. He brought her back to Trina and then stood, raised his hands, and blessed them all.

"Let us go forth, people of God. Let us go forth in joy, in the delight of spring and the bounty of love. Let us go forth and be good to the earth and to one another. Let us bless this union with prayer and encouragement. Let us bless this child with protection and community. Let us bless this place with our honesty and our eagerness to reach out. And let us bless this town with our willingness to welcome all.

"For, like all towns, we are a gathering of weak and strong, male and female, young and old, frail and robust. We are different, choosing to pray in many voices to a God with many names, choosing to sing many songs, dance many dances, and yet we are the same. We try and we fail and sometimes we succeed, and we cheer those around us doing the same. We mourn. We dance. We love. We are Holy Family Church, so let us go forth rejoicing, for in this place and with one another, we will find all that we need to be able to love generously and completely."

And taking a branch of lavender and dipping it in the same water he had used to baptize Alexandria, he sprinkled drops upon the heads of all who were gathered and then, with great authority and vigor, exclaimed, "Now, let us eat!"

The party, the First Annual Pie Town Festival of Holy Family, held under tents in front of the church, went on for hours and late into the evening, when the old ones drifted off and the young ones fell asleep on blankets near the feet of their mothers. A band played salsa and cowboy ballads. Oris spoke of his love for his daughter and toasted his newly declared but long-ago received son. He even danced a slow song with Fedora Snow, whispering something in the old woman's ear that made her blush and kick him in the shin.

There was green chile stew and tortillas, cornbread, fresh tamales and tostadas, natillas and flan, and much to everyone's surprise, lots of pies, including the unanimously declared winner of the pie contest, Francine's Banana Cream Pie. One bite and Bernie King was reconsidering his original notion not to become involved with her while Fred and Bea suddenly realized they could actually rethink their dessert menu at the diner.

"It seems as if," they said after declaring Francine the winner, "Pie Town will finally and once again serve pie!" And they presented her with the blue ribbon and immediately discussed a promotion and raise with their new dessert chef.

Just as things were winding down, Trina left Alexandria with Danny and Christine, who was proudly flashing an engagement ring of her own. The young mother took a few flowers from the centerpiece from the bride and groom's table and walked to the back of the church to see where a special plaque in Alex's memory had been placed. It was a small designated area behind the sanctuary, a little space where spring bulbs were planted and a small marker stood naming the boy and recalling his faith. It was a perfect square of memory. She stood alone and then dropped to her knees. "I wish you could have met Alexandria," she said as she placed the flowers in front of the plaque. "You would have liked her." She stayed kneeling as she was. "She's a funny girl." Trina glanced down. "Your mom came by to see me," she added. "Not long after you died. Not long after I got back." She smiled. "I like her. She seems to be getting herself together." She sighed and pulled her knees out from under her and sat down. She looked up at the sky. "You did good, Alex Benavidez. This town, me, George, Alexandria, Roger, Malene, your mom . . ." Trina paused. "You did good." Just as she spoke these words, she reached down to remove a small rock close to her feet and felt two feathers drop right beside where she sat. She picked them up, holding them both in her hands.

She stayed where she was for a minute, smiling. She then got up and walked over to Father George, who was dancing the rumba with Millie Watson. Sticking a feather behind her ear, Trina took the other and placed it in his front pocket. He reached for it and seeing it, seeing what it was, knowing where it came from and what it meant, surprised everyone, including himself, when he threw back his head, held the feather next to his heart, and laughed right out loud.

FORTY-THREE

"Look, Lady," he said, using the name he still gave his great-grandmother, even though she had given him other ways to call her. "It landed right where she sat, right beside her." The boy smiled and flipped, tumbling across the breeze. "I knew this would work out," he said as the woman drifted behind him. "I knew he could make them come together and that she should be here. I knew the two of them were meant to be married and that she would have a daughter. I knew this town could pull it off, even if you did have to nudge a little."

"Only a little," she said and smiled. "You are a very smart boy." The lady paused. "And what about the other one?" she asked. "What about your mother?"

The boy considered the question. "Not all angels come when they're called," he answered. "But we can always hope they hear their name and know that they are loved." And he flew high and flipped while the lady watched, still smiling.

"I like it here," he replied, dropping down,

spreading his arms, and sailing gracefully. "It's a good place."

"Yes," she answered. "It is a very good place." And she threw out her arms as well, letting the wind catch her as she joined him at his side. "This is my home. This is the land, the people, the gathering I love."

The boy grinned.

"This is Pie Town."

Recipes from Pie Town

Hot Buttermilk Cornbread

2 cups buttermilk
3 cups creamed corn
2 cups cornmeal
1½ teaspoons salt
3 tablespoons baking powder
4 eggs, beaten
¾ cup olive oil
2 cups grated cheddar cheese
8 ounces diced green chiles

Preheat oven to 350 degrees. Mix all the ingredients together except the cheese and chiles. Pour half of the batter into a greased 13-inch baking dish. Place the chiles on the batter and then sprinkle on half of the cheese. Pour in the remaining batter. Add the rest of the cheese. Bake about one hour. (Serves 12)

Oris's Famous Cowboy Beans

4 cups dry pinto beans
2 slices bacon, cooked and broken
into small pieces
1 small can (4 ounces) diced green chile
1 medium onion, diced
2 cans crushed tomatoes (14 ounces each)
1 bottle dark or amber beer
1 teaspoon garlic
½ teaspoon cumin
1 teaspoon salt
pepper to taste

Soak beans for 8 to 12 hours, drain, and rinse. Place in a large pot on the stove, cover with water, and add all the rest of the ingredients. Bring beans to a boil and then simmer, covered, for about 2 hours. (Serves 10)

Bea's Green Chile Stew

2 pounds lean ground round, cubed
1 tablespoon olive oil
2 medium or 1 large onion, chopped well
2 cloves of garlic, minced
2 vegetable bouillon cubes
1 can (14 ounces) pinto beans
2 medium potatoes, diced
4 cans (14 ounces each) chopped tomatoes, with juice
4 small cans (4 ounces each) chopped green chile
2 cups water

Brown the ground round over low heat in the olive oil. Add the onions and garlic. In another pan, cook the bouillon cubes in the water. In a larger pot, mix the remaining ingredients, then add the dissolved bouillon and cooked ground round. Bring to a boil and then simmer for 2½ to 3 hours. (Serves 8)

Posole

2-pound pork loin
1 vegetable bouillon cube
1 large onion, diced
1 cup water
4 small cans (4 ounces each) green chile, diced
1 can (16 ounces) stewed tomatoes, with juice
2 cans hominy (32 ounces each), drained
1 teaspoon garlic powder
salt and pepper to taste

Boil the pork loin until tender and then cut into small cubes. Set aside. In another pan, dissolve bouillon in boiling water. Add onion, chile, tomatoes, hominy, garlic powder, salt and pepper, and then pork. Simmer for three hours. (Serves 10)

Francine's Banana Cream Pie

⅓ cup all-purpose flour
¾ cup white sugar
¼ teaspoon salt
2 cups whole milk
3 egg yolks, beaten
2½ tablespoons butter
1¼ teaspoon vanilla extract
4½ sliced bananas
1 9-inch pie shell, baked

Combine flour, sugar, and salt in a saucepan. Cooking over medium heat, add milk, stirring constantly until boiling, and then continuing for about three minutes. Remove the saucepan from the burner. Add egg yolks to the mixture and place the saucepan back on the burner. Stir for three minutes. Remove from burner, add butter and vanilla extract, and stir until smooth. Place sliced bananas in the cooled pie shell. Top with the warm pudding mixture. Bake for 12 to 14 minutes at 350 degrees. Chill for at least an hour before serving. Add banana slices on top for decoration.

Barb's Biscochitos

3 cups sugar
2 cups shortening
4 eggs
dash of salt
2 teaspoons soda
4 teaspoons cream of tartar
5½ cups flour
1 tablespoon anise seed
cinnamon and sugar mixture

Mix first 4 ingredients together until blended. Stir in soda and cream of tartar, then the flour. Mix in the anise seed. Shape dough into balls and roll in mixture of cinnamon and sugar. Bake at 350 degrees (or 325 degrees convection oven) for 12 to 16 minutes, depending on size. Be sure to take these cookies out of the oven before they're brown. They get crunchy when cooled, so if you like them soft, eat some a couple minutes after they come out of the oven!

From Barb Hively, owner of Cravin' Cookies and More Bakery, Albuquerque, New Mexico

Pie-O-Neer Pecan Oat Pie

¼ cup butter
¼ cup sugar
½ teaspoon cinnamon
¼ teaspoon cloves
¼ teaspoon salt
½ cup light Karo syrup
½ cup dark Karo syrup
3 eggs
¾ cup old-fashioned rolled oats
1 cup toasted pecan pieces
pie shell

Cream together butter and sugar. Add cinnamon, cloves, and salt. Stir in syrups. Add eggs, one at a time, stirring after each addition until blended. Stir in rolled oats. Cover bottom of pie shell with toasted pecan pieces, reserving a sprinkling for the top. Pour mixture into pie shell, sprinkle rest of pecan pieces on top and bake in moderate oven (350 degrees) about one hour, or until knife inserted in center of pie comes out clean.

From Kathy Knapp
Owner of Pie-O-Neer Café, Pie Town,
New Mexico

Author Insights, Extras & More . . .

From Lynne Hinton

Reading Group Guide

1. New Mexico is often described as three cultures living together: Native American, Hispanic, and Caucasian. Which characters in the book represent these three cultures, and how?

2. Pie Town is a very small town. What are the advantages to living in a small town? What are the disadvantages?

3. What is the role of the angel, Alice, in this story? Who needs the angel most in Pie Town? Is it Alex or someone else?

4. How would you describe Father George? Were you surprised by his secret?

5. At what point in the story did you think Trina might be pregnant? Do you think she was treated fairly after people found out? Where do you think an unmarried and pregnant girl would get the most support, in a small town or in a more urban setting?

6. Despite its name, there are no pies in Pie

Town. What significance does this have in the story? Do you think there will ever be pies in Pie Town?

7. How does Pie Town illustrate the idea of "community"? How do you define community?

8. What ultimately motivates the townspeople to help Father George rebuild the church? What does the church symbolize to the town? Why did Alex think it was so important for Pie Town to rebuild Holy Family Church?

9. Why does Alex never seem to be mad at his mother for leaving? Do you think children forgive more easily than adults? Why or why not?

10. Do you prefer cake or pie? What's your favorite kind of pie?

FINDING PIE TOWN

BY LYNNE HINTON

About fifteen years ago, when we were dreaming of moving to New Mexico from North Carolina, my husband and I were traveling through the southwestern part of the United States. On the trip from Albuquerque to Phoenix, we stopped in a little settlement known as Pie Town. I remember thinking what a quaint and funny name for a town. As we drove through Pie Town, we noticed a small restaurant and decided to stop and, with a name like Pie Town, have some pie. Imagine our surprise when we were told there was no pie. "No pie in Pie Town?" I thought, and that notion stayed with me.

People have often asked how I get an idea for a story, what interests me, how do I start. And the answer is something like the situation of finding no pie in Pie Town. I began to think about how often names of places or ascribed roles tempt us to make assumptions. We assume a small town will be welcoming and easy for newcomers to integrate themselves into. We assume a church will be a safe place, a loving and warm place. We assume mothers will be present for their children, and we assume children won't die. Once we think about it, however, we realize that life is rarely what we expect. People behave in ways we never could have guessed, and life is certainly full of surprises.

Having served as a pastor of several churches, I am often intrigued by what church members think about themselves. Most church people will proudly announce about themselves to any visitor that they are a "loving" place, a "welcoming and hospitable" place. And yet, in my experience, this is not always the case. Yes, churches can be quite welcoming and hospitable to the longtime members, the families who are connected to the area, the children who grew up in the church. But for newcomers, churches can often feel alienating and cold. As communities, as churches, as towns, as people, we are often not what we appear, and we are not always as good as we think we are. It was this irony that interested me when I began this story.

Now, many years after my first visit to Pie Town, I have discovered that there is a place that serves pie. The Pie-O-Neer Café, open now for more than ten years, has become quite successful. The owner, Kathy Knapp, has found a great place for herself in Pie Town, and I'm happy to have included a recipe from the Pie-O-Neer. I hope you enjoy it! And if you're in the neighborhood of Pie Town, New Mexico, please stop by and have a slice. Tell them I sent you!

LYNNE HINTON is the award-winning author of thirteen books including the Hope Springs series, featuring the national bestseller, *Friendship Cake*. She has also written a mystery series under the name Jackie Lynn. Lynne received degrees from the University of North Carolina at Greensboro and Pacific School of Religion in Berkeley, California. An ordained minister in the United Church of Christ, Lynne is available for speaking engagements and offers writing and spirituality retreats in New Mexico. You can contact her at www.lynnehinton.com. You can also find her on Facebook at Lynne Hinton Books. Lynne lives in Albuquerque, New Mexico, with her husband, Bob Branard.

Center Point Publishing
600 Brooks Road • PO Box 1
Thorndike ME 04986-0001 USA

(207) 568-3717

US & Canada:
1 800 929-9108
www.centerpointlargeprint.com